afterWORDS

after WORDS

Real Sex From Gay Men's Diaries

Edited by Kevin Bentley

 alyson books
los angeles | new york

© 2001 BY KEVIN BENTLEY. AUTHORS RETAIN COPYRIGHT TO THEIR INDIVIDUAL
PIECES OF WORK. ALL RIGHTS RESERVED.

MANUFACTURED IN THE UNITED STATES OF AMERICA.

THIS TRADE PAPERBACK ORIGINAL IS PUBLISHED BY ALYSON PUBLICATIONS,
P.O. BOX 4371, LOS ANGELES, CALIFORNIA 90078-4371.
DISTRIBUTION IN THE UNITED KINGDOM BY
TURNAROUND PUBLISHER SERVICES LTD.,
UNIT 3, OLYMPIA TRADING ESTATE, COBURG ROAD, WOOD GREEN,
LONDON N22 6TZ ENGLAND.

FIRST EDITION: DECEMBER 2001

01 02 03 04 05 ▪a▪ 10 9 8 7 6 5 4 3 2 1

ISBN 1-55583-656-9

LIBRARY OF CONGRESS CATALOGING-IN-PUBLICATION DATA
    AFTER WORDS : REAL SEX FROM GAY MEN'S DIARIES / EDITED BY KEVIN
    BENTLEY.—1ST ED.
        ISBN 1-55583-656-9
        1. GAY MEN—SEXUAL BEHAVIOR. 2. GAY MEN—DIARIES. 3. GAY EROTIC
    LITERATURE. I. BENTLEY, KEVIN.
    HQ76.25.A37 3001
    306.76'62—DC21   2001034082

CREDITS
• COVER DESIGN BY LOUIS MANDRAPILIAS.
• COVER PHOTOGRAPHY BY JOHNATHAN BLACK.

Contents

Once again, for Paul

"Myself, February 1915"

Anonymous photo postcard, author's collection

Introduction

My first diary was a little turquoise five-year model with a clasp lock and a tiny key I bought with my allowance in the summer between fifth and sixth grade. In it, I kept a businesslike inventory of who "butt-fucked" whom during frequent sleepover parties with neighboring boys on the army base. Before the summer was over, I'd gone back and scored out the most graphic verbs, and when school started, my diary fizzled out.

I next kept a daily diary in a 4-by-7-inch leatherette datebook for most of 1970, when I was 14. Gone was the brisk accounting of the earlier volume. Though I was committing acts with a neighbor boy (also 14) I revisit hotly to this day—and suffering agonies of private shame over them as I steeled my nerve for high school—the voice in this diary is that of a giddy Pollyanna channeled with colored marker pens. Peering through the innocuous celebrations of shopping expeditions to Kmart, the beauty of our new orange shag carpeting, and our elderly dachshund's antics, only I can readily see—in lines like "Spent the night at Mick's last night and we slept out in his backyard. Then I came home and slept all morning"—the sexually athletic all-night games that left me red-eyed, exhausted, and remorseful the next day. "Mick slept over. Thank goodness he didn't stay for breakfast. I just wanted to shower and sleep." Friday and Saturday nights I was fucking and sucking and getting fucked up the ass by a horny straight boy; by day, I was calling girls from phone booths and asking them to go steady.

My diary-keeping halted soon after I started high school and stopped having sex with other boys, and it didn't begin again until I fell in love and had sex with a straight male friend at 18. I've kept a diary ever since.

After I'd grown up and moved to San Francisco, I loved nothing better than marching home in the early hours of the morning, sticky in last night's rumpled clothes, lips swollen and cock chafed, to sit at the table with a cup of coffee and record my latest adventure. Gary, a longtime heart throb of my 20s, used to yell sarcastically over his shoulder as he bounded down the stairs to a waiting cab, "I bet you can't wait for me to leave so you can write all this up in your little diary!" The truth is, sex made me want to write, and I wanted to write about sex.

Gay men's urge to write (and read) about sex has been key to the booming erotic anthology market, from Boyd MacDonald's brilliantly unvarnished accounts (my lover and I hadn't been together long before discovering we both owned copies of *Flesh* and *Meat* disbound with time and devotion) to the annual crop of *Bests, Flesh and the Words,* and *My First Times.* We write about our sex in letters, diaries, and stories. This is surely a reaction to that time for all of us when we couldn't write these experiences down, or talk about them, or even let ourselves *think* them. Many of us knew what we wanted very early, but couldn't imagine actually having it: hot, eager, reciprocating male lovers. And when we finally did have sex with another man, we were often so stunned that we had to get it all down on paper—just to believe it ourselves, to fully comprehend it, to never forget it. Many gay men, whether or not they keep a diary or consider themselves writers, have squirreled away in the bottom of a drawer a notebook filled with the white-hot details of an early mind-blowing sexual encounter or affair.

Gay men think more about their sex lives than heterosexuals— before *and* after. They don't fuck with their eyes shut and block it all out as soon as they pull up their pants and tuck in their shirts. They talk it over with friends, and often they write about it, pondering, savoring, and preserving. This volume collects excerpts from the real diaries of gay men writing about their sexual and romantic lives: what happened, how it felt, and how they felt about it. Just as an old snapshot of a sexy, shirtless man does more for my erotic imagination than a slick porn video, for me, six lines of real sex described in a letter or diary are often hotter than the staged encounters worked into the plot of an erotic story. Some of the diary passages that follow uniquely capture a particular milieu in modern gay history. In every case they give us access to the unadulterated event—in writing that is naked, voracious, and above all, honest.

As these entries show, the erotic diary needn't just be a catalog of exploits; it's a place to ponder one's developing sexual identity as well as a romantic memory-house, both celebratory and nostalgic. These frank accounts range from the details of last night's bathhouse romp to poignant recollections of 20-years-past lovemaking. As I've gotten older my diary's usefulness in remembering and interpreting the past has grown; in reading and writing in it, I reflect on who I was and who I am. (It's worth noting that most of the smuttiest passages in *Meat* begin with lines like "This happened many years ago in Chicago....")

Reading over this volume, I realize how much remains untouched, yet how much of importance *is* recorded here: insecurity and the youthful anguish of coming to terms with our unpopular desires, the yearning for love and physical contact, the sheer joy of a passionate night with a stranger, the life-affirming power of sex. These pieces bear witness to the confusion and difficulty of finding love and sexual companionship at any age—for the young man just leaving home, the 30-something man reeling from a breakup, or the middle-aged man on his own. I read the published diaries of gay men—Isherwood, Orton, Rorem—in part to see how another gay man looks at himself a decade or two ahead of me. There are few thoughtful road maps for gay men, and even fewer for gay men past their youth. We wonder in adolescence if there's ever been anyone like us, and we don't lose that need to compare our feelings and experiences to those of other gay men as our lives go on.

My aim for this book was to deliver real, down-and-dirty depictions of gay sex—but I also hoped to find writing with humor, pathos, self-revelation, and insight. I found diaries with all of these things, narrated by voices of horny crowing and tender astonishment. The dateline may be New York, Fire Island, San Francisco, Russian River, Los Angeles, Toronto, Paris, London, Urbino, or Johannesburg. The setting may be a bar, backroom, bath, tearoom, hiking trail, college dorm, the Y, or even a bed, but it always comes down to one love-struck or fucked-out man sitting at a desk or table, writing honestly to himself in his diary:

> He was here last night. I have to talk about that. How nice it was. The nicest lovemaking I remember. The flowing, the same calm I used to feel with D. as I pushed up into him. Buried myself within him. Rocked slowly on my knees, as he lay on his back, eyes closed, jerking off. Squeezing his nipples, as he came in a white gush, and then I came with-in him at the sight of his coming, his semen floating like dew on belly hairs, running over his curled-up hand. The end of his cock so soft and red, pressing out like a flower from the bud of foreskin.
>
> —Andrew Ramer, "My Older Man"

Kevin Bentley
San Francisco, 2001

Jack Bissell
Diary of an Upstate Boy

1982, SUNY College at Oneonta, New York

John: I think I scared John this weekend before I left Albany. I didn't want anything to happen. I just wanted to rub feet and feel him near me. He is so beautiful. In all these years I've never felt this kind of love. John, I miss you and wish we could talk, really talk. I think I should write to you and just let it all hang out. I love you, and I hope you can understand that. Even if you don't love me. I'm simply telling you this because it is a large step in my life, and it took someone like you to make me see that I can love, that I am not a freak with warped desires.

Chris at Oneonta campus: I thought Chris was so amazing-looking the first time I saw him. He is so good to have, not only because he came to terms with his attraction to me, but that he could say it. We're going to live together this summer!—and all that will mean...

1983, Oneonta

Chris: To experience anal sex, to be really fucked up the ass— oh, how sweet! ...How really happy this time is—right now. Here I lie awake, soothed, with beautiful sleepy Chris on his side, breathing lightly, audibly. We talked tonight, sat on Tablerock Cliff. That place has been good to me twice inside a week—bless it. It is blessed. I feel like Siddhartha, seeking enlightenment.

Months later with Chris: Megan. Lovely Megan. Chris likes her—I'm right. Now I believe what I never wished to see before—all his struggle was internalized—he was never there for me.

1984, art school, Urbino, Italy

Claudio the tease: Claudio held me the other day in the piazza and we danced and stood close together like lovers and his cock moved and grew hard behind me. I did not pursue him, but for that day I felt a very pure warmth and fulfillment, and am rather glad only for that—and so public a display of affection!

Alone in my room: I think often of death. Maybe I will die young, I don't know…. I want to live in groves of small dark trees and touch the strange and luminous blue of today's sky.

On the train in Greece: A couple of boys I just passed were so incredible and dressed to the tough-boy/pretty-boy hilt. Little studs. My own Christopher must be getting ravaged down in Athens. I wonder what he does on his own. What a butt that just went by—a rugged Mediterranean kid. I swear, these kids. If you act sexy in the States or dress that way, you must be a fag. *Fuck* the States. I can't wait till I find Chris, that cutie pie.

With Chris in Istanbul: I'm just thinking that we are so lucky to be here together. It goes beyond that we have lived together, that we have traveled, that we can trust and entertain one another and care for one another…. As I write this, I look at his out-of-this-world control, balance, and beauty. The curve as in a high-classical statue of Apollo, the turn of the hip and the angle of the thigh, the mass of flesh just full and curled enough to show a healthy inviting vibrance.

Sometimes I can hardly stand that I love Christopher's body so much when I'm dealing with his person…. I'm going to jump him now.

1985, SUNY College at New Paltz, New York

Chris: (After a visit to Oneonta campus.) His skin is as soft as a baby's, really supple, and covers a fleshy meaty sort of build, albeit slender in form and proportion. The back of his neck and shoulders are incredible. I was in love with the touch of him. He wanted just the sex.

Fantasy of Marco: Marco, do you love me? Should I put my hand on your crotch without your wanting me to? Would you turn from me in repulsion, cast angry backward glances around the corners of apartment buildings to avoid me? "You had no right!" you shriek from the top of the World Trade Center.

No right. We decide. We act. I have done wrong before, having overstepped the boundaries of what some call respect. But I think it is going for exactly what I want.

Federico: I came home to find Federico from Urbino in my bed. Upon hearing me come in, he wakes up. "Ah, Jack, 'ow are you? Well, it looks like we 'ave to share the bed since I did not bring with me covers." The Greek ideal of physical beauty in the proportion and articulation of the male figure comes into my mind, while Federico sits in the blanket smiling. *"Vieni, Giacomo."* Warm hug. We share this bed. And then it happens. The embrace, the look into one another's eyes, and the kiss that we have anticipated, not without anxiety. But in the instant of that touch—boom! It is incredible. We make tender love for a short while and sleep, to wake together in sunlight, smiling, in one another's arms. Erect dick. Federico.

Relationships: I spend all my time plotting and planning, setting up strategies, whether for paintings or work or especially for romantic encounters. It's a deadly trap for an artist, and one so anxious for love. Why must I prevent love from coming to me? It's like the way I both fight off and depend upon my parents—that's how I deal with relationships. Someday I will come down enough that I can be approached, not be so defensive or in need.

1986, Bellmore, Long Island

Chris: It's strange that tonight I made contact with C.B. after so many consecutive days in which he appeared in my thoughts. I've felt the loss of his camaraderie anew, this time with less of the despair and cloying anger I had experienced during the lengthy process of our separation.... What have I wanted all this time? You. I miss you, Chris.

1987, Williamsburg, Brooklyn

Glenn: We met at Uncle Charlie's bar.... Something did happen, and we talked about taking steps, safe sex, needs. Good things. And we were hot and silly for one another. I saw him for a while, and was building up huge plans and being possessive and sentimental.

Glenn, I am so mad. In your search for the Big Romance you realized I was not the one, but you didn't have enough respect for yourself and faith in me to end or define things in a more direct way. God damn the punishment I've received in your cool departure.

1988, Williamsburg and Manhattan

Jerry: I do feel fulfilled after the recent great trip to Montreal. The basic tenets of my need were met so well in Jerry's closeness, his unbridling (he put it to me!), and his confidence. I think I am on my way, and for however long it lasts, he is the best I've found, the most substantial, a sweetheart, a great friend and lover.

At Jerry's loft: There you are across the room, reading, on this fourth hot, still night in June. There is a languor to your repose and a pointed attention too. Your arm narrows to the wrist in utter grace, Michelangelo in Fruit of the Loom underwear.

1990, Manhattan

Regret: Jerry really exploded against me. I had lost patience and said something cutting: "You'll never get close to me." But he hit me hard when I closed him out of the loft bed. His Aries lunar eclipse when unrealized describes a fit of rage, but the rage stems from other feelings of fear or loss.

1992, Manhattan

Clark Gable: I had such a sad dream last night of meeting Clark Gable. God, he was stunning to look at, not a big guy but very somber and silent. And I had to ride, I think, on a bike, holding his waist, with my mouth against his cool cheek. I kissed him there, and he rubbed against me, letting his slick hair get tousled. And he looked at me smiling, but with the saddest eyes I've ever seen.

1993, Manhattan

Chris unresolved: Seeing old friends from Oneonta at Central Park with Jerry today brought back these feelings of bitterness toward Chris. Back then I felt the taste of humiliation, desire, rage, and above all need…. I remember the last time, when he came to see me in New Paltz. I put a stop to it after that—didn't want to see him on those unfair terms. But on that last night, we were together like dancers beneath our sheets. We knew where to look and love, where to touch. We were like a pair of angels who spoke with no words. That is what I have from you that I still cherish—the best that ever happened to me with a lover to this day.

[Undated page]

I think I remember the first time I had sex—sex that was explicitly clandestine and sexual, erotic. It was too big—I wouldn't let him put it in. I got twigs stuck on my hands and knees, leaves in my hair. I couldn't resist the feeling of arousal and languor that remained long afterwards.

And the first time I made love in bed softly, slowly, with someone I trusted and whose touch and look and laugh thrilled me. We stayed together over 16 hours—lucky us—and watched a light snowfall, and were like puppies at teat, all warm, belly to belly.

Today I lie awake, alone. Light hits my room through a gray Saturday sky, and I've pulled back the cover to look at my body in this light, and remember.

Jim Buck
Fall, 1996

September 5

I've been on campus less than a week, and I've already got the tearoom schedule down—including which to use when. Funny that I've trawled this whole city in search of decent fucks and I've never ventured here. Gold mine.

The library's tough. Fourth floor's best—little or no traffic. Saw a security guard in there today; I ripped a fart so he'd think I was legit. Too bad he wasn't interested. From the view I got of his dick at the urinal, he was pretty well hung. Fat head, dark shaft. No dildo model, but more than enough for me. Looks like he'd taste good. He zipped up and left. Maybe farts scare him.

More action in the basement of the foreign language building. Way too busy in the middle of the day, though. Mostly homos looking for some JO action, but why risk it? I'll try late at night.

September 7

Michael has finally pissed me off. Whining about the fact that I went out with Tori last night instead of him. I asked if he wanted to come along, but he said "No, you'll just be talking about old friends and people and places I don't know." Well, too fucking bad for him. I see Tori about twice a year. If he can't understand that he's gotta take the backseat every once in a while—hello? like I do when we're out with Dan—screw him. If he wants to call me, fine. I'm not calling the motherfucker myself.

A three-month-long headache nearly over.

September 10

Hot fucking damn! Big score at the gym today. Little blond freshman I'd spotted my first day on campus gives me the eye in the locker room, walks off to the steam room. Just finished my workout, so I undressed and followed him. I stopped off in the shower for a sec. Took a stall so I could see the steam room door. He looked out, saw me. I gave him as much of a show as I could. Not too much traffic, except for an older guy three stalls down. Prof-type.

Walked to the steam room half-hard. Just held the towel in front of my crotch, didn't bother to wrap it. Still no traffic to speak of.

The steam room's black, so it's kinda hard to see when you first get in. Eventually I spotted him in the corner, though. Walked over, sat down next to him. Before I could even start cruising him, he leaned over and took me in his mouth. Fuck! I wish I coulda given head that good when I was an undergrad. He was all over it, taking me all the way down, rubbing my nuts, jacking himself off. A one-man band. He had me on the brink in about 20 seconds. I could feel his precome dripping on my leg.

But it wouldn't be sex in a public place without an interruption. The steam room door squeaked, and cockboy sat up, and I started talking to him about the Hapsburgs. He just sorta nodded and mumbled the occasional uh-huh. He obviously hadn't had Western Civ.

The interloper was the guy from the shower. 50-ish. Nice build. Had all his hair. He sat across from us. Dropped his towel and holy shit! That man was hiding some meat!

Freshman wiggled a little like he was going to go, but I leaned against him to keep him there. The older guy started tugging on his nuts, and five minutes later he was full-on hard. I forced blondie back on my dick, and he went right to it. I motioned for the other guy to come on over so I could suck him off myself, but no dice. Too scared I guess. Probably straight.

Two minutes and I was ready to go. I moaned kinda loud and pulled out of the kid's mouth and jacked myself off. I stood and sprayed on his chest. He shot all over my leg. The other guy just groaned, and I turned to see a big load fly halfway across the room. Looked like a big spitwad. Someone could've slipped on it.

Funny how you can have sex in a steam room and everything's

fine, but once you're done, it's suddenly unbearably hot. Like you didn't notice before, but now it's 5 squillion degrees. We all left quickly. Freshman looked like he wanted my digits, but the soccer team had finished practice and the locker room was suddenly crowded. After I'd packed up I waited for him but he'd disappeared.

September 15

No real action. Too busy with my TA duties and study. Note to self: John Donne sucks. But the prof's kinda hot—if he weren't so fucking pretentious. Metaphysical poetry my ass: what he needs is a good old-fashioned butt pounding.

September 23

D Day, Hiroshima, Nagasaki all at once. Michael called, took me out for sushi. I saw some friends at another table and walked over for a chat. Michael stayed at our table.

So I probably stayed too long. Michael was pissed when I got back. Started complaining about how I ignore him. He's partially right, but I expect my friends (including boyfriends) to be able to take care of themselves now and then. Mr. Rogers I'm not.

Didn't talk much during dinner. He was polite enough to wait 'til we we'd left the public eye before starting in on me. And a lot of what he was saying was true, but I didn't care. At that point I just wanted out. I dropped him off and said goodbye and made it abundantly clear that was the last time I'd be seeing him for a while.

Fuck him.

At home, I jacked off to straight porn. What's my fascination with Ron Jeremy? I think it's just his cock. So big and fat and fuzzy—just like him.

September 30

Saw Michael on campus. I was coming out of the bathroom in the basement of the foreign language building. He tried to be a little catty. "I didn't know you were studying French." "No," I said, "Greek." He wandered off, probably toward the library. I feel bad for him and for us, but I don't have the energy to fix it.

No action. Janitor doing his cleanup routine.

October 3

Hot cock action today, but it gets complicated. Rundown: (Mostly not real names—I'm just making 'em up—stereotypical so I can keep 'em straight in my head.)

Abdul: 21-ish, thin, dark, probably Turkish, skinny circumcised cock, kinda preppy, nervous;

Ralph (real name): Late 30s, works in library (I've seen him), red hair, pale, short stubby cock, excellent cocksucker and bottom, stocky baby-bear type;

Chip: 18 or so, very preppy, brown hair, tan, Abercrombie & Fitch clothes, not really cute, but looks like he's got a good body (swimmer?), probably into guys his own age;

Carl: 21-ish, average build, good body, very dark black guy, cock of average length but thick, total freak for sex, doesn't seem like a bottom, but probably would if the situation were right.

Three stalls in use: B, C, D (A's taped off for repairs this week); two urinals: E, F. When I walk in, Chip's in B and Ralph's in C. I grab D, drop my pants, start stroking. Look through hole at Ralph. Very hard. (I guess he'd already scoped out Chip and knew he was OK.) I keep looking, he sees me. Drops to knees. The floor was filthy and probably hadn't been mopped in weeks, but when you're horny, you do what you gotta do and hope Spray 'n Wash can fix everything later.

I reach down and grab his dick. It's fat and oozing juice. He's moaning like it's the best hand job he's ever gotten. I hear B unlock, and Chip scoots around to look through the crack in the door. I look up, get a good look at him; he does the same.

Main door opens. Chip goes back to B. Ralph sits. Abdul comes in, steps up to F. I look through the hole on that side of my stall. His dick's just hanging there. I can see up to his nose. His head turns in my direction. I back away from the glory hole, checking my shadow on the floor to make sure he can see I'm not looking at him. Nothing like some asshole homophobe running to the security desk to ruin a fag's day: "Mama, he's lookin' at me! Wah!"

After a couple of minutes with all of us just sitting there, I look back again, and Abdul's raring to go. I signal Ralph, and this time he stands up, shoves his dick though the glory hole. I suck on it just to get it wet, then start jacking him off. I hear Chip unlock his door and come around to the front again. He looks in, sees me pulling on Ralph's meat, then sneaks a look at Abdul. I lean back as far as I can without letting go of Ralph and peek at Abdul. He's clearly looking at Chip.

The door opens again: Ralph sits down, Chip zips over to stand next to Abdul. Carl walks the length of the room, peeking in my stall and Ralph's. He lingers at my door, eventually takes B.

Ralph's so horned up, he doesn't even wait to see if Carl's cool. Within 30 seconds, Ralph's finger is tracing the rim of the glory hole begging for my dick. He wants a taste of me. I give it to him. His mouth's hot and wet, and I don't feel a single tooth. I know he has 'em, but he's doing a damn good job of hiding the things.

I can't hear what Chip and Abdul are doing, but my guess is that they're beating off. That's what I hear anyway. (Overlooked Zen question: What's the sound of two cocks jacking?) The beating gets faster, and I hear both sigh. Then the urinals flush and zippers zip and they're done. That's what I like about tearooms: quick and easy. You don't have to serve anyone breakfast after you've fucked around in a public restroom.

We keep still while Chip and Abdul wash their hands and exit, just to make sure no one comes in while the door's open. When the coast is clear, I put my dick back through the hole, and then I get the treat of my day: Ralph backs his tight ass up on my dick.

It's a little touch-and-go at first. He's shorter than me and keeps pulling my dick down. I'm chafing against the bottom of the glory hole. I wince a little loud, and he hops off my dick for a second and puts his backpack down and steps up on it. Perfect height.

Carl gets a good look at things, and he's pretty turned on. His door opens, and he comes over to look through the crack at me, and my dick sliding in and out of the glory hole. I can see he's jacking off a nice dick. I'm getting pretty hot, and I probably wouldn't do it if I was thinking right, but I lean over and open the door. His pants are to his knees, so he just kinda waddles on in and shuts the door behind himself. I reach out, grab his cock. I think for a second about having him fuck me while I'm fucking Ralph, but I decide that's a little too decadent for this early in the semester. Maybe later...

Carl squeezes by me and hops up on the toilet seat so I can lean over and suck his dick. Nice and hard, sweet flavor. Little bit of sweat-stink. Very hot.

Another interruption. Door opens, I pull outta Ralph, face the toilet like I'm pissing. Carl squats with his feet still on the toilet seat. I open my windbreaker as wide as I can to hide Carl, just in case someone glances in. I guess Ralph sits back down.

The guy who walks in almost runs to the urinal, unzips, and there's a really long, tense pause. I don't want another guy in the scene right now. Three's perfect. But then I hear the guy sigh big time and piss hitting the urinal and he starts to whistle something stupid. Farts a couple of times—really loud and stinky. Almost enough to turn me off. Carl's laughing with me, though; that helps.

Guy flushes, leaves. I get hard again, stick my dick back through the glory hole. Ralph rides me, and I suck Carl. Ralph gets louder and grunts, and his ass gets tight and I know he's just come. He pulls off my dick—clean as a whistle. Good bottom.

Ralph sits down and collects his thoughts. Carl fucks my face, I jack off. In a minute or two, Carl's grabbing my head and pumping jizz down my throat. Salty taste I love. Makes me come like that. Look down so I can aim between his legs (nice jeans, dark).

No time to whisper sweet bullshit nothings. He hops down, goes to the urinal, pisses, leaves. Ralph and I leave together. Chat a bit. Turns out he's looking for a tennis partner. We're set for next week.

October 9

Went to the movies with Ralph tonight. Saw Michael. Spoke briefly. He was with the blond freshman gym-boy cocksucker. Small fucking world. I glared at the kid just to fuck with him. He tried to ignore me, but I know he was nervous. I think he likes me better than Michael. Maybe that's just my ego, though. My cock's bigger anyway.

Michael sneered at Ralph. He doesn't go for the bearish types, thinks I'm a freak. If he knew Ralph's ass, he'd shut up and how. Wonder if that kid's ass is as good as his mouth. Maybe in a month or two I'll finagle a four-way out of this.

Joseph Manera
Pinballing

June 23, 2000

I'm home for another week or so. I spent the greater part of the day driving around aimlessly by myself. Solitary road time can be overrated: the trip was neither romantic nor lonely. No twangy falsettos commiserated with me on the radio, no roadside billboards advertised uniquely American experiences. Everything was a half-hearted green—not quite summer yet and taking its sweet time getting there.

My unintended destination was Burlington. The last time I was there was three summers ago, slinging brushes and swinging ladders for my summer house-painting business. I had flashbacks of how terrible I was with Massachusetts directions then, how I fell off my chair at the first Student Painters' managers' seminar, and how that summer I rolled all of my problems out like sticky pizza dough and force-fed them to everyone around me. When I drove past the Burlington exits on Interstate 495 in June of '97, being alone on the highway was maddening. I'd speed home at ungodly hours, a tunnel of inky blue sky surrounding me, and think of all of the stupid things I'd do to get people to notice me.

I had no reason to travel to Burlington today, just a nagging desire to flee from home. My dad checked the Nissan's odometer tonight and asked me how I managed to put 200 miles on the car in just one day. He's been nosy lately, asking me pointed questions about where I'm going, what I'm doing, who I've seen, what I'm putting into my body and how much of it. I told him I was looking for sneakers but that everything was too expensive, so I just drove around and around. He nodded. I don't think he believed a word I said.

The plane tickets finally came in the mail this morning. I haven't thought of this move at all, really, but with college just over, I feel like I need to do something dramatic. This should qualify.

I'm in that sloppy haze of doing and not thinking. It's hard to escape from it. I've been a real-life whirligig these past few days, no doubt inspired by mom to some extent. She's been especially twitchy lately. Her latest mission is to load my room with ridiculous, impractical items that will never make it with me to San Francisco: jugs of extra-virgin olive oil, big empty water bottles, four hammers. What does she think I need this shit for? Fortunately, her bustle has distracted me enough to ward off any crippling fears about boarding the airplane.

People are saying I'm courageous for moving away from comfortable things—washing machines that don't require quarters, cousins I see twice a year, ready supplies of elastic bands and aluminum foil and toilet paper. Of course, it's easier saying goodbye when you don't feel like you have much to say goodbye to. I've been contemplating the existence of this "not much" lately. Where did this lack come from? It's not so conveniently attributable to the places I've been. It's too easy to blame Hanover, N.H., and Cranston, R.I., for a dearth of satisfying activity. I'm afraid that this "not much" is somewhere in me, is me, and has coiled itself inside my stomach to stay.

June 24, 2000

I got my laptop in the mail today and promptly tore it open and installed AOL. It's probably a good thing I didn't have Instant Message at school. One 70-year-old guy sent me a photo of his prick, all gray and wrinkly like an elephant's trunk. He had a link on his profile to a picture of himself masturbating. He was curled up, with such an awful grimace, his body arched like a Halloween cat.

Otherwise, not much today. …I tried to see a movie with Lisa, a sneak preview of *The Perfect Storm*. The trailers are full of *GQ* men wearing grizzle the way some girls slip on their mother's pumps. Fortunately, or unfortunately, the movie was sold out.

Lisa and I tried to have one of those big talks we're usually so good at having, but we just ate Ben and Jerry's and chatted about how we both need to go to the gym but are ultimately much more content wolfing down gobs of mint-and-cookie-dough ice cream.

I think Lisa is aware of me editing my feelings in front of her. Lately, all she can do is comment on how quiet and secretive I've been. But what can I do? I'm horned out of my fucking mind and don't really want to tell big sis how I want to jump the UPS man and lick his calves.

June 25, 2000

I had some success with AOL. I'm meeting a guy tomorrow night. We didn't chat long, but I like him. Reasons:

* He didn't ask for a picture of my wiener.
* He didn't ask about the size of my wiener or the shape of my wiener or whether my wiener hangs right or left on full moons.
* He didn't ask me to take out a ruler to measure my wiener or to stick it up my ass.
* He's 32. I prefer odd numbers, but I do like to challenge myself every now and then.
* He managed to be funny without using those pesky smiley faces—colon, dash, closed parenthesis.

So I don't know if this guy is something special, or if I'm especially pathetic. Hopefully it will be a good time.

I told mom and dad that I'll be seeing Sharon tomorrow night. *"You know, Sharon from high school? With the thing she always wears in her hair? You know, SHARON? Shazz!"* They said of course they know Sharon, a sweet girl, really, although they've never laid eyes on her.

June 27, 2000

I met Todd last night. My first impression of him was that he was handsome and together and probably wouldn't like me. He has ridiculously blue eyes, which I thought were colored contacts at first, but then he put on a pair of glasses. He was a bit frazzled when I walked in—he was searching for his keys—and he barely acknowledged my presence when I slipped through the door.

Todd's apartment is small and tidy, and he has had photographs he took in Italy enlarged and framed. He's a very respectable amateur photographer. The picture I liked the best was of a village at night with all these sparkling lights and a man, barely visible, sitting on a bench in front of a building lighting a match. You can see his thumb because it's the same pale yellow as the streetlights, but only after detecting it are you able to map the rest of his body.

Todd leaves the television set on all the time (the History Channel) but never watches it. I asked if he was trying some osmosis experiment and he said no. It keeps him company, he said. I admired his forthrightness but felt embarrassed for him and for myself when I've done such things to stave off loneliness.

We went to a Greek restaurant on Thayer Street and sat outside. Everything I ate managed to find its way out of my mouth. I can't be trusted to consume food in public. I was blabbering on so much about school and San Francisco that chunks of gooey lamb and rice splattered on my plate periodically. The only thing to do in such situations is to call attention to it, so I did. *"I'm a slob! A pig! Look at what a dirty little piggy I am! See that? Oink. WOW!"* Very classy. But I didn't want Todd thinking that I was so coarse that I didn't realize gyro was forming a two-way street between my mouth and my plate. For his part, he smiled and nodded his head. He didn't scowl, nor did he engage in any long, throaty, feigned laughter.

I bumped into an old lady after I excused myself to go to the restroom, and she said "Hey, watch it, buddy," which is such an ungranny thing to say. Todd laughed, and I thought maybe he was beginning to find me charming.

* *

He has an easy sense of humor. He talked about how he used to be a waiter, and he mocked the Brown University kids that would walk into the Florentine Grill wearing thrift-store threads and then order $100 bottles of Cabernet. We spoke about our hobbies and interests. Todd likes this television show I have never seen where all of the characters fuck like beautiful, rich folk are wont to do and then gather together at the end of each episode to say terribly clever things about their experiences. Our topic of conversation turned to turn-ons. Todd said he's a kissing slut. I was pleased to hear that, but it sounded like saying you're a soda alcoholic.

He told me about how he used to be a camp counselor, and how he used to really, really, really, REALLY love it. "Really?" I asked. I was expecting stories of fucking in tents and guys in little puce shorts eating out each other's asses, but all of his anecdotes were about "team building." He told me this one story about a kid who was a mess at the beginning of camp—wiped his nose with his sleeve, brought a math workbook to lunch, and was generally such a hopeless dork that I immediately identified with him and wanted to hear that he turned out OK. He did. The kid was kissing groovy chicks and riding a motorcycle by the end of the summer. Just like *Grease 2*.

Todd and I took a long walk afterward, and then we both needed to piss. I started to skip every fourth step or so. It felt appropriate. I was happy, and skipping and happy go hand in hand. Tra-la-la! I wanted to hold his hand but didn't. Todd thought he knew of a park nearby where we could sneak a leak, but it turned out that the park was about three miles away. So he talked about history, and I admitted I don't know much about history. Or geography. Or biology. Or much of anything. I asked him what his favorite time period in history was and he said medieval. I got a vision of him in tights and one of those large plumed caps. It wasn't such a bad image.

We went back to his place and talked more, about art and Rhode Island and being queer. I called my house at 11 to tell my sister to inform my parents that I was alive and would probably be home after they fell asleep. *"That Sharon is such a talker! Shazz! Shasta!"* I sat on Todd's couch and said "so" and "um" a great deal, the sounds separated by seemingly infinite stretches of ellipse. When he finally touched my thigh, he tilted his head in a manner that suggested I needn't have worried about whether or not he wanted to touch me. "I just wanted to be sure," I said. I wrapped my legs around him and pulled him into me. He seemed a little surprised.

Todd's kissing is triple exclamation points and every kind of positive hyperbole. Nice and rough, but he didn't rape my tongue. Properly placed, like someone gave him a map of my mouth in advance, checking off all of the fun places to visit. Not sloppy. Smooth. Not too much saliva. Moist. Not too slow. FAST! He didn't try to reach my tonsils. He just worked his tongue inside and outside of my mouth like he was trying to sew my lips together.

He scooped me off the couch and started unbuttoning my shirt while he walked me toward the bed. I worked on removing his pants, then his sweater, then the rest of it. Everything except for his underwear. I grabbed Todd's hand and sucked his fingers and watched him get hard under his boxers just from that. He kissed my belly. I was ticklish and almost fell off of the bed. I grabbed his hair in clumps when I kissed him in return and fell back into the bed in a ball. He slithered on top of me so that my knees touched his chest.

There was comic howling outside, the neighbor's dog. I thought it was funny, but this racket put me at ease, like I was in a bed in a home where I belonged. I put my lips on Todd's dick. He lay back and grabbed the sides of the bed tightly. He squeezed the insides of my thighs, right below my cock, and found his way inside of me so expertly that I didn't remember him even trying to get in.

We both came twice. He was sleepy when we were through. He said he wanted to see me again for sure. I wanted to stay but couldn't. I left at around 3:30 in the morning and wondered where all of the other cars on the highway were going.

I sneaked into my room quietly at 4:00. This is the high school student I never was: slipping into and out of strangers' beds, tiptoeing through my house to avoid waking my parents, planning the story I'll tell about my evening instead of the truth. I lay down in my second bed of the night, this one big and dry as a desert, and fell asleep feeling like a very adult teenager.

June 28, 2000

Realization: Todd is the first mature man that I've been with. No chicken shit or bullshit or any of the other varieties of shit. No bizarre sexual fetishes. No wild mood swings. No canned laughter.

I called Todd and asked if he wanted to do coffee. We met at the Starbucks near his apartment. I was talking about my dad and asked him about his. His dad died when he was 8. He told me about being raised without a father, and he was entirely unsentimental about it while still speaking of the man with a great deal of warmth in his voice. Twenty years later, he says he doesn't think of him all that much, but that when he does he feels like there's a hole in him somewhere. This made me insanely attracted to him. A handsome, smart, well-adjusted man that has experienced and bravely dealt with tragedy.

On the flip side, I wonder if Todd thinks I'm anything more than a charming diversion. I want him to think I'm more. Speaking to him today I wanted him to respect me more than anything. I played out a little scenario in my head where Todd introduces me to his friends, and smiles when I say smart things and laughs when I say funny things. All of the people in my daydream were wearing sports jackets or casual summer dresses. They'd make comments like "a fine young man" and "you've got yourself a pot of sugar" to Todd in my presence. They'd say hushed things to Todd, too, their heads bowed down. "What a butt!" they'd whisper, thinking I wasn't able to hear them. Oh, but I was!

It was a beautiful picture with beautiful people. I just had no idea who any of them were.

June 30, 2000

I met Todd in the city last night after he was through with work. He was tired, and I became more aware of something I had noticed the first time we met: He has a serious, pained face that seems to collapse into a frown when he thinks no one is looking. Exhausted from work, he made less of an effort to disguise this today. Or maybe he just feels more comfortable with me.

We duplicated our first date. We ate dinner, walked, and then went back to his place. But this time there were long, rough patches of silence in the conversation. Todd is starting to hate his job and his apartment and Providence. All I could do was listen.

At his apartment, Todd grabbed the collar of my shirt, led me to his bed, and threw me on it. He unbuttoned my shirt quickly, my pants more quickly, and fell on top of me fully clothed. I had to struggle to free up my hands so that I could unbutton his shirt.

His body pushed mine into the mattress. It felt like he wasn't looking at me. I couldn't tell if I was supposed to be upset or excited by his disregard. My body opted for the latter.

I'm in love with Todd's body—the way it stretches, the thickness of him; how when he takes off his shirt, you know that he had massive, spreading freckles as a kid. How his hands are big and warm. How he digs into my flesh like a bear scooping honey. He makes me feel wildly, preposterously sexy.

We came at the same time. I lay on his bed naked while Todd sat up, his back to me, his shirt hanging open. He looked grumpy. I asked him if I did anything wrong. It took him what felt like a full minute to say no.

July 1, 2000

I saw Todd again last night. It's the last time I'll see him until I return home for Christmas.

Todd said so many things that I disagreed with but allowed to roll by unprotested. We were talking about things that make people unhappy, and he said that people are always able to control their moods, that it's only a matter of will power. What surprised me is that his saying this didn't make him any less attractive to me. I momentarily hated him for it, and I hated that I was willing to shut down parts of myself so easily. I'm ashamed that a fair share of my eagerness to please with Todd is due to the fact that he's so good-looking. I'm more than a bit of a hypocrite. I complain about men I'm attracted to not being attracted to me in return, more often than not assuming that it's because I'm not classically handsome. Then I meet an attractive guy who seems to like me, and I edit myself like a moth-erfucker. I argued with Todd weakly, just so I didn't feel like I had completely willed myself away. I said that sometimes people just feel like shit BECAUSE. There's no explanation for it. It comes on you like a drive-by shooting; sometimes you get one bullet, and some-times you get 50.

I let my age show.

As if this weren't distressing enough...I told Todd that he was the first guy I could stomach giving a blow job to since what happened last summer, and he shot me a look that suggested I shouldn't have volunteered this information. I've replayed scenes from that experi-ence in my mind a lot lately—being forced to do things I didn't want to do, appalled at how my own lack of confidence and common sense got me into that situation in the first place. I thought it would feel good to finally talk about it with someone. I didn't go into detail. It just made us seem that much more impossible. I'm going away anyway, and now he's going to start seeing me as pitiful, a victim. I feel like the whole impression of intelligence, humor, and sexiness that I've worked to build for him and for myself has been obliterated. Do I actually possess these things, or am I cobbling together quick, pale substitutes to mask being their opposites?

When we got back to his place, I put my head in his lap for a little bit and then started to run my fingers through his chest hair. He told me it was late, that he was tired and I should go home. It was 2 in the morning. He would E-mail me in San Francisco. He wished me luck. *"I admire you. I really do. I think you're a lot like me."* It sounded like: *"You're a kid. And you're confused. Look out for drive-by shootings, Joe."*

Driving home I realized that I'm nothing like Todd. At all. And I am not OK with this.

July 2, 2000

I talked to Lisa tonight about Todd. I wanted her perspective. She listened and didn't say anything for a while, and then remarked "Gee, you must really like him." Why should this sound like such an unusual thing?

Lisa asked about our future, and I said I would love to keep in touch with him and so on and so forth, but I don't see this happening at all. I'm almost afraid of meeting him again. I came close last night to telling him I could easily fall in love with him. I held myself back. I assume he doesn't feel the same way.

I'm starting to question if Todd actually even liked me. Looking back on my entries these past couple of days, I'm appalled at how little perspective I have on him, and how I've spent so much time obsessing over my feelings and my perceptions of the experiences. I don't know this man very well. I know that I enjoy him. But maybe I should be looking for something else.

I had a surge of panic in the car today that hit me fast and hard. I started thinking that if I were to stay in Rhode Island, Todd would eventually stop speaking to me altogether and begin regarding me as a pest. I can picture him looking at me contemptuously, serious face turned mean. He has it in him, I think, to completely cut me down.

Lisa thinks I'll meet thousands of guys as cold and beautiful as Todd in San Francisco. I don't like this, that there could only be so many types of people, that thousands of Todds and thousands of Joes are pinballing off of each other, colliding and parting and never quite getting anywhere. It's funny, I guess. I know I've been hit, I just don't know what hit me.

I'm glad I met this Todd and not some asshole Todd, if this is the way things are to be—a multiplicity of Todds, a multiplicity of Joes. I already miss his body, his presence. I want to see him again and let his mouth go exactly where it wants to, so that I can smell him on my skin and have a diary of this experience on my body. And right now I want to have that with *this* Todd, and not with any other.

Doug Jones
Quick Black Ants

In a box under my bed I keep my journals, including the one I wrote as an 18-year-old exchange student in Italy, in 1982-1983. It is a pretty blank book of the kind that fill the racks near the cash registers of our better card shops, much worn and completely full of abstract musings. It did not contain what follows. At some point during that introspective and isolated year, I started keeping, in a freebie day diary from a bank, a secret journal. I only filled a few pages, which I tore out when I left, discarding the binding. I found the secret diary pages in a bag of loose papers dating from the same period. On them I agonized over things I had previously grappled with, aided by Vaseline, in the flesh. For while I'd had sex—quite a bit, in fact as a boy—that winter words substituted for acts, invading even my fantasies. One of the few actual events mentioned in my journal, an open-air screening of Visconti's Ludwig, sticks out in my mind for what I didn't write. As the first on-screen man-to-man kiss of my life lit up above me with all the force of an explosion (I can feel it still), a friend leaned over and hissed, "I knew it! A fag! I can smell 'em a mile away."

In spite of the way these barely edited, undated entries end, I didn't have sex the entire year.

* *

And so I begin. Writing is such a commitment, as if by expression a thought comes into existence, becomes concrete. I feel the need for this, though: We'll call it my fag diary. In it I will at last commit to and explore the facets of my homosexuality. So am I resentful that society rejects what I am? Or am I secretly glad, since it justifies my own rejection of society? Justifies—or precipitates? I don't know. I can only say I'm glad I've begun. It's as if I'm finally giving birth to another part of myself, letting myself be born.

Am I hoping that by evacuating all of this I might be rid of it? That as if draining off pus or squeezing a zit I could cure, or be cured? I think I accept it. It makes me what I am—but so do good teeth and skinny shoulders. HOMOSEXUAL. I AM HOMOSEXUAL. It's so hard to write it. I guess some things are hard. Something strikes in my stomach as I read it, as I write it, sometimes as I feel it.

Is this my defiant act of coming out of the closet? Such a stupid term but then I tend to be biased—most of those terms offend me. *Gay* is one thing I am not—to me it connotes a lifestyle that, if a little radical, would still restrict me as an individual, just as any social group label does. If this is my exit out of the closet, at least it is controlled. I have a choice. It's just that now there is not only me but another expression of me, a concrete expansion.

I sometimes feel what is obviously lust in the classic sense. I just want to grab a guy and stick my cock up his ass. Even as I do it, I have to force myself to write those words, and they shock me, but I enlist honesty as long as it serves me, and beyond that there's always silence. A little shock hits me when I come home & see this book.

My fantasy for the day: A spectacular-looking, spectacularly dressed guy got on the bus and stood, as if unconscious, all the way to my stop. I later imagined myself stepping forward, tilting my head, and kissing him full on the lips, maybe putting one hand on his shoulder and the other in his crotch—which is all rather unusual since kissing is not usually something that "turns me on"—I sort of consider it reserved for love. In fact, before I actually did it (kissed), the idea rather revolted me. From this I created a dream: that I kissed him but could awaken no response, then took out his cock & balls— an impression of largeness & heaviness—I sucked, and again no response, and then I'm kissing again, and from his mouth bursts semen, or on a parallel course his mouth finally opens, and from it into me quick black ants, small & senselessly busy.

Will my fear lead me to destroy this? Should these things be written? For an American sex is such a huge "last frontier"—perhaps this is the only way to exorcise that element from myself.

Is anyone guilty of my existence? An inevitable progression from a certain point, but are my shoulders any more suited to bear the guilt? And "if they knew," no one would want to hurt me, but oh, how it hurts to learn so innocently, so unconsciously early, that you can't be what you are. The jokes and disgust that you cannot take personally but do, because you feel that way in part yourself. Should I be happier that I was taught to hate myself? Denial the teacher, forceful but true, sharp—if one does not, cannot, understand what one has unless he is without, perhaps you can only learn what you are when you can't be it. I don't know, but to sink into resentment is such a common error—or worse, that of K.C., vengeance. He told his parents that they had failed, but by placing the blame, he lost perhaps forever the chance to understand. By placing the blame he too receives an equal share. He should understand no one is to blame; we are all guilty. Oh, what Greek tragedy, what a tragic flaw. Bullshit. Face your enemy. Walk into fear. My only tragic flaw is that I'm human.

Those deceptively baggy pants that sack upward and then clasp around tight at the top of the butt; those two little curves—as if carved there, as emphasized by wet material.

The Italians are a people made for sex. Christ, racially inherited sensuality.

It's fascinating to be an object of attention, female sexual interest, but I can't help being a bit clinical, because it just doesn't do anything for me. And at this point it's a disadvantage (I think) looking younger than I really am. Christ, it doesn't seem to matter. I often feel as if I'm invisible, but I suspect it is mutual fear. Everyone is afraid to commit himself, to make the admission, and I understand because I am too. Staring at asses while on the bus, at faces with 5 o'clock shadow. Frustration.

Attraction is such a fascinating thing. (Why? Is it mutual? Physical? Spiritual? How can you so securely deny the value of first impressions in the negative sense and be so willing to accept them in the positive?)

I see in myself certain characteristics that could age into sissy effete fagginess—the tendency to arrange things, close cupboard doors—and beyond that I have a fear of aging alone, 40–50, like Cory, and losing the physical appeal so necessary to the homosexual game—a game I don't even want to play. It remains to be seen whether or not I must.

An interesting reaction. One of the (very few) sexually appealing males in the school comes toward me. I can't even look at him.

I can see it as if a scene in a movie: a subtle stylish double-take as the guy with a face like a pig stands up to reveal, in down-home terms, a whopper. Grey corduroy pants, Christ, that's the only thing it could have been but what a cock! How can you be sure of things like that? Go up and ask if you could borrow his newspaper, then point? The stunned expression on my face must have been visible to all.

I've just never been comfortable in those intimate male atmospheres, perhaps because I'd rather fuck some of the "boys" than recount my conquests.

A bearing—one of containment—smooth and controlled: the set mouth, the smooth-smooth walk, hands placed somehow specifically in a position of closure. I wonder if it's defensive.

It's true, if with minor exaggeration, that I have the girls licking my shoes—the only problem is that I'd rather have the boys licking something else.

Watching *Ludwig,* I feel a great deal of empathy—fucking servants and actors: it must have been horrible; absolute power that was actually absolute servitude—to have been given that sort of power and borne the expectations that came with it.

Sex at this point is the urge, the need to have an orgasm, a little reward of tawdry pleasure. Sex with D.W. was a small step above masturbation—essentially the same thing, but with more realistic sensation. I want to make love, to give & give. With K.C. it was different, but came at a time entirely too emotionally threatening. It was probably a mistake, but I didn't feel that disgust, the need to get away—my spirit has always known my compromise. It has always known: I felt guilty not because I was doing an unchristian thing, but because I committed a sin against myself—and there is no higher god. But the times I enjoy masturbation are when I am making love to myself, when I enjoy myself for what I am, not pretending anything.

I sit in a group of people and there is always someone good-looking. Just sitting there, fascinated by jawlines & 5 o'clock shadow & eyes & cheekbones & backs & hands & asses—mental rape.

Is Marcus really flirting with me, as he seems to be? Why did I start to get a hard-on as I shaved?

How many years has my obsessive drawing of female (rarely male) nudes been an outlet for my sexual (i.e. homosexual but disguised) desires?

Had a dream with D.W.—pretty sad.

What has changed now with Marcus knowing and gone? I can't tell, but tonight on the bus there was the guy I saw twice while Marcus was here; my God, he is the most beautiful male I've ever seen. Wow.

Those two guys (gays) whom Marcus & I sat across from in the café—what a price they were paying for their "freedom," their eyes, those hurting eyes. They looked bruised from the inside out, or like holes into a dark place of pain—denial. I wonder if I came off as a cock tease? They never smiled. My God, what's it worth when it's all so sad? Are my eyes like that? And is it my imagination, or does my bus man have them?

God, he's beautiful. I was struck from the moment I met him, those pale sea eyes that put you into a tilted distant place, a place he came from with such ease, but the feeling remains that more of him is there. And the hands—he has such a masculine (totally unfaggy) grace, except when he's standing and adjusts his crotch. Christ, that drives me crazy (not lust—it's so threshold pubescent).

Today I ran onto the bus from Mario's bar, and there he was in the backseat. I haven't been so shocked—my God, I almost died. And I was so close, and when I got off the bus he was looking back out at me (?) and I couldn't look directly back. Oh, God.

Andrew Ramer
My Older Man

Monday night, 4 October 1976

It is already too late to go back and capture the eerie, wonderful sense I had as events unfolded. From moment to moment, when something happened I would say—"Oh, yes, that is what happened next. Of course." As if it were all preordained and then forgotten, like a dream.

Sylvia and I were sitting on the couch, her legs on mine. We were talking and drifting the way two people can who, complete strangers, have found themselves sharing a lonely beach house for a week, cooking, cleaning together. She's a coworker of my neighbor Rebecca, who told me about this place. I arrived on the 19th. Sylvia was there already. We became an instant husband and wife. There was no sex. I drifted toward it. Knew it could happen, happen easily and be a nice event. But I felt it was not important, and we stretched apart, more reluctantly on her part, I think.

She: [*Yawn*] "I'm so tired. I have to go to bed." But not getting up.

Me: [*Yawn*] "Oh. I have to go all that way home alone." Standing in the doorway for a very long time, before I went down the hall to my little room.

But we became close in an easy sort of way. The shopkeepers acted as if we were married, and we did nothing to protest. The married role acted as a bridge over our discomfort.

So on Saturday the 25th we went to look for houses together. And the realtors acted as if we were a couple, although it was Sylvia who was looking for the rental for next summer. She hadn't wanted to look beyond meeting with the woman who had shown her our house. But I (what was it to me?) persuaded her to try other realtors. There were four more at that end of Fire Island. We talked to two, both of them

28

older women. One fat, washed out, and riding a giant tricycle. The second, hair half-dyed red, for whom every house was "superb," "truly magnificent," "a fabulous house."

The third realtor wasn't home, so we went to try the last one. A wooden gate. A fence on the street. I remembered hearing voices behind it one night and saying to myself—"A gay fence."

So we went in. Across the deck. French doors. Chairs, couches in a half circle facing them. Three people talking. Two men. A woman. One man the realtor. Bearded. Dark. Open shirt. Smile a little bit too big.

Later Sylvia and I talked about him. Seems he was the mirror image of the great love of her life, and she was certain that he kept looking at her. Not realizing they were business eyes. When she left to go back to the city on Sunday she gave me her card to give to him. To ask him to call her if something turned up.

So I went Monday afternoon—what did I know? With her card. With a pad, a pen—and for luck, Oscar Wilde. "Oh, what are you reading?" Who knows?

The gate was open. He was home. I planned to pop in and out. Didn't sit down. His too-nice smile a turnoff. But he asked me if I wanted coffee. He exchanged his business smile for a warm one. And we talked and talked. Why did I talk so much? Squirming as the coffee rushed through my empty stomach. And I had to piss. And our talk danced out across the air. Taking cautious, curious, tiny chances.

He: "I like to walk. I walk in Greenwich Village a lot." (Oh, the Village.) "And go dancing in Cherry Grove." (Oh, the Grove. Gay? But still no indication.)

Me: "I keep meaning to go out there, but I've never made it. Friends of mine are staying there." (A lie, later recanted.)

Life, self, sense of self. I mentioned the upheaval. Going to India. Not going. Later I wove back to it and said, "He and I were going to India." He and I. Still his face was quiet, and he sat there in his underwear: white boxers and white undershirt. Would a straight man do that?

And finally, when it seemed as if both our bladders would burst, he got up, asked if I was gay, to which I answered "Yes."

"Great. Fantastic," he said, a boyish smile turning his bearded face into a sunflower.

As he went to piss, I sank back into the hours of waiting. Of waiting, after David and I broke up, and he went off to India without me. I heard myself telling Cathy and Ellen—"I wait. I just wait. I always wait. And then something happens. Never quickly. Always oddly. Someone turns up. As if all the waiting were an unfolding."

So had I slept with Sylvia, she would never have given me her card to give to him. Without her card I would never have returned alone. For a chance. How many faces have I passed up? How many smiles?

He went to piss, and I thought about waiting. Looked around at the beautiful home that I sat in. Embracing. Familiar. A part of him.

Time moves from place to place. But I cannot sort out the time into perfect chronological order. It exists as a pearl exists, round and glowing.

A sense of him, and a calm unsettling sense that he and his house were always a part of my experience. I could say—I will never be the same for having met him. I will be changed. And yet I felt as if I had already and always been changed in meeting him, as if I'd always met him, and always knew it. That coming to this place meant I had always been here.

There are no connections. Only the purity of moments remains. Tumbling in bed. Sexuality diffused. Ungenital. Clutching. Nuzzling. Holding. Warm. Close. Frustrating and yet not caring that it wasn't HOT.

Touching. Freedom of touching. Silent. Riding bicycles over sandy paths. Laughing as they bog down. Walking. Riding over an empty highway; me frightened as he rides beside me, wanting to touch.

On the beach as the sun sets. The sea lit in orange and green. Hugging in the sand. Living what had been a dream of possible, but not likely. Only not a dream. But real. Quiet. Warm. I spent the rest of my vacation with him. Will go back this coming weekend.

Tuesday, 11 October

Pills. Special K did he call them? I, the old puritan, gave in. Drifting across wine and the bed. As if the world had turned to water. Giving myself into it. Tumbling. Falling. Feeling the mind twist and untwist. Spinning as if I were a top. Changing faces. Being man woman fish. Man woman fish. Growing a face in the back of my head—woman. Red lipstick. Orange hair. Then my own face. Twisting. Spinning. Twisting from one to the other. As below a great merman's fin writhed and twisted on the bed.

A bridge. Twilight. Bicycles. Him. The sun a soft wet giant orange disk settling slowly behind the graceful bridge lines.

At night I could not sleep. Wrapped in a blanket, soft as satin, I came out to the living room. Still dark, but the dawn was slowly creeping up. Spreading frail pastel fingers through the dark pine and willow trees. And there were four French doors between us. Each pane a window onto magic. A trembling Japanese screen. Alive. The light glowing on the floor. Ribbons of light stretching out to us. Quiet. Wrapped in a satiny blanket on the couch. Everything hushed. Everything trembling. All seen. All seen before. As if from a dream so real. And so unreal.

Or now, lying naked on the deck. Legs entwined. Sun embraced. Hot. Too hot. I move over in the shade and write.

a deck

bend down when entering
beneath pine bough
rise up
in a forest

from our bed
arisen
the white of me sown
spent lingering
in his slumber

i rose
i rose above him
i sank into his ass
with sweat, with sigh
with desire

i rose out of bed
his beard
a pillow on the pillow
face ruffled
lace trembling breath

as i held him
there was no him
no i
there was holding going on
there was oneness
i had to open my eyes
to see what part of him
some part of me was touching
shoulder—no, cheek
hand on mine—no, leg

the body used itself
without being itself
arm went beyond arm
lip beyond lip
head beyond head
two hot thick chocolate syrups
flowing across each other
over the bed

he sleeps
and now i write
pen moving back

into our loving
as it scatters cloud-lines
on the page
scrawl to children
words to readers
memory

a tree trembles
from two birds
the sun
sultana
peers at me through veils
i put the pen down
i return to him

Sunday, 24 October

Five uninterrupted days of being together.

Monday, 1 November

"Poppers," he called them. How amazing. One sniff in each nostril, a feeling of dust in the throat. A cough. And suddenly, the two of us are clutching, hugging, writhing across the bed like two enormous snakes. Pressing, holding, slimy, slippery, delicious, and wet. Endlessly wet. Two water creatures, every cell of our bodies like octopus suction cups, drawing, pressing, clinging to each other. Wet. Endlessly wet. And then suddenly exhausted. Falling back. Tossed up on the beach of time again. Arms around each other. Panting.

He asked me what I thought of him. "Tender, warm, manly, gentle, a little weird," I said. "What do you think of me?"

"I think you're beautiful."

My dream—to be beautiful: I always wanted that—and when he said it, I thought—*How nice, but what else? Is that all you think?*

Sunday, 7 November

Where does desire come from? Why do certain people excite us, while others leave us cold, indifferent, or perhaps a little curious? What is it that makes me like Ron? I have always asked that question and gotten no answer—but oddly—never asked the most perfectly obvious question—what in Ron makes me like him?

His looks. His smile. The all-at-once mature and childlike quality of his behavior, and the way it moves across his face like clouds over a field, changing color from mood to mood. His lips tightening, turning up into a little knot when he is hurting. Cocking his head and showing a 7-year-old's smile, full of trust, curiosity, and caution. As if the boy in him were completely frozen, pure and intact, to reemerge at certain moments from a cool, detached, and overly friendly, capable face. He'll seem so dull, and I'll ask myself what am I doing here—when all of a sudden some bit of wisdom will pour out, polished as marble, clear as is possible. And his house—not every man is so fine, so sensitive an artist as to be able to make such a house, where wood, trees, windows, light, all combine to show off the best of each other, the best of space. We are so different—and yet so what? It is too soon to be thinking of marriage. Time only to be thinking about being together.

Wednesday, 10 November

Ron called last night. How embarrassing after so intense an eight-day time together to not be able to recognize his voice on the phone. Oh, on the phone he sounded like 34. So old, without his face, without his smile to fill him out.

How nervous I am, how scared, to be alive, to care. To take chances with an organ as fragile as the heart. The unknown is terrifying, but it is, I suppose, the only real thing. To admit that there is no way in the world that I could know what is going to happen between us. And if I did—why do it? I'd already have the knowledge. No—life is composed the right way.

Saturday, 13 November

Already the nervousness begins. He was here last night. I have to talk about that. How nice it was. The nicest lovemaking I remember.

The flowing, the same calm I used to feel with D. as I pushed up into him. Buried myself within him. Rocked slowly on my knees, as he lay on his back, eyes closed, jerking off. Squeezing his nipples, as he came in a white gush, and then I came within him at the sight of his coming, his semen floating like dew on belly hairs, running over his curled-up hand. The end of his cock so soft and red, pressing out like a flower from the bud of foreskin.

But now he called and maybe he will come. Maybe not.

Monday, 15 November

The weekend went by so fast. Too fast. After the anxiety of Saturday night, with its storm warnings inside and out, Sunday morning arrived. And although I waited for the phone to ring and Ron to say, "I changed my mind," it never rang, and at 8 A.M., on schedule, he arrived. The ride out was so fast, and beautiful. The clouds so thick and sun-glowing. We went food shopping. Boarded the ferry—but from the moment we arrived time seemed to compress itself. I think I enjoyed myself, but it all went by so fast I felt gypped. As if I'd prefer the slow heavy movement of depression, plodding through time, so that I'd feel as if I'd gotten my money's worth of every agonizing moment.

I painted for a few hours while Ron showed houses. Laying out colors. Experimenting, feeling the less cerebral pleasure of creating without words. What I made was dull and uncraftly, but I enjoyed it. And I enjoyed painting Ron a new sign. We made love. Watched television. Ate. But later in the evening he fell into a mood he would not talk about. So I went down to the beach. The moon was out, almost full, and hit the water in such a way that it looked like mercury pouring in. The sky was clear, so easy to see. I felt almost as if I were really seeing for the first time. The shadows of trees in a streetlight, falling upon the sidewalk, leaping in the wind—only a shadow and yet so full of life. I nearly cried from it.

Today rushed by, clients in and out. No time to be alone or talk. And then I had to leave early to catch a train

Monday, 22 November

He was here, and he is gone. I wrote him a letter saying how raw and vulnerable I felt in wanting to know him. He said he wants to know me also. But he also said he was so fucked up, and I might get hurt. And I said I wanted to try and know him anyway.

Saturday, 27 November

As we are eating spareribs in Minsky's after several Black Russians and a joint—he says to me, "Sometimes you're so cute, I want to eat you up." "Please do," says I. And we walk home in the pouring rain, huddling under my umbrella, set off from the world in a tenderness we would not otherwise allow ourselves in public. Behind a wall of rain, a little nervous at first, following footsteps with our ears, and then falling into a silent closeness, his arms around me, mine around him, his head on my shoulder, my head resting on top of his.

Making love had a kind of awkwardness to it. It felt all right to not be "good." My cock fell out of his ass just as I was about to come. I couldn't get it back. I came between his legs. So what.

I like him. It's easy to be with him. "You don't have to do anything to please me. I don't want you to. Just be yourself," he said.

Monday, 29 November

I wake up thinking of him. What a delicious, dangerous energy. And is he thinking of me? He who hasn't called as I haven't called him

I don't want just a relationship. I think there is more than that. Relationships end when the ease of relating stops. I want more than that. I want a marriage. A structure large enough to safely include relating and not relating without it collapsing.

Sunday, 5 December

Ronnie and I were lying up in the loft above his living room. A place we had never been in together before. We were lying in each other's arms, clothes on, penises pressing into each other's crotches, hugging each other, pressing against each other, rubbing cocks against each other in a hard continuous rhythm. And I felt something building up in me. A warm expanding feeling that built up within me. A deep, internal radiating feeling that kept time with my increasing breaths and sighs, and then suddenly seemed to build up and burst within me, in what I can only describe in the words I used to Ronnie after the intensity of it passed. "I felt," I said, "as if I had come all over the inside of my body."

Such a strange, nice, comfortable, uncomfortable weekend. We talked several times about living together. About my coming out and working with him. And I think I am entirely capable of separating the fantasy of it from the potential in it. Admitted I wanted to do it, but not yet.

Sunday, 12 December

So another chapter in my life is over. Ron: "I don't feel romantic about you anymore." I clung to hysterics for a while, guilt for a moment, but it all flowed well. And of course, I should have known it.

We had a joyous time together, and if I hadn't made all those fantasies, it would have ended sooner and been sweeter. But I always hope and dream. Inflate reality with my fantasies, which doesn't work.

I would say it's the most adult affair I've had. Am I making progress at last? Moving to a place where I can control and experience my emotions, instead of being a blind slave to them?

Don Hatch
The Met Rack

1/3/60

Olsten's called, left a message. They have an assignment at Cooper Union, light typing and filing. I'll take it. They pay doodly, but they're dependable. Who knows? A few days of temp work, and I can blow myself to a bottle of cheap Chianti; a few more days, and I can get a candle to stick in the empty bottle.

Got off to a lousy start. Due downtown at 8:30 and didn't hit the deck until 7:15. No time to walk, had to take the subway. The train was jammed when I got on, and it got more crowded at each stop. I clung desperately to the pole by the door so that I could get out fast without being trampled to death. I was beginning to feel a bit testy when I noticed a very pleasant feeling of warmth and pressure against my crotch. What a nice way to start the day! And on the IRT of all places.

I looked up into a good-looking but expressionless face. I grinned encouragingly. I mean, why not? I'm not the type to frown at a time like this. He grinned back and thrust his crotch forward—hard. Hello there! Now there are two warm and friendly lumps getting acquainted.

By now we're rolling into 42nd Street. The doors open, and it's sardine city. My pole buddy and I are now so close together that it's hard for me to get my hand on his zipper. Suddenly, our hands collide. He's beaten me to it. His great stiffy is in my hand, and he's working on *my* zipper. Now that's enterprise!

He's uncut too! It's seldom that my foreskin gets to meet another. Suddenly, it occurs to me that this could get very messy. The motion of the train, the rapid hand action, and his hot breath tell me that the inevitable is about to happen. Now I know why these subway poles always feel so slimy.

He grunted, rather loudly I'm afraid, and I felt a warm, gooey jet shoot up my arm. This inspired me, and just as I was about to let go, my pole buddy miraculously produced a handkerchief and shoved it between us in the nick of time. I'm sure it helped, but I hope it's not bragging to say that it was hardly adequate.

Fourteenth Street. The guy winked, said something I couldn't hear, and got off along with about 30 other people. There I stood feeling flushed and vulnerable. A quick look at the front of my pants told me that I'd have to find some warm water and paper towels before I reported for work.

Look what I've been missing with all this healthy walking. Wonder if rush hours on the IRT are always so entertaining? Just in case, remember to stuff a few paper towels in your pocket tomorrow morning—at least.

1/6/60, 11 P.M.

Down, boy! You are not going out tonight. Audition tomorrow, and the rest of me needs sleep, even if you don't. Gotta put my best foot forward and break away from this office temp routine. So no 42nd Street fleapits tonight, no tubs, no bars. Just sleep.

Oh, all right! You're on—but you're doing a single.

11/7/60

Went to audition for Cape May Playhouse this A.M. They're doing mostly musicals—not my strong point, to put it mildly, so I was more nervous than usual. Gave a shaky rendition of "You Have Cast Your Shadow on the Sea" (always figure nobody remembers this old chestnut, so it's safe for me to desecrate it), did a few tap steps, read some lines from *The Boys from Syracuse,* and got off. Can just imagine what was in those notes they scrawled. "Acting OK, can dance a little, can't sing for shit." Don't call us, we'll call you.

Am in no mood for a party tonight. Jerry is celebrating his second year in *Hello, Dolly!* We've had our ups and downs (and even a short run of tops and bottoms), and he's still my best friend, so I'll be there. Maybe it will cheer me up after all.

1/8/60

Jerry's party was a bust. He promised construction studs from *Skyscraper,* but all we got were the same tired waiter queens from *Dolly.* Tried to hold on for at least an hour. I did, after all, have an excuse to leave early—these gypsy fruits don't have to get up at the crack of dawn.

Then they started playing silly games—everybody getting nicknames based on their personalities. Naturally, they had to be female names. I hate this sissy shit! I made my excuses and got up to leave, but Jerry wasn't having any. He wasn't about to let me get off scot-free. "On your knees, slaves. The Empress Lascivia Whorina is leaving us."

I opened the door and turned to glare at him. He flashed the sweetest, most guileless smile. He's really very cute and loves to kid. Not a mean bone in his body. I forgave him. I was just tired, cranky and—yes, a little jealous. These people are making a good living doing what they love, while I'm slaving for peanuts in a temp job. I turned my back on him, grumbling "Call you tomorrow."

Some willowy twinkle-toes skittered past me, said he was leaving too—did I mind if he tagged along? I was in no mood for idle chitchat or anything else for that matter, but I shrugged and said OK. He must have read my mind, because he said, "That's all right. You're not my type either." We had a good laugh over that one, and pretty soon we were getting along famously. Even the long wait on the subway platform seemed to fly by. His name is Bruce (of course), and he got off in the heart of the Dance Belt (where else?), but not before he told me about supering at the Metropolitan Opera. You don't have to show up until 10:30 for rehearsals. The pay is low, but it's cash on the line at the end of each day. If you can show up every day for rehearsals and every night for performances, you can make as much as $80 a week, tax free. He says they always need big guys.

I'm to meet him at the stage door at 10:15 tomorrow.

1/9/60

Called in sick at Olsten's. Practically a blizzard out there, so don't feel too guilty.

Met Bruce at stage door. Not too late, considering the weather. Things moved very fast from then on. Bruce introduced me to Stanley Levine, assistant stage manager in charge of supers. Got rushed downstairs into a large, overheated communal dressing room, where I met an amazing assortment of guys ranging from drag queens to Brooklyn stevedores. Strangely enough, the queens can take opera or leave it, while the dese-dem-and-dosers dote on the stuff. Then we were herded upstairs and onstage, where we learn from some guy with a megaphone that today we are a crack regiment of Babylonian soldiers. The opera is *Nabucco* by Verdi. The music is wonderful. The discipline is downright military, and the theater is spectacular, very impressive.

Some of the guys are also impressive, as I found out when we all stripped for costume fittings in the P.M. Many glad eyes, much flirting, grab-assing (and grab-cocking). It's hot down there in more ways than one. Everyone hangs out in various stages of undress, and there's an atmosphere of sexual tension you could cut with a knife. I think I'm going to be very happy here! Will call Olsten's tomorrow to tell them to take me off the roster till further notice. Don't call me, I'll call you.

1/10/60

Had a long wait before they were ready for us onstage this A.M. We sat around with our Chock Full O' Nuts goodies and got acquainted. The guys who are old hands at supering are split into clannish groups. The queers and the straights keep pretty much to themselves. But the nice thing is there seems to be no animosity between the two groups. In fact, there are some amusing crossovers.

Case in point: Angelo, a pixieish Italian kid with a creamy little body, lots of teeth, and the butt of death came bouncing down the stairs with loud cries of *"Ciao"* and *"Buon giorno!"* The hairy Brooklyn contingent cheered, whistled, and blew kisses at him. Angelo took all this with many bows and grins as he paraded through the dressing room. He opened a large battered metal door at the rear of the room, threw a wicked smile over his shoulder, and walked into the darkness.

A macho, muscular type rose from the cigar-smoking corner, and a big cheer went up. With many slaps on the ass and shouts of encouragement from his buddies, he strutted through the doorway and shut the door.

We heard some muffled giggling and falsetto screams of *"Aiuto! Aiuto!"* from behind the door. Everybody just grinned and began to talk of other things. Must find out what's behind that door.

Went to lunch with one of the supers—Tad's Steak House on 42nd. Heard rumors that the steak is actually kangaroo meat imported cheap from down under. Who cares? Tastes fine, and with baked potato and salad for $2.99, it can't be beat.

My new friend is Sam. Now this guy *is* my type. Tall, rangy, broadshouldered; well-knit, as they say. Sam doesn't talk much—very Gary Cooper, and I think this is going to be a one-sided romance. But I intend to cultivate it for all it's worth.

Back to work in the P.M. Rehearsals for *Don Giovanni* are going on topside. Sam and I have been tapped to carry some diva across the stage in a sedan chair. Piece of cake, we think. We get extra bucks for this, and later we find out why. This is one very large soprano! We made it, but just barely. When the fat lady got out, we dashed into the wings to have a good giggle. Sam is loosening up. There's hope yet.

1/12/60

A.M. coffee klatsch. Lots of dishing and I discover that everyone has a nickname. Christ! Nicknames again. Angelo is Aiuto. Bruce is called Bruce the Sluice (don't get that one), and Sam is Lonesome Luke. (Not if I can help it.) I'm still too new for *my* moniker. They haven't yet taken my measure, as it were, but they say they're working on it.

Later, Bruce took me on a tour of what's behind the metal door. It leads to a catwalk that runs under the stage. Used for quick access from stage left to stage right and vice versa. Management insists that it be used whenever possible, because people running behind the backdrops onstage make them billow.

Running off into darkness back of the catwalk is a maze of rotting planks and struts that support the scene loft. This old dump is truly decrepit. Rumor is that they plan to tear it down and build a new Met somewhere uptown. Bruce went bounding off into the shadows, jumping from beam to beam. I followed—carefully, because there were gaping holes in some of the floorboards. Far below, Bruce said, was another sub-basement. The only light came from a few naked bulbs strung over the catwalk.

I heard a voice call out "Watch your step." No kidding! I stopped to get my bearings. I heard sighs and moans all around me in the dark and I could just make out a few figures in some very interesting postures. Holy smoke! This place makes the meat rack at Cherry Grove look like a Sunday School picnic!

Didn't take long before my eyes became accustomed to the dark, and soon I was leaping over those beams like a sex-crazed monkey.

1/15/60

Getting into the spirit of things, I have dubbed the place the Met Rack. I spend most of my waiting time there, and I have plenty of randy company. If a stage manager calls to gather the supers, there's always some wallflower hanging out by the door to holler "Olly, olly income-free!" to warn us that we better zip up and get our asses on stage pronto.

The game here is to make eye contact with your chosen victim in the dressing room, make a few subtle gestures—vigorously rubbing your crotch while rolling your eyes toward the metal door is very effective—and then lead the way. You might be followed, you might not—those are the breaks.

I've been given a nickname now, and I write it with pride: the Phantom of the Opera.

1/17/60

Elektra tonight. Sam and I (together again) carry a slave girl over our heads. The victim is a sassy, amusing gal from the Met ballet. She's to be sacrificed (offstage, fortunately for her) by that crazy bitch, Clytemnestra. It's a short bit, then down to the Met Rack for fun and games. Maybe it's the skimpy rags we wear as slaves and the Texas

Dirt body makeup that makes everybody look hot, but the guys seem extra horny tonight. Got to the dressing room and looked around for Sam. No sign of him there. Can it be that "Lonesome Luke" is looking for company? The metal door is open. Here I come, ready or not.

Orgy night in Ancient Greece. It's slaves' night off, and they're making the most of it. Must be developing cat's eyes because I can see pretty well now—well enough to see that most guys have stripped off their rags. Crazy thought crossed my mind that they better be able to find 'em when they go back to the dressing room, and there better not be any stains on 'em. They may be rags to us, but they're costumes to that dragon lady in wardrobe.

Then I stumbled into him. My heart leapt, and so did another part of my anatomy. This was going to be the night—I was sure of it! A pale ray of light from the catwalk reached just far enough to spotlight his back. I'd know that ass anywhere. I reached out to stroke it and felt it moving, pumping very fast. He looked over his shoulder. His teeth were clenched, and his eyes gleamed in the dim light. It was not a particularly friendly look. "I'm busy right now," he said.

In spite of the darkness, I could just make out a long, lean back stretched out at a right angle to Sam's crotch. The back was moving rhythmically in tune with Sam's forward drive. I knelt down and saw that whoever it was had the muscular legs of a dancer. He was gripping his ankles with his hands. I should have left, but I had to know who it was. I moved in closer. He looked down between his legs, grinned goofily, and said, "Hi." It was Bruce—the Sluice.

I felt deflated—in every way. I mumbled something inane and beat a hasty retreat.

The showers are usually fun on a Texas Dirt night, but I decided to clean up at home. Time to give the old pecker a rest anyway.

2/12/60

Auditioned this morning for Champlain Shakespeare Festival. The Bard's my bag, and it went real well. I'm a cinch. Hear Vermont is at least 20 degrees cooler than NYC in the summer. Good to get out of town for a few months. Nice change.

Felice Picano
Fire Island, 1975

September 2, 1975

Miss Destiny's up to her old tricks again—in the past week she has been working on so many little bringdowns. But I refuse to buy any of them; not to mention the accumulation they might all add up to. Even tempered, I remain.

The biggest of the bringdowns was the sudden and terrible news that I must leave my beloved Fire Island Pines weeks earlier than I had assumed. Our lease expires 9/15 and we cannot get an extension on it, as the owner claims to be using it beginning then.

This turned out to be a double blow. Not only do I have to return earlier than I wanted to the city—which I now have very mixed feelings for—but also I will have to do it somewhere in the middle of the typed revision of my novel, bringing up the possibility that the arc of the work experience would be totally destroyed.

No need to worry on that account at the moment. Although I am typing and revising every day—up to chapter VIII today—there are enough little problems to spoil any sustained and concentrated sweep toward the conclusion. Not authorial problems so much as mechanical ones. My electric typewriter has begun to fritz—the *f*'s and *v*'s aren't striking right. I suspect all it needs is a good cleaning. But the only nearby repair service—across the bay in Sayville—just moved this weekend. As a result it won't be for another two days that their cleaning vats will be set up. So the week will be just like the last one—heavy typing with lots of problems.

Yet another bringdown was unrelated to any of the rest—and totally gratuitous—a spontaneous case of nonspecific urethritis made its appearance on last Friday morning. I was not astounded. My health has been ghastly all this year; I am prepared for just about anything these days short of terminal cancer. Still, for it to come then—on the eve of the final and hottest weekend (not in weather but in personal terms)—seemed like a very bitchy stunt. Especially as I was looking (& dressed) quite the best I have been all summer: a fact suddenly noticed by scores of men unavailable all season, now suddenly vying for my attention.

I rose above it—I must say. And then the damn thing appears pretty well healed: yet it did put restraints on my weekend. More about the ups of the weekend will follow.

I should have known it that last week in May; the closing for the summer of Flamingo—Manhattan's best disco—but I didn't. It was only the past weekend that I knew for certain—but it is certain. The '60s are finally laid to rest, and with them the regalia of the sudden flowering counterculture consisting of drugs, nonviolence, anti-government demonstrations, violent activities, mass concerts, and floating mysticism.

The '70s are officially upon us—for half a decade already—but only this summer have the '70s revealed what they will bring forth—and it is quite as new, exciting, and counter a culture as the '60s were.

If you were in Cancún with Lee Radziwill and Truman Capote, you missed it. If you were in San Francisco you probably heard about it. If you were gay and European, you managed to touch it during your vacation. If you were young and straight and hip—living in L.A. or New York, you tried to get near it—most likely you didn't.

Because it was happening on Fire Island from Memorial Day to Labor Day. It was on and off; it was elusive but so present you couldn't miss it. It was gay, not as in gay lib. Or *Women's Wear Daily* fashion, but macho, humpy, dancing, boogying, sexy, druggy good-time gay. It was the summer of '75, and it made certain what has been slowly happening for the last five years—it put its stamp on it, so hard that even the media got the message.

Essentially all it is, is dancing in a discotheque. But around that simple statement an entire culture—with its appurtenances, its rituals, its delights and terrors, its gods and goddesses, and its priests and priestesses—has been built. It is now the only exciting mass-entertainment leisure pursuit taking place in the country—and for that reason alone it is worth taking a look at.

It is also based on complete illegality. The music played is stolen—i.e. no royalties are paid to ASCAP, BMI, or the performers—it's all pirated on tapes. Those tapes run anywhere from half an hour to an hour and a half. They are specifically designed to fill an evening with dance—to get up mood, tempo, pace, relaxation, tension—in short all that can make people stay on a dance floor for three to five hours a night.

Pirated tapes have been around for years. So have been places where they were played. These were usually very, very private clubs. The first was The Loft, the granddaddy of all discos. The second was The Tenth Floor, set up by two acquaintances of mine—David Brury and David Sokoloff. This also was a private club—with seasonal membership. Ray Yeats was the DJ during the winter and spring. During the summer, he DJ'ed at the Sandpiper, F. I. Pines' local dance place. Members were allowed to bring guests. Who paid to get in. On New Year's, on closing nights, many guests were invited for blowouts.

The initial membership was limited to about 150 or so of these three men's friends. They all had common attributes: They were young gay professional men who used drugs, were heavy into sex, knew and (often) slept with each other, and spent their summers out at Fire Island.

By the second year, even with tighter controls, The Tenth Floor had become a Frankenstein. So many people wanted to go that membership trebled. The place was always jammed—but what was bad was that the original familial atmosphere was gone. There were too many new faces—uptown, female, too old or too young, too fancy or too shabby faces—for the regulars. They stopped going. Even the lure of money wasn't enough to keep it going—the dance party ended there.

It was picked up at other places—but not until 1974-1975 did a Manhattan disco pull together all of the elements divided since 1972-1973. This was Flamingo, a huge loft on lower Broadway. Significantly, its entrepreneur had been a member of The Tenth Floor in its heyday. He knew the same people. So, they were gathered together again. Oh, they had been sporting at Le Jardin in a midtown hotel—but that was public and got media-blitzed and celebrity-conscious too quickly. You cannot be a celebrity in the new culture—at least on the dance floor you can't. You must be willing to let go of that hard-earned ego trip to become part of the one. This is not to say celebrities don't appear—but they are immediately assimilated—often the real celebrities grow out of the dance itself.

When Flamingo closed for the summer, 12 West picked up the midweek crowd. It is more centrally located for the scene—along the Hudson River strip—a strip under the now-closed West Side Highway from 23rd where all the heavy leather bars are—Spike, Eagles Nest, the Strap—down to Christopher Street past other bars, Peter Rabbit, Danny's, the Stud, the Barracks, right to Keller's where the leather scene first took off 10 years ago. Every street down there is heavy cruising ground. There are open and closed places for sucking and fucking. There is West Street for car pickups. It must always be remembered that while the essential activity of a discotheque is to dance, the underlying purpose of the place is to meet people to fuck.

Sex then is necessary—or at least the promise of sex. All the good discos have spectacular dancers who are also "hot"—i.e. good fucks before, after, and sometimes in between the dance numbers.

Meanwhile, the summer dance scene got hotter and hotter itself. Fire Island—and especially its twin cities, the Pines and Cherry Grove (known affectionately as Sodom and Gomorrah)—is one of the most active, alive, chic, and sexy free places in the world. It is no surprise then that disco dancing should really take off here.

There are two discos in the Pines and two in the Grove. The Botel, where Tea Dance takes place daily—rain, shine, hurricane, or earthquake—is the afternoon disco. Despite the fantastic music of this year's DJ, Robbie Morgan, The Botel still hasn't been able to take off at night. During the week, and even with Barry Lederer's schizoid playing, the Sandpiper is it. The reason, of course, is partially layout. The Botel is lousily laid out for dancing; the Sandpiper is better, but still not perfect.

So imperfect that this year the Grove's Ice Palace became *the* spot. Newly designed, the Ice Palace is now the best discotheque in the world. It has high ceilings—formed attic style so that the mirrors and lights slant up, meet, and reflect, refract down. It has a spectacular light system, head-thumping strobes, and a long bar and a horseshoe bar. It has a huge outside terrace and a smaller deck. It has two dance floors, with split-second delays in the lights—very trippy. In the double DJ box are not one, but two DJs: Bobby and Vincent.

Last Saturday night, when the music finally turned into Ray Charles at 5 A.M. (the bar was closed at 4 A.M.) the crowd applauded Bobby DJ for 15 minutes. Along with Luis Romero (at Flamingo), Ray Yeats, and Vincent, Bobby is one of the new priests of the culture—the perfect DJ. He can shape his music so it slides into shades of excitement that will keep your legs and hips shaking long after you've passed your exhaustion point. Last Saturday, he molded the last half-hour of his playing into what can only be described as transcendental music—like Mahler's Eighth Symphony it could go no higher without attempting to bypass itself.

A terrific environment and a great DJ. But that isn't really enough. For this is a mass entertainment, a unified entertainment. What it needs is people to fulfill it.

And it gets the best. Pines and Grove dancers fill the place at midnight and don't leave until long after the music has stopped. Although there are sometimes straights, and often a dozen or so gay women, the real group is made up of macho gay males and beautiful women. TVs are allowed, of course—La Potassa and a few others are there—but their business is to add flash, not sex appeal. Also, they've got to know how to boogie.

Because that's what's on. Sex and dancing. A midwestern Baptist or even Episcopalian minister would call it "lewd and lascivious dancing," and he'd be right. Shirts off, muscles lubricated with sweat, torsos spinning and flashing, two or three or more bodies pushed together, men French-kissing, sucking nipples, dry-humping, it's undeniably sexy dancing—like a ritual courtship dance, a promise of things to come.

Clothing is tailored to the dance. Shirts have to come off—the place is too hot not to take them off. Last week it was 55 degrees and windy on the terrace. Within, not an inch away, it was 95 degrees and humid. Heavy, solid shoes; close-fitting, suggestive pants; T-shirts or bare torsos. Accessories include: tambourines, whistles, chemically glowing necklaces, popper cases, drug containers, roach clips hung around the neck. Inner accessories include any and all drugs—the strong hallucinogens especially—but also MDA, THC, PCP, hash, liquor, coke, grass, speed, you name it.

But it is only an accessory. Just as the sex is only a promise. For the new culture is dance, dance, dance.

Why is it becoming a culture? There are several reasons. First of all, gay culture remains the most intriguing, mysterious, frightening, and alien culture in the Western world today. It is huge, growing every day. It is extensive—everyone seems to be gay. It is powerful—not only in the arts but in industry and business. Second, it is completely oriented toward pleasure—sex, primarily, but also every other sensual gratification. Third, it offers anonymity, freedom, and astounding promiscuity. Last of all, it is a culture that is not assimilated yet—and possibly unassimilable by the great masses of the Atlantic world. The reason, of course, is that it does not deny or argue; it ignores and builds on its own. As a group, gay men have built a half-dozen superstars in the entertainment field—Streisand, Redford, Minelli, Midler, LaBelle, Barry White—and more. It is powerful, closed, and highly elitist. If you are in—and you can be very easily—you are a brother. If you're out, you're a "straight," often a "redneck."

At its best, gay culture is attractive, fashionable, intelligent, mobile, and extensive (coast to coast and Europe too) and very, very alive.

It is therefore no surprise that the disco craze of the '60s (*Twist and Shout!*) didn't take off; but the current disco trip is. Naturally, discos are popping up everywhere—but the taste—what is played, who plays it, what is worn, what is danced—takes place in two or three places: Flamingo, Ice Palace, and Sandpiper. Recording artists whose careers were dying have tailored themselves to the gay beat boogie—as a result not only LaBelle, but also Frankie Valli and

Dionne Warwick have hits now. Then too, since gay culture has no racial or ethnic prejudice, Latin, Black, and even Hebrew music have been assimilated into the rock beat. There is a new richness to the texture and sound of the mix. And since a disco tune can go on for five to ten minutes—the old ABA rock formula has been killed. Songs like "I'm a Free Man" begin with a long orchestral prelude, change rhythm for the vocal, go back to orchestral interludes, and change rhythm again for the vocal/orchestral finale. In short, the music itself has begun to find new experimental forms of expression not available in two- or three-minute minute tunes.

All of this is apparent. But on a hot night in a good disco, something else happens too—and it is the experience especially that has set the new culture apart.

Let's see what the ingredients are—music, lights, people. But all of them raised to some incredible exponential extreme—music and lights by artistry, people by artificial stimulants and, most importantly, by energy.

Dance—the dance of the cosmos—the universal energy—the primal flow of atoms in ordered rhythm. Primitive peoples dance in order to proffer their energy up to their deities. And on the Ice Palace dance floor, sweating faces fall back, as the eyes glaze over with what can only be called ecstasy—the mystical encounter of body with soul with something much larger than either.

The source of energy is simple—hundreds of men and women in the prime of their physical life dancing as hard as they can. You can feel the energy, almost see and sometimes touch it. And, if you've been dancing for an hour or so, and you ought to be fainting, all you have to do is pull in some of that energy around you. Believe me, it's there, palpable, free to be used, strong, and mostly refined—totally usable, easily grabbed onto for another few hours' boogie—and if the vibes are right and the drugs and music are peaking together—usable for what I have to call a mystical experience—like Shiva dancing the destruction of death.

A religious cult? Possibly. Though no one will ever admit it.

A great untapped natural energy source? No doubt about it.

A night in heaven? Yes, and in hell too! For all previous realities are destroyed in the cosmic dance. Who knows but we queens may be swinging our tushes right into Nirvana.

David May
Something Sensational to Read on the Train

17 October 1978

Called Robby on Sunday and made a lunch date for yesterday. I arrived on time at 11:30 A.M.; he was running late. He showered/shaved while I read. Then he walked in and lay down next to me where I was reading on his bed. He kissed me. At first it was pleasant. But later when he fucked me, I became so anxious that I lost my erection. I never fully got it back either. He tried to jerk me off but couldn't even get me hard. Then we began foreplay all over again. I became almost completely erect and fucked him. I faked the orgasm. I felt like shit.

13 February 1979

Paul from New York: of Greek descent, dark, heavy stubble, *very* hairy. 43 years old; looks more like 35. Not at all condescending. Appreciated both my maturity and naïveté, and was threatened by neither. Beautiful man. Not very tall, but a very sexy body. A nice face: the lines are deep but few, not a mesh of fine ones—very masculine. We fucked.

His whole body is brown and hairy—all over. His cock (of average size) was a youthful pink. It was so beautiful I had to suck it. I loved sucking it. I drove him wild, licking his balls, cock, and crotch, rimming him. I took his whole cock into my mouth and swallowed every drop of come. Wanted more of the same sweet juice. Then I fucked his hairy, round ass.

"Do you want to fuck me?" he said. "Let's see if you fit. I'm tight as a…"

He kisses like no one I know. He came toward me with an open mouth, like he was going to eat me. His rough-bearded face scratched mine. He would hold me down and lick my neck, driving me up the wall, or lick my navel and suck my cock alternately. (Later: "You didn't know about your belly button, did you? Watch that navel!") Threw me all over the bed. We would crush each other with our arms and legs, all over each other, often making love in wrestling positions. The sex was better than anything I'd ever had with Robby. Rough but never violent. Gentle at times, abrasive at others. He called out my name and grabbed my arm as I brought him to climax with my tongue and mouth. "Take it! I'm coming! Take me!"

Then today he invited me to New York this summer—and Fire Island!

25 June 1979

Yesterday was Gay Freedom Day. I was freed, in a matter of speaking, reaching new depths of degradation, seeking out still-untried (by me) paths to sleaze, losing myself to moral decay as I had never done before. After the parade we went to the Castro and had dinner at the Neon Chicken. I had two Dubonnets before dinner while we waited upstairs to be seated and two glasses of wine with dinner. So I was pretty tipsy when Cary and I left the restaurant. We walked along Castro Street, which was packed with men. We somehow managed to get into DJ's and onto the dance floor. They were playing Donna Summer's "Hot Stuff" when we came in. When the song segued to "Bad Girls"—we had walked down 18th Street after leaving the Neon Chicken singing and dancing to "Bad Girls"—a leatherman started feeling my ass and groping me as we passed, his buddy humping me. I grabbed the crotch of the first man.

"You *are* a bad girl!"

Then I humped his buddy.

The dance floor was packed with bodies wiggling like living sardines in a can. I groped ass to my heart's delight, getting the same. (Earlier at the celebration I had seen two leathermen. One of them— tall, young, and quite good-looking—being jerked off through his jeans by the other—not so tall, young, or good-looking as the first— who stroked him with one hand and pinched his nipple with the other.

I was turned on by the exhibitionism of it, being a voyeur.)

A man of about 30, maybe 5 foot 4, bearded, and moderately good-looking, started dancing in front of me. The floor was so packed that people had come between Cary and me anyway, and I supposed that the man was dancing with someone behind me, though I couldn't be sure. I had noticed him cruising me earlier, but hadn't paid much attention to him since I was with Cary and wasn't going to follow through with anything. Then he reached out and felt my chest. I returned the favor by rubbing his torso. He pinched my nipples. I pinched his. I looked over at Cary, who was laughing, and decided to see this thing through. We as yet hadn't stopped dancing.

We progressed to groping buttocks and crotches and, finally, kissing. Then he grabbed my hand and, without saying a word, led me to the men's room. (Cary asked for the poppers as I passed him on the dance floor and I gave them to him.) We went into the only stall, which had no door, where we kissed and fondled each other, still saying nothing. Then he started to jerk us both off. When he came, I bent down to take his come in my mouth, and it dribbled over onto my moustache and chin. After that he asked my name. I told him and asked his: Serge. He was French. I explained that I was spending the day with my friend Cary but that I'd like to go home with him another time. He said no, he couldn't because he had an "old man" (whom I saw later: much older, probably a sugar daddy). We kissed and parted. I was amazed with myself. I couldn't believe what I had just done.

Later on we stopped at the Locker Room on Polk Street. I went back to the peep shows. There was a sign that read HUSTLING AND SOLICITING FORBIDDEN, but there were a lot of men cruising and a couple of what looked like hustlers. I went into a booth and saw, for a quarter, a bad JO film. Very sleazy. We went home after that. I am now ready for baths and backrooms. Am I jaded yet?

29 July 1979

Went to the Twin Peaks to meet Robby at 11:30 P.M. He didn't show up until after midnight. We chatted a while about this and that, then in walked this fellow, Kevin, who worked with Robby. I always thought him attractive and pleasant enough, but never really knew him. He sat with us. I offered him my extra King Tut ticket, since Robby didn't want to go with me tomorrow. He said, "Yes," and I handed it to him, not wanting to make a big deal of it or demanding that he go with me. He thanked me with a kiss. After a few minutes I decided that I might want to go home with this man, so I pretty much threw myself at him.

After the bar closed we all went to Robby's flat on 16th Street for port. We were talking about music, and I mentioned my love for Laura Nyro. Kevin winced, and when I asked him why, he said, "I was just fantasizing about a relationship with you, but I used to live with someone who played Laura Nyro all the time. I couldn't stand it again."

Later on I made some indiscreet comment about bondage or rough play, and Kevin looked at me with renewed interest. Robby remarked that I shouldn't have said whatever I said, because Kevin would make me prove it. I perked up. As it turns out, Kevin is very into S/M and bondage.

I eventually ended up at Kevin's place on Liberty Street. Since both of us were drunk, we tried getting some sleep before having sex. But we kept playing with each other, caressing and talking dirty.

"What do you like?"

"Everything," I said, thinking that he meant fucking and sucking.

"No you don't. If I hit you in the wrong place, you'd be upset."

He had some hardware by the bed: handcuffs, rope, et cetera. I was a bit intimidated to see it but said only, "I'm just beginning to explore the rough side of it."

When we finally had sex the next morning, there was a lot of hitting, scratching, slapping, and such. But no bondage. I now suspect that he wanted me to establish limits while I was waiting for him to bring it up. Next time, if there is one, I'll bring the subject up, ask to be allowed to explore new horizons.

The next day he made several references to my age (23 to his 29). He somehow thought me very young for the range of my experience.

He also said that I was a pill but would grow out of it.

29 August 1979 (Provincetown)

They closed the A-House at 1 A.M., so I walked over to the beach behind the Boat Slip, which my little book told me was cruisy. It was. I approached several people, all very nice, but no luck. One older man I cruised off and on, hoping he'd approach me. He reminded me of Paul, only not nearly as hot. One fellow explained to me about the bushes: There were only so many, and people had to wait in line. People were sucking each other off pretty casually, and I was missing it! I made my way over to the bushes and cruised the older man again. He had followed a pretty young blond all in white, and I followed him. The blond was a little put-off, not knowing what was happening. The older guy asked me what I was up to.

"Cruising," I said.

"Really? I wish you had said that three hours ago!"

We got to my room at 3 A.M., so it was only *two* hours. He was very nice, intelligent, a teacher (an art teacher, I think), and he had a huge cock. He fucked me royal then sucked me off, spitting out the come. We talked a bit, and he left. I might see him on the beach again tonight.

31 August 1979 (Cherry Grove, Fire Island)

Getting here was not fun. I missed my flight from Provincetown to Boston because I had a hard time getting up with only 2½ hours sleep. I was up late again fucking with Don (as his name turned out to be). Huge cock. It took both my hands to cover the shaft, still leaving the head. Don told me I was an exceptional lover and very beautiful; he liked the way I kissed.

After dinner tonight we went to hear some singer named Karen Akers at the Monster. Then we went to the Sandpiper to dance. Then to the meat rack in the Pines. After fooling around in the bushes at P'town, I was pretty much ready for what went on, but it was still all very new to me. The first thing I saw/heard was one man face-fucking another. The fucker was jockish-looking in a sleeveless T-shirt.

The cocksucker was a beautiful man we'd seen earlier at the Sandpiper. After the fucker came, he sucked off the original sucker, who either pulled out early or came quickly (I think the latter). Then they both pulled up their pants and wandered off in different directions.

Whenever two people started making it, others gathered around, feeling up the two, pinching tits, maybe even sucking the cock of the cocksucker. One man sucked my cock but wasn't very good, so I pushed him away and pulled the fellow sucking his cock onto mine. I face-fucked both of them. After I came, he kept sucking. I finally lifted him up and left him with the first cocksucker. Later on I ran into Paul as he was sucking off a lot of men while getting sucked himself. Face-fucking definitely seems the norm. I looked for someone I'd like to suck. The guy I found was so drunk he couldn't come. I left him undone. I did a lot of looking because I love to watch. I respect this sort of departmentalization because it's honest and to the point, no time wasted.

I decided later that I wanted to come again, so I waited for one cocksucker to finish another man and put his hand on my cock. After a moment of playing with my cock, he knelt down and started sucking. He used poppers as I face-fucked him. A handsome, muscular black man came along and started playing with my nipples. We kissed. I licked his face. (My first sexual contact with a black man. I told Paul about him later, and he said that he had done him too.) I realized that I wasn't going to come because it was still too soon after my first orgasm, so I pulled out, stuck the black man's cock in, and left them.

Paul said right off that I shouldn't feel obligated to him as my only sexual partner, which is good because I don't.

4 September 1979 (New York)

Fire Island is all it's reputed to be. Quite decadent. We went to the meat rack every night except last night because we had to wake up early. I woke up with the clap. First time and I'm very upset about it. Paul said that it's just a souvenir of Fire Island. Meanwhile, he has been put out of commission by a torn foreskin. One of the boys in the meat rack was pulling too hard on it, not realizing how sensitive it is.

Saturday night we were at the Cherry Grove meat rack until the sky began to grow light. I was invited home for a four-way, which was interesting if not terribly satisfying. My first experience with group sex. I came crawling in at 7 A.M. Paul only laughed. Later, Paul woke me up making love to me. My mouth had opened to receive his tongue before my eyes had opened. I told him it was my favorite way to wake up.

21 September 1979

One of Paul's games was to kiss me, inserting his tongue in my mouth, but withdrawing his mouth from mine if I responded in kind. Every time I returned the gesture, he pulled away. It was a sort of power game, I think, and felt rather kinky at the time. I get excited just thinking about him. How that man can make me whimper.

21 October 1979

When I woke up this morning, it was very cold. I could only think of how nice it would be to have another body there to share his warmth with me, to share my own with him. I then decided that I should fall in love again.

5 December 1979 (New York)

Paul, Paul, Paul. I almost love him. We've had sex four times since I've been here, but only once when it was really exciting, really fun, to where I was making enough noise to worry Paul about disturbing the neighbors. But he took delight in my ecstasy. He mouthed my throat, nipples, navel, abdomen, and genitals; slapped me; pinched me. I went down on him, then fucked him. Again, I almost enjoyed eating the come. I told him how much I enjoy sucking his cock, which is so rare for me.

6 December 1979 (New York)

The first time we had sex on this visit, I was too tired to really respond. He fucked me. The second time, I had to do all the work, and I got the feeling that he was only doing it as a favor. The third was great. The last time, this morning, I started it. We only jerked ourselves off, like the second time. He spent most of his energy giving me very visible hickeys and throwing me around. But he had told me on Wednesday that he just wasn't horny, that he had been very horny the week before. Bad timing.

We also went to a backroom bar after the opera on Tuesday night, the Half Breed on 8th Avenue near 68th Street. We stopped by for a drink. There we were in a Levi bar in our opera drag. We felt out of place. Paul had never been there before, either. There was a sign that read STABLES pointing to a stairway down. Paul went to pee and investigate. He was gone about 10 minutes while I watched our things and felt progressively more uncomfortable. When he returned, he explained that there was indeed a backroom. Then it was my turn. I tripped down the dark stairs and moved about with deliberation through the half-lit and red-lit rooms before cautiously entering the dark room. Men leaned against the walls and watched me. I found a place to stand and stayed there listening to the sounds of sex (slurping, breathing, the doing and undoing of pants). Soon someone came up, undid my zipper, took out my cock, and sucked it. When I got close to coming, I began to breathe louder and make noise, knowing I'd get more attention. I did. Men stroked my tits and butt. It became a community effort, like back at Fire Island. I loved it. When I returned, Paul asked me if I'd gotten done. I told him yes, of course. My experience at Fire Island's meat rack had trained me well in the attitude of the stud, the dominant participant in depersonalized sex. Another new experience. So sleazy. The blackness made for an even more intense depersonalization. After sex, I simply put my clothes back together and walked up the stairs. So very, very simple. Beats jerking off.

31 December 1979

"I'm sure you've been in this position before."

I laughed. Said it was the best line I'd heard in a while.

Add Father Jimmy to the list. My latest lover is a Jesuit priest.

Nordic extraction, he said. Handsome and bearded. A gentle but nonetheless enjoyable lover. Had only a single bed, however, and I had to go home and sleep alone after we had made love. Seduced me with a fine Liebfraumilch. Already aware of his intent, I helped him along.

13 January 1980

Saw Jimmy again. He called me up on Thursday night saying that a meeting had been canceled and he'd been freed for the evening. Could he come over? Of course. I opened a bottle of wine. He got physical. We moved to my room and made love.

I am mystified by it all. He told me how pleased he was to see me at mass on Christmas Eve, how he enjoys "sharing it" with me. Me? It is a puzzle. I understand why others like me but not why he likes me. I can only think that it might be because I am so apart from him and his profession and his day-to-day life. Does that make me in some way exotic to him? Or merely safe?

4 March 1980

Safeway on Market Street. So many men. Better cruising than at a Greenwich Village laundromat. I love being here. Got sucked off last night at the Locker Room peep shows. After I came, the man seemed somehow distraught. I left without a word. Good looking, though. I wouldn't have minded getting to know him.

6 March 1980

Met Robby at the Elephant Walk before lunch today, where I also saw Randy Shilts. He was better looking in person than on TV.

7 March 1980

Rolling in the gutter. A three-way with a leather-jacketed *hung* fellow named Jim and a pathetic, self-loathing alcoholic named Wayne. Met the two at the Locker Room. They both said that the place was trashy.

I said, "Yes, I love it!"

They didn't understand. Wayne had a bruise on his face—whether from an attacker or a trick, I don't know. Jim tried fucking me but wouldn't be gentle in his entry, and I got angry. So I fucked Wayne while Wayne sucked Jim. Jim was hot, but Wayne was pretty sad. I left before they'd finished, called a cab and took off. Came rolling in around 4 A.M.

When I refused to let Jim turn me into a fuck hole, he just made me a partner in doing it to poor, pathetic Wayne. Wayne was very drunk and behaved like a popper junkie. He spilled the poppers (mine) all over Jim's bed.

It was all so sordid: "Take it like a man! Take it, bitch! Get on all fours because I'm gonna fuck you!"

16 March 1980

Met a man named James Meade. I like him.

24 March 1980

Much romance after the opera. We ate a cold supper I'd prepared ahead of time. Then we made love. Quietly at first. Very enjoyable. The nicest sex since my first night with Paul. There were a couple of times I wanted James to slap me hard across the ass but was scared to ask him. I didn't think he'd be into it. He'd mouth my neck and ears, or my pelvis and torso, in a way that made me quiver and moan. I did the same to him, and he accused me of having a mean streak. I told him he'd done the same to me.

"I didn't notice any resistance," he said.

"Only because I'm a masochist."

23 April 1980

Met Robby at the Twin Peaks, where I had three Campari and sodas. I was drunk by the time we left. He asked me where I was going when I kissed him good night in front of his flat, then invited me to stay the night. I did. We hugged and kissed before falling off to sleep. Around dawn when his roommate, Don, got up to get ready for work, we had sex. Wonderful. He fucked me, and I came with only a little encouragement. Then we went back to sleep as Don left for work.

12 May 1980

Julian. His place after work—and after dinner and a lot to drink. We shared a joint.

"Are you going?"

"Yes, I'd better be off."

"Do you want to stay?"

"No, I…was that a pass?"

"Sort of, I…I'm not sure."

"You're not sure?" I put on my jacket and stood up, looking down on him still reclining. "When you're sure, let me know."

"That's just it. I won't be sure until I try it."

I felt very uncomfortable, wanting to but not sure of his motivations.

"It's not that I don't find you attractive," I said. "It's just that I don't know what you want or expect. But I would like to."

"Then take off your jacket and sit down."

I did. I lay on the floor and looked up at him sitting on the couch. I explained that I didn't want to get started and have him back out, nor did I want to spend the whole time wondering whether or not he was enjoying it or just going through with it for me. I also wanted to get a little more stoned. He opened a bottle of German wine. It was awful, but we drank it—Dutch courage.

"I hate sweet wine," he said.

I agreed.

He suggested a shower first, thinking that a good way to warm up.

"You see," he said, "I want to get fucked."

"Why? No, actually, I do understand. I've read about you, about straight men wanting that."

"I've read about you too. I want to see if I like it. Maybe I'll wake up tomorrow morning and say, 'Gay sex is not for me.' Or maybe I'll say, 'Gay sex is wonderful! Let's do it again!'"

His Sheffield accent made me laugh.

"I wonder if I'm bisexual," he said. "I mean, I like men—gay men—

and sometimes find men attractive. It's just that…"

We went to the shower. I touched him tentatively. His body is much nicer than I expected. His cock is lovely, large and uncut. We nuzzled each other. He fondled me roughly but sensually. We kissed. He held me tight, tighter than I him. He ate my neck. (He *knew*. I'd told him that I love it.) He bent down and sucked my cock.

"Was that good?" he asked.

"Wonderful. You've never done that before?"

"Never."

"You've a beautiful cock."

"Thank you."

I sucked his. The water splashed over me. As I gave him head, he washed my hair.

"Do you still think I'll back out?"

He kissed me once more. The hot water ran out, and he turned the shower off. I checked to see if he was clean. He was. We toweled each other off and ran to his bed.

We wrapped ourselves in each other under a quilt on his bed, barely more than a cot. It was rough and exciting.

"Are you always this rough, or is it for my benefit?"

"Partly for your benefit. But I *am* a rough lover most of the time. I can be very tender too, though."

Then the time came to get down to business. He sucked me, playing with my cock and getting it good and hard.

I mounted him, rubbing my cock into his buttocks. This excited him, and he wrapped his legs around me. I sat up and started to open him with a finger. He was tight. When I got to the second finger, he said that he needed to go to the toilet. I let him go, even though I knew what was happening from my own experience, a trick the body plays on virgin buttholes. He came back, and I knew at once that it was over.

"You're not really into it now, are you?" I asked.

"No. I guess not."

We lay in each other's arms. I tried to give him head to get him hard again so he could fuck me. No luck.

"I'm afraid I'm not into it at all now," he said. And then, "I'm sorry. I've led you on…"

"No, I…"

He explained that he hadn't been satisfied with his relationships (sexual, emotional) with women and hoped I was going to make it better, show him the light, make bells ring, and so on. We talked more. I already knew I'd be leaving, though. I never expected to be spending the night with him. I told him that it was all right.

"You didn't use me," I reassured him. "I've been used before, and you didn't use me." I left him my number so he could call me, should the need arise.

1 June 1980

Lethargic and in lust. His name is Yves, and he is from Quebec. About my age, an architecture student on break, visiting friends in San Francisco after a semester in Mexico. And he draws. Today he drew me by the pool at his hotel. Handsome, sexy, and very nice. He told me I am sexy—or sexier—when I speak French (I eat flattery like French fries). We shared a joint this afternoon and I am still a little stoned. And tired. Crashed at 2:30 last night and had to wake up at 7 A.M. for work. We've yet to fuck in a bed. First in a car by the beach. Last night in a truck. So naughty. Never did it in vehicles before. What I won't do.

Met him Thursday night. He kept telling me I'm beautiful.

"Bel homme." Or, *"C'est bon, David. C'est bon."* Said that David was a beautiful name and that it fitted me. "You're skin is beautiful like that, so pale."

His accent is so sexy, as is he: olive skin, growing a beard, beautiful green eyes. He smiles a lot, laughs. Appreciates. A wonderful, considerate lover.

But he has flown home.

11 June 1980

Night before last Father Jimmy called. A film? Sure. After the movie Jimmy asked what I'd like to do next. Wine and cigars at his place?

Sure. When there he asked if I wanted to spend the night. Why not? A good fuck, better than ever before with him. I was very relaxed. He pulled out of me and began to jerk off.

"Get back in there! Finish inside of me!"

I am not passive when passive. Nice sleeping with him. Left after breakfast feeling better about him than I have in ages.

1 October 1980

Bob, a bouncer from Monterey. Offered to love me "to death." I took him up on it. I thought him hot, and he was/is. Like a picture by Tom of Finland: That brooding mustached face, the finely muscled body, brown silky hair covering the chest and torso. Large cock.

"You're making me come," he said as I reached my own climax, his strokes battering home deep within.

The Joy of Fucking. We came together.

And another Bob on Sunday night. Went to the Jaguar for the first time, where we met. He came over to me in the video room and asked me home. I was whisked off in a sports car to Diamond Heights. Dare I complain?

He fucked me royal and well. I stayed the night.

"You have the distinction of being my first trick from the Jaguar," I said.

"I'm not a trick."

I didn't ask.

5 January 1981

Got me some unhealthy love. Black-gloved spankings and lots of dirty talk. And there may be something else to it: a boyfriend? His name is Jan, and I first met him months ago with Robby—on Gay Day last summer, I think. I've seen him around a few times since then, but we hadn't really spoken much. Then the other night I ran into him at the Twin Peaks with Robby's boyfriend Marc (who was mooning over Robby, who was mooning over Andy, who was fuming over Marc.) So Jan ended up coming home with me. Such a night! I was sore for days! Then again on Saturday.

"You want it?"

"Yes."

"Yes, *what*?"

"Yes, Sir!"

Smack!

"Thank you, Sir!"

And bent over his knee. Never have I felt so fulfilled.

14 January 1981

Just called Jan. Will be seeing him Saturday night. Talked dirty on the phone.

"Take out that gorgeous cock and stroke it!"

Last weekend I went out on my own. Ended up at the Jaguar. A pretty boy named Tom asked me to fuck him, and I did without giving Jan a second thought. But I do think of him a lot, or at least our sex play: I fantasize about new, less wholesome games to play. I am so excited thinking about it now, I won't be able to sleep.

18 January 1981

Last night was so wild. And this morning. And this afternoon. I was ravished. The same sort of games, only played with a great deal more earnestness than before. I was punished for my presumptuousness. Scolded and threatened. My ass, back, and thighs slapped to a dull purple. I sobbed, clenched my teeth, bit a pillow.

Once I gasped, "Please, Sir," only to be told, "You can take it!"

And I could. I did. New limits. My ass was fingered to stretch. I know he wants to fist-fuck me, hopes to slowly lead me to it. Once I cried tears because I was afraid that I'd done wrong, but it was all right. He made it (or me) all right again.

I screamed: "Fuck me, Sir! Please fuck me, Sir! I can take it, Sir! Give it to me, Sir, give it all to me! I can take it, Sir!"

Once he asked whose ass he was fucking.

"Mine, Sir."

"What?!"

"It's your ass, Sir. All yours. You can fuck it whenever you want to, Sir."

He did. Drove me wild.

This afternoon I lay on his bed, my feet up, with a robe of his loosely wrapped around me; a pose I've taken for years that no one has ever responded to before. He ravished me, fucked me for the third time. Easy at first but so hard at the end when I begged him to shoot. So hot. Asked if I had pleased him.

"Yes."

Would he continue to train me?

"Yes."

His pubes had been shaved.

24 January 1981

My birthday party.

James: "David hasn't been spanked yet. He needs his birthday spanking."

Everyone else: "Oh, yes."

Me: "No."

Larry grabs my arms. I want to resist but don't.

Jan: "Yes."

I can't deny him. He bends me over his knee counting to 25 with an extra slap and a kiss to grow on.

Then on Thursday night I went out and ended up at the Jaguar (sort of by accident but not really.) This time I wanted to top, but everyone's hands were all over my ass. Was sucked three times, the last so good that I finally came in seconds. When I got home I undressed and, feeling a little blue, lay on my bed in the nude contemplating masturbation when the phone rang. It was Jan. I was overjoyed.

He apologized for not staying the night of my birthday party but wanted me to come over now. I looked at the clock: 9 P.M. I thanked him for sharing my birthday with me.

"I'd like to give you another spanking."

Of course. We agreed that I'd be there in half an hour.

I arrived five minutes late, already afraid that he would discipline me for my tardiness. He opened the door, and I was at once taken aback. The apartment was candlelit, otherwise completely dark, and he was in leather (save his jockstrap). Completely in leather.

I entered and just stood there. Said hello. Wanted to touch him but didn't dare make a move. I went to the table and removed my jacket, laying it on the table with my umbrella. He approached, held me gently and kissed me. How was my day?

"Fine. Thank you, Sir."

"Happy birthday."

Thank you, Sir."

Then he told me that I could take off my clothes and leave them on the chair. I did as I was told.

He went into the bathroom and made some bathroom noises. He came back to where I stood naked. Held me again.

"You've showered?"

"Yes, Sir."

"Have you douched?"

"No, Sir."

"I think you should."

"Yes, Sir."

"Have you ever douched before?"

"No, Sir."

"OK. Everything will be fine if you do what you're told."

"Yes, Sir."

The bathroom was steamy. He glistened in his leather.

The enema was not so gruesome as I feared nor as pleasurable as I had hoped. He asked if I was full. I said, "Yes."

"Does it want to come out?"

"Yes, Sir."

"How is that going to happen?"

"I don't know, Sir." (I didn't!)

"You're going to have to beg, aren't you?"

I tried begging, poorly.

"I don't think you mean it."

I was getting uncomfortable.

"Please, Sir, please! Please let me release the water, Sir!"

"All right."

I released the water. He washed me off and stuck the hose back up my ass. The second time I was filled even fuller, which I didn't hold all of when he pressed into my abdomen with his fist. As punishment, I had to take a third, very full bag that I had to fill myself.

"What sort of punishment am I going to give you?"

I knelt down in the tub, trying hard to hold all the water in.

"I don't know, Sir."

"Fantasize."

"You'll whip me with the belt, Sir, and make it hurt more than I want."

"No, I don't think more than you want."

I cried out in pain.

"What's wrong?" he asked coolly.

"It hurts. The water wants to come out. But I can hold it, Sir. I can hold it as long as you want, Sir."

I was told to release it. I did. He put his boot on the edge of the tub.

"Kiss my boot." I did with great pleasure.

"Lick it."

I did so with equal pleasure.

"You're going to lick all of my leather aren't you?"

"Yes, Sir. May I start with the chaps, Sir?"

"You're not done with the boot yet are you?"

"No, Sir."

"You haven't even touched the other side."

"No, Sir."

Again, I did as I was told.

Then he told me to clean myself up, dry off, and tell him when I was ready. When I was clean and dry again, I opened the door and told him. I was told to bring in the candles from the bathroom. I did, placing them on the bookcase as ordered. Then I licked his other boot and the left side of his chaps. I was told to stop licking the leather and to start on the jockstrap, to get it "good and wet." Then I was allowed to take his cock out with my hands. I kissed the head.

"Did I say you could do that?"

"No, Sir. Please forgive me, Sir."

I was allowed to kiss his balls, then suck them. Then the head of his cock, then all of it. He forced my head down on it, making me choke. Asked why I was choking, I apologized by saying I didn't know how to swallow such a big cock. At some point (which I can't remember now) he started to whip my ass with his belt while his dick was still in my mouth. I took it well, savored it even, until his lashes reached under my buttocks to my balls. I cried out involuntarily.

"Whose ass is this?"

"Yours, Sir."

"Then why are you pulling it away?"

"It hurts, Sir. I'm sorry, Sir."

He continued the whipping and I, no longer relishing the pain, called out, cried, and continued sucking his dick.

I can't remember exactly how it happened, but he was standing over me again. Not knowing what to do, or if I'd displeased him, I began sucking his cock. He knelt down next to me, held me and asked if I was OK. I held back a sob. I was horrified and in agony.

"You...! You...!"

"Go ahead, cry. Tell me."

"I'm frightened. You..."

"I took you farther than you wanted to go."

"Yes. You slapped my balls with the belt. It hurt but I wanted to take it. I wanted to take all of your pain, Sir."

We lay down together.

"Am I your Master?"

"Yes, Sir."

"If I'm your Master, do you know what that makes you?"

"Your slave, Sir."

"A good slave tells his Master everything, doesn't he?"

"Yes, Sir."

"A bad slave is a slave left on the wayside. He isn't even a slave."

I held him tighter.

"Now I can't stretch your limits if you don't tell me, can I?"

"No, Sir."

I refilled his wineglass, prepared and lit a new cigar for him. Then, as ordered, I sucked his cock, almost gagging. He must have forced my head down for me to choke like that, but I don't remember. We got into a sixty-nine position. I sucked his cock as he spanked and rimmed me.

It must have been about now that he told me to take off his boots. I did so lovingly, kissing the boots as I put them carefully aside. Then he fucked me. When we changed positions (as is his wont) my ass disengaged from his cock. This displeased him. I hung my head. He ordered me to lay down on my tummy. He grabbed his belt and started snapping it.

"What does that mean when you hear the belt snap like that?"

"That you're going to whip my ass, Sir. Because I need it, Sir."

Again, I enjoyed the pain. He pulled out my cock and balls from underneath me where they could be gotten at easily. He never touched them. Trust. I began to flinch, asked him to switch cheeks.

"I'm not done with this one yet."

A few more strokes. It really began to hurt again.

"Why are you flinching? Do you need for me to stop again?"

"Yes, Sir."

We lay down again and he held me.

"This is now the second time I've had to tell you. Tell me when you need to stop. A good slave tells his Master."

"Yes, Sir. I'll try to be a good slave, Sir."

"You're not a slave yet."

"No, Sir."

We fell asleep in each other's arms. We awoke a little later. I helped him out of his chaps, kissed them and his vest as I laid them aside. As I lay in his arms again, he said, "You'll get your cock and come later."

"Yes, Sir. Good night, Master."

Later he woke me in the usual way, his fingers up my ass, and fucked me, coming before he meant to. He held me, his cock still up my ass, as I jerked off. He apologized for coming so soon.

"But you got me so excited I couldn't help it. Like you're supposed to."

"Thank you, Sir."

"Thank *you*."

At some point during the night, while I was on my knees, he wrapped the belt around my throat. I was excited and terrified. I've a long-standing phobia of being choked. Later on, sobbing, I asked him if he'd please not do it anymore.

He agreed, saying, "You need to tell me, or how else can I know?"

Then I kissed the belt, again with great pleasure.

The next morning my ass had bruises and welts. It's still bruised. Yesterday it hurt to sit down. He called me last night to check on me before he left for the weekend. He said he'd call me tomorrow. I miss him. I want him. I'm not in love, though. I trust: something akin to love.

28 February 1981

I met Randy Shilts a week ago at the Brig.

Shilts: "How're you doing tonight?"

Me: "Just fine."

Shilts: "Just fine, huh?"

Me: "Yeah."

Shilts: "Yeah? Children starving, social unrest and turmoil in the world, and you're just fine?"

Me: "Yeah. I *was* going to say how much I enjoyed your last article in *Christopher Street*. But fuck you, you arrogant son of a bitch."

Shilts: "I didn't think you knew who I was."

From then on things were fine. He spilled my soda, and I mopped it up with my handkerchief.

Shilts: "What color is that?"

Me: "Dark blue."

Shilts: "What side was it on?"

Me: "The right."

Shilts: "You know what that means?"

Me: "Of course."

Shilts: "That's the side I'm interested in."

Me: "Yeah?"

Shilts: "Know what I like? I like to tie boys up and spank them till they call me 'Daddy' and 'Sir.' I bet that turns you off."

Me: "No."

Shilts: "No? Can I buy you a drink?"

I proceeded to explain that I'd gotten a note from the clinic on Friday. (I didn't know yet that it was just a follow-up check. I had just assumed the worst.)

Me: "So I've got something, and I may have given it to my Master."

Shilts: "You've got a Master? How do you feel about having a Master?"

Me: "I like it. It fulfills a need."

Shilts: "I'm a Master sometimes..."

It was arranged that I would call him. I did. He remembered me. He came over last night bringing his own beer. I called him "Daddy" and "Sir," and sucked his balls and cock, and let him spank me, whip me, tie me up, and fuck me. It was fun but lacked the intensity of sex with Jan. As he left, he told me that he was one of the most interesting people I'd ever meet.

7 April 1981

Jan called. I started off the conversation being off-hand and flippant, ended with "Sirs" and "thank-yous." Quivering and undone. He knows what his Mastery does to me. Jan has grown a beard, and it's very handsome: gray and black. I'll feel his beard on Thursday night.

11 June 1981

This man, Mick, was pleased with me. (He must really like me: He bought me a slave collar on our first date.) Took me out to show me off, rearranging my jacket before we went into the Brig. I got to wear his motorcycle jacket, which made me feel like a child in one of Daddy's shirts. I did look good in it, though. Sweet leather.

I am not to be his slave for a while. I am just his fuck hole until he finishes training me. He said that I'd been much better trained than he had anticipated, that it would be easier to call me slave than he had thought. He called me pretty, made me feel cared for. I felt very calm at the end of the scene. He brought me home around midnight.

24 June 1981

Last night at Hamburger Mary's, as I was paying the bill at the bar, the bartender/cashier handed me my change with one hand and pulled at my slave collar with the other.

"Who's the lucky man?"

I nodded to the dining room and said, "He's in there."

The bartender smiled and so did I. When I sat down again I told Mick. He suggested that we show off and we went into the bar. I told him which bartender (blue tank, black leather armbands, cute) it was.

When I got our drinks the bartender said, "That's him with the hat?"

"Yes."

"You're both hot."

I told Mick, swollen with pride.

28 March 1982

Met a man last week named Steve. He was well-hung and long-lasting, talked dirty and played Daddy. I was a good boy. He worked my nipples like no one had ever done before, giving me pleasure/pain like I've never known. He'd fuck me until he was close to coming, then withdraw and kiss me and/or work my tits. This went on for an hour and a half. Heaven. When it was over, he hopped out of bed like it was nothing. I lay on the bed, spent. He wants to get together again, to do something "besides just fuck."

24 August 1982

I met Brad at the Cauldron two Saturdays ago. We played—had a good time. He fucked me, spanked me, and fucked me again. So I told him I'd like to play with him again. He said, sure, the next weekend (last weekend) would be good for him because his lover would be out of town. I played it cool but gave him my number. When he called on Tuesday, I verified that he was involved in an open relationship and that our liaison would in fact not be clandestine.

Last Saturday at 9 P.M. I arrived at his apartment. He greeted me in full leather. Very exciting. His beard is lush and beautiful. He is muscular and furry. His left nipple is pierced and he has a Chinese dragon tattooed on his left shoulder. We talked for a while before playing. His leather pants had a codpiece. I licked the codpiece and then, when he removed it, sucked his cock. I did my best to give him head, going down as far as I could and trying to control the gag reflex. Once, when I choked, he pulled my head back and kissed me. He fucked me while I was tied to the bed.

"You like Daddy's cock up your ass, don't you, Boy? You like feeling Daddy's leather?"

"Yes, Daddy, yes. Fuck me please, Daddy. Thank you, Daddy."

The session was short and sweet, but lacking intensity, for which he apologized, explaining that he had been studying all day. We sat around and talked, eventually getting back to sex and fetishes. I got turned on and asked him to play with my hole while I got off. He happily obliged. As he slipped a finger in, I handed him his leather cap. He smiled and put it on.

While he played with my hole, he said things like "Come for your old man. Let me see you come."

He poked my prostate right on target, so I stopped jerking on my cock and let it happen: I came like rockets. Then I asked him to notify my next of kin.

3 October 1982

Saw Brad in front of Safeway today. Some men look better by moonlight. I almost didn't recognize him but for his beautiful tattoo.

Meanwhile, at the Catacombs Friday night I played only with Bear. Had a great time. Was assertive, communicative, and allowed the scene to be fluid. We were the only ones in the playroom at first but eventually acquired an audience that included women and straight men getting off on us. I was taken where I wanted to go, and all so seamlessly. I felt so safe and content when it was over that I was close to tears. Felt high from the intensity of the scene, from the eroticism of it. Got to bed around 2:30 A.M. and woke up two hours later with a raging hard-on. I absolutely *had* to jerk off then, and again in the morning when I woke up at 10 A.M. *Had* to. Will play with Bear again in the near future.

6 December 1982

The Catacombs again on Friday. Played with Guy. He tied me very securely, arms and hands, bent over the motorcycle in the playroom, and spanked me all over with his hands and *my* belt.

"I like hands and belts," I'd said.

"I didn't wear a belt tonight."

"I did."

He left several bruises, which I (as always) feel rather proud of.

Then I played with David Lourea, a smaller dark man who, it turned out, has a wife: bisexual. Our scene started around ass play but ended up centered around bootlicking. He fucked me in such a position that I could lick his boots while he was plugging my hole.

"I'm coming, Sir. May I come, Sir?"

"Lick my boot harder, harder!"

I came beautifully.

Then: "Kiss the boot goodbye now, like you mean it."

He told me later that he had never been so excited by having his boots licked before. I told him that he had never been with anyone who enjoyed bootlicking as much I do before. Exceptional play.

20 September 1983 (San Diego)

On Friday night I went out to the Loading Dock wearing a leather vest and black hankie and slapper on my left. Met a handsome man named Rich Jamieson. We went from there to the Hole. When he asked me where I wanted to go next, I asked him, "Do you want to play?" Yes. So I played with his nipples, and we kissed, locked mouths. Oh, for a cannibal's kiss! When we got to his place, I showed him my toys: riding crop, slapper, tit clamps. I topped. Put him in a collar, a first for him. Used his handcuffs on him. Put on my new gloves. He ate my jockstrap, sucked my cock, licked my boots, took my pain, asked for more, and got fucked. When I took the collar off of him, and after we had showered, he fucked me. His cock was *enormous*. *Hurt!* But no complaints.

I spent the night with him in his apartment on Loma Portal, the fan on all night drawing in cooler air from the window and circulating it softly over us, our bodies covered by a single sheet. Beautiful image. The next morning he told me that his roommate had been standing by the door, jerking off while we fucked.

4 October 1983

I want to describe Rich in more detail—particularly his face. Half Polish, he has what he calls a pug nose, one I find very cute, even handsome, in profile: straight, upturned, and present. He's freckled everywhere, even his lips, and has pale skin that burns, then tans. Beautiful coloring. His hair is dark with red highlights from the sun; his beard and moustache are auburn with brown and blond. Predominantly dark red, his body hair varies in color; part of his pubic hair is red, the rest brown.

But what I really want to describe is a certain expression of his. Whenever we kissed our cannibal kiss, he'd sometimes pull his head back, lower his chin, and give me something like a child's sly smile. I've been thinking of that expression for a few days now, and I guess I've only just realized how charmed I am by it.

22 October 1983

Brad last night. Used me as a footstool, a fantasy of mine I'd never mentioned. Had only told him that I needed humiliation. Good sex as well. Used lambskins, which felt very close to natural. He spent the night with me as his lover had a date over at their place.

1 November 1983

Rich arrived on Friday night.

I put the collar on him Saturday night. He was disobedient.

"Whose ass is this?"

"Yours, Sir."

"Whose cock is this?"

No answer.

"Whose cock is this?"

I squeeze it harder. No answer.

"Whose cock is this?"

I squeeze even harder on it. He gasps in pain.

"Yours, Sir."

"Why didn't you answer me the first time, Boy?"

I'm still squeezing his cock.

"I don't know, Sir."

I spit in his face and roll him over onto his stomach.

"Count, Boy."

Three very hard swats with the length of the riding crop.

He told me later that he wanted to see what would happen; when he saw how angry I was, he became frightened. I then explained to him that punishment might involve having the collar taken from him—rejection. He promised that it would never happen again, that he was sorry.

Very hot. Very real. The exhilaration of ownership. And he is so hot. I suppose I'm in love.

15 November 1983

The moments with Rich that I most enjoy remembering are the quiet ones: once in San Diego, when we were lying on the couch listening to Billie Holiday for a while, his head on my lap; another time here, while he was collared and sitting between my knees as I sat on the couch. We were taking a break in the scene, listening to Culture Club's new record. Him naked and mine.

18 November 1983

I think it first all came into focus when I was 11 or so, when my best friend Leigh and I went to see *Wild Angels* with Peter Fonda. Much of it, like rape, was implied rather than shown, and I was simultaneously frightened and excited by it, beyond anything I could remember. Soon, quite by accident at first, I started to jerk off, and then to jerk off wearing black leather gloves, fantasizing about violent sex with men who were virile, hairy; who had moustaches, sideburns, and stubble. And tattoos. And then men raping me. For years I buried it all: loving men, S/M. I wouldn't think about the later for years, not until Robby slapped my buns, got a little rough. Then I wanted more, craved it, though it would be 2½ more years before Jan brought me out into S/M, slowly and with careful deliberation. I will always be grateful to him. A Master, I eventually learned, isn't the monster I was afraid he'd be, but only a part of me, someone to love and cherish, a means of coping with internal dramas and demons.

26 November 1983 (San Diego)

Spent last night with Rich. We cuddled all night long on his waterbed. His left tit is pierced. It will look even prettier with a gold ring in it. The pain was still all there in his eyes, and I wanted to ease it. "You need lots of affection tonight, don't you, Boy?" "Yes, Sir." I held him tightly. Then I made love to him, fucked him both last night and this morning. Left marks on his neck. I always feel the need to mark him.

"Now everyone will know you have a Daddy who takes care of you."

23 December 1983

After Christmas shopping today I stopped to see a leather porn flick at a porn shop on Polk Street. Always a pleasure. Was at the Catacombs last Friday night. After I topped Chuck, whipping him within an inch of his life to the "Hallelujah Chorus," Ta whipped me, forcing me to beg on my knees so everyone could hear: "Please, I've been bad and need to be beaten." Left a lot of pretty marks. The next day at Cynthia Slater's tree-trimming party, she and I went into the bathroom where I dropped my pants and showed her the marks. She liked them. She keeps calling me a sweetheart and a good boy.

"So responsive. I like the way you yell."

Chuck called me the next day to say that his fanny was a checkerboard from my riding crop.

4 March 1984

Topped Mick for the first time last night.

He said, "You've become the person I always wanted you to be."

17 March 1984

Last night I did the Catacombs with Mick. We played differently than we did before (role reversal aside). He asked to be tied up, gagged, blindfolded, and abandoned. I was happy to oblige. Used my new sign: DO NOT TEASE, TORMENT, TOUCH, FEED, OR SPEAK TO THE ANIMAL WITHOUT ITS MASTER'S PERMISSION!!! I got a host of compliments on it. A *hot* party. Fucked Chuck again—this time with a condom, which I felt better about. Called me a "real man" again and complimented me on my prowess. Yes, I *am* good sex.

19 May 1984

Met Yoni at the Eagle after answering his personal ad. I figured he wasn't husband material in about 10 minutes. So, when he kissed me at the Brig and forced me to my knees to lick his codpiece, I accepted his decision that I needed to be tied up and went home with him. If I thought there had been the potential for a real relationship, I'd have demurred last night and held out for more when I knew him better.

Gags, blindfolds, masks, and hoods are his specialties. Safe sex, whips, and hot wax: such a jaded boy. I noticed that there were two different whips used on me without even looking. He gave me a ride home at 2:30 A.M.: such a gentleman.

2 July 1984

After the Parade and going to the dance to see Sylvester with Cary (just like old times), I went to the Academy. Did a very short Daddy. Didn't get his name. It could never be repeated, anyway—safe sex: a condom, no rimming (I refused him the pleasure of "kissing Daddy's asshole") though he begged for it. Proud of myself for sticking to safe sex without breaking the rhythm of the scene.

19 July 1984

Out with Yoni. We capped off the evening with a little public humiliation. He put a collar on me, took me into the Brig, bought me a Calistoga, told me to stand up by a pillar and walked away for a few minutes. Men cruised by me, looking me over. I kept my eyes toward the floor. A major turn-on.

30 October 1984

Leather and S/M as well as my identity as a leatherman are of increasing importance to me. I'm reading Mains's *Urban Aboriginals*. The further I read, the more I see S/M as valid, as my own experience. Also borrowed Grumley's *Hard Corps* from Cynthia. Such are my interests. Also, the more I play, the more I see S/M as essential to my emotional well-being. I crave the sensations of power, of pleasure and pain.

4 November 1984

Did Folsom Street with Pete Hopkins on Halloween. Out until late. Felt like who I was/am: a leatherman, and a hot one at that. I asked Pete why we weren't lovers. He said that he was afraid of me, afraid that I'd release what he wanted to keep locked up: He'd rather stay frustrated. Last night I went to a party at the S/M House (née the Catacombs) with Yoni. He left pretty marks with a braided cat-o'-nine-tails. Feels so good to submit. Lots of humiliation, both there and later at the Brig. I was very happy by the time he dropped me off.

23 November 1984

Lunched with Yoni. Such an enigma. I find him handsome, charming even, more so than before. We talked about dominance and submission, safe sex, group play, altered states. Play in general. I told him how deeply I felt connected to him at the S/M House a few weeks ago. He concurred. The conversation made me want to play. Then he called me not half an hour after he'd dropped me off here.

"I get the impression that you're ready for something more."

"Yes, Sir."

"Yeah, I think you better call me 'Sir.' You'll be hearing from me."

Mike Hippler
When It Rains, It Pours

January 9, 1980

...M. wasn't particularly exciting this time either, because *I* was so high and couldn't keep it up. Also, because we know each other too well now, and I just couldn't get real hot and bothered about it. How do you shove your dick in a friend's face and say, "Eat that big juicy cock, you asshole!"? It works sometimes, but not that night. We should have fucked earlier.

I had the same problem with L. from work before Christmas, only that time he was the one who couldn't get used to the sexual situation with a coworker. He just wanted to cuddle; I wanted to fuck his ass silly. Nobody came, and I ended up not even having to be sly and quiet when I came home, since B. was out partying that night. Probably fucking too, but I know as little about his nightlife as I can these days, and the same holds true for him knowing about mine. We get along better that way.

Of course, there have been other tricks along the way, but just because I have avoided mentioning them in my journal doesn't mean that now, when I have finally decided to open up and be truthful with it again (and damn the consequences if B. finds out—he probably ought to know everything anyway), I should feel compelled to spill my guts out and relate every little sordid detail concerning my sex life here on paper....

One last little story, however. One Sunday before Christmas while B. was studying for exams, I took a bike ride to Buena Vista Park (not my first visit there) and encountered the fattest cock of my entire life. I was so horny, I grabbed the first thing I saw when I hit the bushes, and although he was *not* good-looking I figured he'd have *something* to offer, and God, did he ever! Such a fat cock, my mouth was full forever. His name was Jim—he works at the Rich Street Baths. (A few weeks later, when B. left me to go out one night, I hit the baths to see if I could grab onto that cock again, but [when I saw him there] he didn't seem to remember me.) After the park I went to work, and after work I went home with someone I met on the street at 2 A.M. While we were fucking under the Christmas tree lights, his roommate, this gorgeous hunk, came in and joined us. I fucked his butch ass in an armchair—this tattooed muscle stud who couldn't get enough of my cock up his ass while I drooled in his mouth and shoved poppers up his nose.

Then there was the gymnast I dildoed to death months ago, the S/M freak in the parking lot, and several others. Sexual escapades can be so much fun—but that's all they are: simple fun. They don't mean so much as they used to when I was in Los Angeles, and thank God for that. I hope, however, that I never take them for granted. I forget how oppressive the world at large is for gay people, living in this utopian gay oasis…. I forget how lonely and isolated gay people can be in places like Covington, Virginia. I remember mornings of intense, unfulfilled longings there, moments of heartbreaking nondirected lust, when all I had to satisfy myself was my hand. Yes, I miss the horses, the cows, the fields and woods—but I almost *never* miss the solitude.

July 11, 1982

When it rains, it pours, and Friday morning M. called me up and asked me to come over and lie on the roof. We hadn't gotten together in several months, so I said sure, and yes, we fucked. M. says he wants us to go to Yosemite together this week on my days off, taking his boyfriend's car, and if he's serious about it, I suppose I'll go. I ought to settle down a little and do something constructive instead, but life is too short to let an opportunity to go to Yosemite again pass me by.

One might wonder how T. fits into all this fucking around. He doesn't, really. I've been seeing him every other night—this week it was Monday, Wednesday, Friday, and Saturday—and the more I see him, the more I like him. He's a dream in many ways. But I'm not going to let my relationship with him interfere with the rest of my life. I'm not going to be monogamous, not just because I'm used to fucking around and I like it, but also because I don't want a relationship so serious that T. becomes everything to me. I want him to be one of my boyfriends—not the only one. I can't picture a serious relationship without all the petty bickering and jealousy I hate so much. Anyway, fuck the reasons, I'm going to do what I want.

I don't want T. to get hurt, though, so I had a serious discussion with him on Friday night after work—our first. I told him how much I like him, and I said that I'd be perfectly willing to let things flow as far as they would, but that I wasn't going to be monogamous. I wouldn't tell him about other people unless he asked, and I would expect him to do the same—exactly what he wants to do. What he wants, however, is me, yet he isn't at all grasping or possessive. He wants to take things easy too.

Having said all that, this next part may not make sense. Last night J. joined T. and me for what we thought was going to be a movie. The movie was sold out, so instead we had champagne, ice cream, and a tiny bit of cocaine at my house and then went bar-hopping South of Market. J. was very horny because his boyfriend, with whom he has been monogamous for four months, was out of town. Consequently, he was looking for a trick all night. Nothing worked out for him, though, so since I didn't think T. and I were going to fuck anyway, I invited him over for a slumber party. Not smart. I knew T. thought J. was hot, and J. thought T. was hot, and when you put three naked men in a bed together, all drunk, you are asking for trouble. I must have subconsciously wanted a three-way, for I put T., who seemed the horniest, in the middle and encouraged any sign of "infidelity." Naturally the inevitable happened, and we all fucked. Very weird— not something I thought T. could do. T. fucked me while I fucked J., then T. took turns fucking me and J., which was a joy to behold. (Nobody fucked T., since he's still inoperative.) Eventually, we all came, and T. and I retired to the bedroom to sleep together. (This all happened on the fold-out couch.) This morning I fixed us all breakfast, and I think everything is OK. T. doesn't seem unduly upset, and I certainly am fine. I hope this won't interfere with the progress of an otherwise tender and romantic relationship.

August 2, 1982 (Gay Rodeo)

I ran into B., someone I had met at Moby Dick weeks ago, a 23-year-old beauty whom I meant to connect with but never did. We exchanged numbers, but he went out of town the day after our initial meeting and had been gone ever since. He asked if he could join me, and I said sure, and before you know it, we were holding on to one another in the bleachers and getting very chummy. Soon we couldn't stand it any longer and retreated to a secluded part of the fairgrounds, where I fucked him silly in a horse stable. Such a fantasy—gay cowboys doing it up against a wall in a horse stable. As it turns out, reality is almost better than the fantasy. B. is a model and a porn star who's made two fuck films, one for Falcon Studios and one for J. Brian. The J. Brian film I saw, in fact—it was *Flashbacks,* the one with Doug and Frankie. B. was one of the two men in the opening sequence, the one who gets fucked on the beach. I didn't recognize him from the film at Moby Dick or at the rodeo, but I do remember his scene in the movie. He's also done a few gay greeting cards and the like, and he sells pictures of himself through *Advocate Men*— nude photos of course. Knowing all this turned me on even more and made our tryst in the stables doubly exciting.

August 7, 1982

I've been trying to juggle two boyfriends at once this week, and I'm not sure that's very wise. But I care for both and can't let either go.

Sunday's brief romantic interlude with B. was so wonderful that I called him back on Monday, and we made a date for Wednesday. I spent most of Wednesday getting ready. After the gym and doing my laundry, I cleaned house from top to bottom and then shopped for dinner: flowers from Neda's, baguettes from Bakers of Paris, truffles from Kiss My Sweet, and Quaaludes from J.W. were all part of my plan to seduce this boy. I hadn't cooked a meal for anyone, much less myself, since I could remember, so I decided to go all out. After setting up all the ingredients for shrimp tempura, setting the table, and then taking a shower, I sat down to wait for B. at 6:30.

At 7:30 he finally showed, confused about the agreed-upon time. By that time I was sure I was being stood up and so was livid, but I got over it as soon as I saw him. Dinner was wonderful, and so was the rest of the night, and when he left the next morning, both of us were in seventh heaven. I was surprised by the ardor of his affection—after all, the boy is a porn star and, as it happens, a high-class hustler to boot, but he seems absolutely enamored of me and ready to throw himself headlong into this affair. I am also amazed at the intensity of my attraction. I love to hold him and kiss him. I like to play with him in the pool, bite his neck, and cuddle at night. Part of it is sheer lust, of course, and a lot is pure fantasy. After all, I hardly know the guy. I realize that I'm partly attracted to the porn star image. But I also like *him,* and the more I see of him, the more I like.

Thursday, after we both ran errands, we got together in the afternoon to swim at his place. We didn't spend the night together, but we did get together again Friday for a little while to swim and play around a bit. He came over after work last night and is coming over again tonight, so we've really been spending a lot of time together, and I have no idea where this is leading.

Minor problems that I should mention: As always, health matters are complicated. Because I fucked him silly with no grease on Sunday at the rodeo, my cock was rubbed raw, and since I haven't left it alone for even a day since then (I couldn't—I've had too many dates), it hasn't healed. So every time we get together, I make him promise to leave my cock alone, and he never does. Also, because I let him shove a dildo up my ass on Wednesday, two nights after T. fucked me, my herpes came back again, so he can't use my ass anymore. (That's no big deal. He's a professional whore and knows plenty of ways to be creative; besides, I like to fuck him the most.) However, it's a drag to get herpes in the ass now *every* time I get screwed. It's just ridiculous. Since Memorial Day I think I've had herpes more days than I've been free of it.

Anyway, I can't believe I'm falling for a porn star. I mean, the man is making a movie on Tuesday with one of my all-time favorite porn idols, Tim Kramer, so while I'm working, B. will be fucking and sucking on the beach at Half Moon Bay in front of the cameras (weather permitting). Then he wants to go to the River with me on Wednesday and Thursday. The film business isn't the only thing. Tonight B. had a date with one of his clients, some rich faggot who took him to dinner at the St. Francis and paid somewhere in the range of $500 to $1,000 for sex with him. I don't really care, I suppose. B. doesn't think I should. "It's only business," he says.

As all this has been going on, I still care for T. I've avoided him, of course, so that I wouldn't have to explain anything. He knows I've been screwing around, but he doesn't know with whom—or that it's been with only one person. I'll tell him eventually, but first I want to see how things go with B. and with him. When I told him about fucking in Reno the other night, the intensity of his jealousy scared me—so I've avoided him even more. I never promised monogamy.

January 2, 1983 (Washington, D.C.)

I left something out in last night's journal. I didn't say that on the first night in New York I had sex of a sort with L., my ex-roommate. I was very stoned and fairly horny. L. was horny too, and as he told me later, he's always been attracted to me. "You wouldn't believe the number of times I've fantasized about you," he said. It almost didn't happen, however—it was very touch and go, and I'm surprised it did happen, because old friends rarely fuck after four years of knowing each other, and I was never sexually attracted to him. But I do love him, and it was a pleasant, if not fantastic experience. (I say sex "of a sort" because we only sixty-nined. For me, sex isn't really sex unless somebody gets fucked.)

Do you know that I find myself more and more reluctant to write about sexual episodes as time goes on? I don't mind saying that I had sex, but I don't like to describe it in detail. But surely that is a backward tendency, so for those of you who must know, L. and I sucked each other's cock until I came in his mouth. Then I ground my balls in his face and chewed on his while he tried to come as well. He was never able to, however, and I wasn't especially interested in achieving that end, since I had already shot my wad. So that was the end of that. Now are you (am I?) satisfied?

I deliberately didn't write about this last night, because I didn't want to begin the new year with tales of sex with yet another person.

Richard E. Bump
The Lost Boys Journals

September 19, 1982

Took the bus to Boston last night. Dozed uncomfortably until I stepped off 55 minutes later. Decided to go straight to Club Baths. It's always an experience unlike any other. Created purely for homosex. No pretense of seeing a movie, drinking, or dancing. Just sex. Lust. Fantasies acted out between strangers of every shape, size, and color. The 1980s version of a Greek bacchanal. Club Boston is large and has a character all its own. There's the smell of BenGay that permeates your nostrils and stays in your clothes long after you leave. A smell that reminds me of locker rooms after gym class or a soccer match, of me at 16, 17, and 18 expressing myself physically on the athletic field with other boys. Feeling like a man displaying my battle scars: black eye from lacrosse, broken finger and frostbite from ice hockey, broken collarbone and torn ligaments from soccer, chipped tooth from roughhousing after a game.

Images—flashes and brief glimpses of people with whom you share nothing but lust and desire. A furtive glance. An unabashed stare. Eye contact. Wordless rejection. Accidental eye contact that lingers. Interest. Lust stirred to be acted upon later. Being admired and desired by men I'm not attracted to. More silent rejection. Eyes downcast. Firmly removing a hand from where I don't want it to be. Looking defiant. Staring coldly. Cruel but efficient. Primal communication in a world shut away from polite society. A night where no one was good enough. I began to doubt whether I would score at all. Then I saw this blond who reminded me of a hot and horny bartender I knew from home. Maybe it *was* him. It was hard to tell in the dim light. I cruised him downstairs, then saw him a few minutes later upstairs in the orgy room. I reached out and stroked his cock through his towel. He responded, and I attacked him with my eyes, my hands, my mouth. He was tall and muscular with a smallish cock that tasted delicious, as I slurped on its growing hardness. I sucked and toyed with his well-developed chest and sensitive nipples. I licked his mouth and bit and clawed at his neck and back. He bent over so I could finger his asshole while we attracted a growing crowd that eventually became involved. I glanced up from his butt and spied a boy I had cruised earlier in the TV room. He was tall and broad-shouldered with a small, tight waist and a shaggy haircut that partially covered his hungry eyes, and he was staring at me and not at the blond whom everyone else was now ravishing.

I began to tease the tall kid with my eyes and cock. He struggled to get through the crowd to me, and when he did the passion ignited. He had a sweet, gentle smile. With one hand, he removed his towel. I had to stand on my tiptoes to reach his lips. We searched for a private corner. Orgies had sprung up around us. He begged me to suck him. I refused, still teasing. We found an empty mattress, where we kissed like two sex-starved, love-hungry young men. People groaned in orgiastic ecstasy around us. We devoured each other with every sense, every way possible. He produced a bottle of poppers, and we became like wild animals fucking and sucking in that dark orgy room. Tension. Near release. More poppers. I come a lot. We kiss. His body jumps and jerks, and he cries out as if in pain when his cock explodes. More kissing. We hug. He calls me "man." I stumble out of the orgy room, sleep fitfully while disco blares on the loudspeakers all night and, exhausted, take the bus back to Providence in the morning, realizing nothing will come of our chance encounter. The baths: You go there for sex, not love.

December 11, 1985

This kid delivered firewood to my house last night, and after he finished unloading his truck, I asked him if he wanted to come in to warm up before he left. He said yes, and we sat down on the floor in front of the wood stove and talked and played with my cats. I got up to answer the phone, and when I came back he was lying on his back, his T-shirt lifted to expose his alabaster-white stomach, his jeans unzipped enough to reveal no underwear, just a few red pubes. I lay down next to him and began stroking the cat that was on the floor between us. He began to do the same. I reached over and began stroking him. My hand ended up down his pants and wrapped around his small, bullet-shaped dick. He smelled of axle grease and demolition derbies and Marlboros. I pulled off his jeans, lifted his legs over his head, and licked his crack, chowing down on his hairless virgin ass. He moaned and squirmed in pleasure, saying no one had ever done that to him before.

We retreated to my bedroom. He wanted to fuck me; I stripped and raised my ass while he stood at the side of the bed. It took him a few awkward attempts to get it in. He wasn't big by any stretch of the imagination, but for some reason it hurt like hell. He fucked me fast and furiously, and said it was better than fucking his girlfriend. He slept naked in my bed and listened to a heavy-metal radio station all night.

February 12, 1989

I had promised to take William out for his 20th birthday: I arrived at his house at 7 o'clock. His mother's car was not in the driveway. I approached the back door; the techno remix of *Phantom of the Opera* was blasting from the stereo. I knocked once, twice, then let myself in. There he was: skintight faded white blue jeans, rolled up T-shirt, ripped-up tank top, black motorcycle boots, and ears full of safety pins. The one in his nose was fastened to a chain, which was attached to another pin in his ear. He was sporting a church full of rosary beads and crucifixes, big and small. On his wrist, my "Rebel" I.D. bracelet and a cock ring.

He took his beat-up black leather jacket outside, spread it out on the driveway, and spray-painted a big white X on the back of it. We made quite a pair and that's the effect he was trying to achieve: him in his punk rock armor, me in Gap jeans, red turtleneck, white cardigan sweater, and military surplus overcoat.

I asked him where he wanted to go. "Someplace gay." We drove to

Thayer Street and walked around and couldn't make up our minds. We ran into one of my clients ,and her jaw dropped at the sight of me and my date. Tongues will wag.

We settled on the French restaurant where he used to work, full of chichi attitudes and conservative East Side patrons. Both of us were so wired, it was as if we were on coke. We ate from the same crock of French onion soup and barely touched our salads and entrées, excused ourselves in the middle of the meal to have a cigarette in the adjoining bar. He began rattling off song lyrics by a group called Suicidal Tendencies: "Fuck you, fuck me. I saw your mother. She was dead...." Charming.

I reached across the table and lightly slapped him across the face just to get his attention. I hit a nerve. He loved it. He warned me to stop. I smiled and didn't stop.

Our waitress wrapped our picked-at food, and we almost left it behind. All heads turned as we left the restaurant, but we didn't care.

We stopped for dessert at the bakery where he works. We shared a slice of banana cream pie and took turns feeding it to each other.

We couldn't decide where to go next. Coming down a bit from our initial high. No place to go. No scene to crash. His house? My house? New York City? The decision was made when I turned left onto Rochambeau Avenue—my house. He wanted to smoke a joint he had stashed in my room.

Ken was home. We made brief small talk with him in the living room. Then off to my bedroom. He found the joint and lit it. Offered me a shotgun. I declined. He's a fucking handful to deal with straight. We thrashed around and wrestled on my bed, and I fucked him through a hole in his jeans. I realized I'd never fucked a man with a chain in his face. Before long, his jeans and the rest of our clothes were scattered around my room. We took turns slurping on each other's cocks, his a bit fatter than mine. Shaved balls. Soft belly. Chewable nipples. Hungry mouth.

He said he didn't feel right spending the night. I decided to take him home, but before we left I pulled my black leather belt out of the closet, the belt with all the chains hanging from it that my uncle had gotten during the war. He almost came at the sight of it.

He said that before he could go home and face his mother he had to make himself look more presentable. He lay back on my bed, and I sat astride him and forced him to submit to me—symbolic rape. One by one we removed the safety pins and crucifixes. I held his belt against his throat and mouth-fucked him with my tongue. I unfastened a big safety pin from his earlobe and scraped it slowly across his jugular vein, then chewed and sucked on his neck for a while. The last piece to go was his nose chain, which I removed deftly. "No one has ever done that before," he said softly. He figured it would be OK if he wore just one pin in his ear. He couldn't get it through the swollen hole by himself, so I pierced it for him. No blood.

He looked like a virgin once everything was removed. Innocent. Defenseless and vulnerable without his armor.

He ritualistically arranged his stuff on my bed, pulled down his jeans again to expose his ass, and I took two photos with my Polaroid to chronicle our date: one for him, one for me. He said he was going to give his to his mother.

It was time to go, but he didn't want to go home. He spoke of not letting many people in. He said, "You're in." He said he often feels confused. He can't control his sexual urges. He doesn't trust himself.

We drove back to the same French restaurant where we'd eaten dinner earlier and ordered tea and another dessert. He propped his feet up on my thighs, then rested his head on my shoulder. He quoted more song lyrics, and a new crowd stared at us. *Fuck them,* I thought. *Who cares?*

I wrapped my arm around his shoulder as I drove him home. He said he feels safe with me. He sucked on my finger.

When we arrived at his house, we took his pit bull, Max, out for a walk. Max pissed on a tree. Billy pissed on the sidewalk. The steam from his piss rose off the concrete as he strutted down the street with a still-leaking dick. We kissed good night. "Drive safe. Use your high beams. Wanna go to a movie tomorrow?"

As I pulled away I turned for one more look. Billy: a whirling dervish in faded denim and black leather, circling, whirling around

Max under a streetlight on a deserted street on a moonless February night. And as that free radical revolved and danced around his beloved Max, who in turn was dancing and circling around him, I think I fell in love with him all over again.

I went home, called him to say good night again, and went to sleep, my hard-on replaced by a smile.

November 16, 1990

A boy I had shamelessly cruised at the Y last night was there again tonight. I concentrated on him, and he showed up as if I had willed him to appear! That's been happening a lot lately. I think of someone or something, and then it happens.

I had finished working out and was alone in the sauna. He entered. We were both naked; I had a towel strategically covering my crotch. He wore a thin gold chain around his neck. There were curly hairs around his asshole, which appeared when he sat facing me, his feet planted on the bench, knees drawn up to his chest.

He had a perky cock with a decided hook to the left, half-erect. We pretended not to be looking at each other, but my stiffening seven-inch cock betrayed my growing lust. After a while I let my towel slip away to see how he would react. Out of the corner of my eye, I saw him casually stroke his dick. Several times he got up and left muttering that he "had to take a cold shower" only to return again a few minutes later. One time I stood as he announced his departure and turned toward him as he passed me in the cramped wooden box that smelled of cedar and teenage B.O. and sweat, and his hand accidentally on purpose brushed my erect cock as he passed by.

When other people joined us in the sauna, we would cover ourselves with our towels and wait for them to leave. And when they did we would silently remove our towels and each wait for the other to make the next move.

At last we were alone again, and I was growing dizzy from the heat, the excitement, and the anticipation of what might happen next. Almost in unison we began stroking our hard cocks—one eye on each other, the other on the window in the door, four ears listening for advancing intruders.

He stood up and draped his towel over his head exactly like the boy in the photo that I had cut out of a porn magazine and hung over my bed. Did I invent him? An image I had jerked off to alone in my room was now before me in the flesh.

He approached the door, and I was afraid he was going to leave again. I couldn't take much more of this cat-and-mouse game. I couldn't take much more of the heat. I thought I might faint or pass out from dehydration. He paused directly in front of me, inches away. Our sweaty bodies were almost touching, his curly brown hair hanging in ringlets around his 18-year-old face. I figured it was now or never, and I reached out and touched his cock. He didn't pull away, didn't say a word—simply reached out and began stroking mine. We jerked each other off, our sweat making the perfect lube. It didn't take long for him to shoot his substantial load onto my thigh. He continued to jerk me, and I groaned as I showered his washboard stomach with my jism. The cum mixed with our sweat, and we headed for the showers just as the sauna door opened and two other guys took our places.

I may never see him again. I don't even know his name. But it was one of the hottest sexual experiences of my life.

January 30, 2000

Joe Sunday: a name like a porn star or a cowboy, a face and body like River Phoenix. Too many teeth, scruffy beard. Big fat dick. He took a long time to come. "I really wanna come, man." He apologized for being "long-winded." Said he should've warned me. I said, "That's OK. It means we get to kiss more." He didn't seem like the kind of boy who would like to kiss: ex-Marine, grew up in Bethel, Pa. Lived in a row house in the poor part of town, the only white family in a Puerto Rican neighborhood. He laughed when he said they were a minority within a minority. He asked me about Perma-Doors. Said he was thinking of putting one on the house that his mother gave him after his grandfather died, a Cape Cod in New Bedford, Mass., with cedar shakes that his grandfather had painted yellow—the one color he can't stand. He wants to put beige vinyl siding and new windows on it, then finish off the basement with a family room and a weight room.

When his family's home in Bethel caught on fire, the whole row of houses burned; the Perma-Door survived the blaze, but his 6-year-old brother did not.

He liked my tattoos, especially the Celtic cross because he's part Irish. People ask him why he doesn't have any tattoos, having been in the Corps and all. He said he has two on his ass, courtesy of his father who beat him with a 56-inch leather belt after he'd let his little brother cross the street when he was supposed to have been watching him—two welts that are still obvious years later. He said he's had lots of friends and acquaintances who have told him that parents shouldn't beat their kids. He said he was grateful he'd gotten regular whoppings from his dad, or he would've turned out worse than he is. He said that today he'd be on *America's Most Wanted,* if it hadn't been for his dad's beatings.

He wanted me to fuck him without a condom or lube. He begged me to let him swallow my come, but I shook my head no. I wouldn't even let my last boyfriend do that, though I had let one guy at the bookstore do it a few weeks ago. We kissed a lot. He tasted like Appalachian coal mines and smelled like tar. His fingernails were black. He works for a roofing contractor. He loves the steam room at the gym. Says it reminds him of California. He says there are only three areas in the country he would live in. He holds up a finger with each place he names so he doesn't lose count: (1) New England, (2) North or South Carolina, (3) California. Arizona was OK, but he likes being near the ocean.

He likes working for the roofing company. One day he could be in Boston, the next day in Caribou, Maine. He likes to travel. He can't explain his Southern twang. He says he never thought he could love a 4-cylinder, but his Dodge is sweet. He drove a '68 Chevy cross-country. That car was sweet too and got good gas mileage. He liked driving on Route 66—drive-ins and dinosaurs and no speed limit. He asked me if I wanted him to fuck me. When he tells me his name, he says not to bother making a joke because he's heard 'em all. He says it's of German origin, and he laughs because he can't figure out why someone would change their name to a day of the week.

He's like a baby in my arms. He doesn't trust meter maids, so he always parks in a parking lot or a garage. I'm parked on the street, it's snowing, and there's a parking ban in effect. While we're making out to "Be My Baby," the club attendant announces over the intercom that the police are towing cars, so I get dressed and say goodbye.

I smell him on my fingers and taste him in my mouth all the way home.

Steve Nugent
He'll Read It in My Eyes

Wed., May 24, 199_

Ken phoned just as I was getting out of the shower, nearly not going to answer it. Wanted me to drive down to Brighton with him in the afternoon—a meeting there just came up. Brilliant weather. I had to ask Joan to come in. She was going to take the day off. A bit pissed with me—wouldn't blame her!

K. thinks his contract will come through for the job in Islington and seems to be getting more confident about it. Not your glamour job, he insists. Just your ordinary bank manager, a BM as he calls it. "I'm actually a GWMBM," he hoots.

Tourists everywhere, packing the souvenir shops. K. to his meeting. Sat in the sun on the stony beach, and then we went for dinner at the Dog and Firkin.

Back home by 9. K. started on how we could be so much better off if he got the new job...have to Tube it more each day but more moola. He thought that after six years we should be lying into a bit of luxury, not always having to be so careful, and he feels he depends a bit too much on me having the store and subsidizing him at times. We finished up a bottle and then did our sex number. Got up later to get a drink of water, and he was naked outside the clothes, so I just sat admiring and holding his half-cocked dick for a while before going back to bed.

Thurs., May 25

Morning. Joe on pager. Lunch at the usual. Worried about how his new job is going. Bill Broyer there giving us the eye, so tried to look businesslike, as he'll probably tell K. that he saw me with some hunky-looking guy. Told J. that I don't want to lose him and at the same time don't want to hurt K., so he got sulky and ruthless and said that it sounded like I really liked K. more than him, so he needed time to "back off." A few minutes later we are in his flat, fucking like animals. He's sooo hot. I can't get him out of my mind. Keep thinking of the look on his face as he strips me and runs his tongue up my body.

Evening. To Jane's birthday party. How old today? Must be 45. She's in a full-length flowered taffeta and kisses everybody all round. K. loves her, so they fuss together. The usual crowd—very dressed up. Jamie Balfour there looking like Keanu in *The Matrix*. Kevin Green, a decorator, pulls me aside to ask who I was with in Granthams last week. I look vague, so he prompts, "The hunky one—you must remember." Since he assumes, with a laugh, that I'm busy with K. in my life, what about an intro? K. joins us right then and listens to me telling Kevin that the guy at Granthams was just somebody was I do business with. "And anyhow, Kevin, the guy is as straight as an arrow." A close one. I'm going a bit nuts inside, though.

Fri., May 26

Can't sleep. Up at 4 drinking milk.

Very busy at the store. Joan sick, doesn't think she'll make it tomorrow. Won't say what's wrong, so assume gyn. (Jesus! Not preggers?) French couple want to buy Picasso litho. but he's a fussy bitch and wants more time to research it. Could do with the sale right now at the end of the month.

With K. at the club for lunch on the roof. Swim first, attempting instant relax. Lie in sun and watch the 3-D sky of blue and puffs of white. Thinking of J. all the time. K. asks me if anything is wrong. I blame the store, a bit worried about sales. He's used to hearing me whine about that. Watch K. in the pool. Looks paler, maybe losing weight. Hair showing thin in the water. Feeling distanced from him. How long is it since I met J., now? Christ, only three weeks.

K. suggests having dinner at Salvados. "A bit tired today. How about tomorrow?" I swear that if I have to sit opposite him, he'll zero in on me, and the way I feel today, I'll probably crack.

Home. K. straight to bed. Fiddled with chat line: golden-brown complexion, dark hair and eyes, 6 ft., 30 yrs., 170 lbs., 33 W, 40 C. Is he passionate? Could he be J.? Tried herbal. No effect, only up to pee later and can't get back to sleep. Where's J. now? What's he doing? People take Prozac for less.

Sat., May 27

Up "very betimes," as Pepys would say.

Venus to vet for checkup. OK. More exercise, less food, putting on too much. Resolve to do park run for her—and me...on weekends. K should do more with her. Maybe I should visit my G.P. too.

To gym 7-ish. Milling crowd of the buffed and burnished. Arms and chest. Pain. I'm getting old. J. says that's why he likes me: wisdom and knowledge and so on. To Celillos for groceries. John Rafter there with muscle boy—what a tosser!

Store busy. J. phones. Lunch. To his place later. He has this thing about humming like a vibrator when he rims, which drives me wild. Heavy discussion follows. Says I should tell K. "Not now." "Well, then he may find out." Thanks, J., so reassuring. K. is very touchy about other guys...always checking me out. J. says that means he must always have been distrustful and that if I look closely at my relationship with K. there'll be a whole lot more that is problematic. Sure, that applies to most relationships. J. is pushing things, I feel. I tell him it's only been three weeks—he backs off a bit and says, "Well, you know what you feel." He's got his "backing off" tone. Truth is I want them both, but they'll never go for that. Haven't really talked about our feelings that much. Always seem to have somewhat panicky conversations about our situation. Love was only mentioned once when we were fucking ("Making love," J. corrects me) when he said that he thought he was falling in love with me, and I shut him up by putting my dick in his mouth.

Movie at the Curzon: *The End of the Affair.* K.'s choice. Tried to steer him away from going to see it, but he insisted. Is he sending me a warning? Afterward he said he liked it but doubted that people went to such lengths for each other in affairs, and anyhow, her husband didn't seem such a bad sort really. I froze. He later said that he thinks the job is for certain now—told by a mole in the bank, so I chattered on about that.

To Jump on Greek St. for drinks and then back here before 11. Coded call from J. Wish he wouldn't do that. Watched movie, fell asleep, K. in bed when I woke up a few hours later.

Sun., May 28

Mum, Godlovethewoman, woke me up at some unearthly hour to invite me down on the spur of the moment, as always, for lunch. Wants me to get to know her new boyfriend and potential husband-to-be. Ted seems as ill-suited to her as her previous three, including my dad. "So how are you and K. getting along these days?" says she in an over-cheery tone. "I thought he might come down with you." "You didn't invite him, Mum." Her knowledge of relationships is confined by her belief that there is a red-blooded man for every red-blooded woman on this earth. Wonder what it would be like to have a mother who would respond to my talking about J. and K. right now—all I seem to think about these days.

Man on the Bakerloo Line cheerfully urinating. Watchable dick was a saving grace. Back by 6. Couple next door having a hi-vol. row that went on longer than usual. Phone rang a lot. Called J. who was on night shift, talked about nothing much, as his coworkers don't know he's gay. K. in Faversham doing his filial duty too.

Mon., May 29

Spotted Judi Dench getting out of a taxi and into the Oratory wearing a huge beflowered hat...a wedding, christening? Funny day for it.

Quiet day at the store. Didn't mind the slack as I need to do some heavy thinking. I'm beginning to feel trapped in this situation. As other people would see it, presuming they have never fallen in love with two people at the same time, I'm an out-and-out slut. I suppose I care what others think. I'm in a relationship with a really great guy who is devoted to me and who respects me fully. J. insists that can be a form of control. It's not ideal, but then nothing ever is. And people comment on how sexy K. can be…and he *can* be, but I've not given him many chances recently. He's not the shrinking violet type and has a big intelligence (not so sure about J. in that dept.), although he has a slightly goofy sense of humor. J. can be really affectionate. I lose myself in him…just flip out when doing it with him. Suppose it's just physical. I know a lot of it is the sex…but he's a super-nice guy too. Am I shallow? The answer could be yes. Is this just a phase? Perhaps it's infatuation with J. and will all go away and leave me back where I was—happy (unhappy?) with K. Now the anxiety I feel is like some great beast that claws at my innards and never leaves me alone—except when I'm fucking J.

K. unexpectedly in the store after lunch. Said that he was on Gloucester, so almost next door and thought he'd just drop in to see about having that dinner at Salvados? He looked around for a while, said the store looked good. I watched him like a hawk. I thought he had something on his mind…and that something could be me. Then he drifted off while I was with a customer. He had just left when J. paged me. He's free for an hour at 5…[*in his stroking voice*] "What about it?" So I'm there in 10 min., and we're all over each other. Wants to see more of me. Now really dreading dinner with K. He's onto something. He'll read it in my eyes.

Robert Marshall
Diary of a Smurf

August 199_, San Francisco.

If he were an ad, I tell myself (as I cross the dark bar) he might read: "5 foot 10, 180, 44 C, 30 W." He's smooth, he's young, he has black hair; I can't read his expression. The way his muscles join: the work, I think, of a craftsman, a perfectionist. When I speak, he responds slowly, smiling slightly. Turns out he's a biochemist who works in the East Bay. Also a classical musician. Likes Chopin. Used to belong, in college, to a Christian fundamentalist group. He's beautiful and *nice*. It's hard to believe he would want me. Leaving the bar, he suggests that we take a walk, and he shows me the park where everyone goes after 2 A.M. I think this means we will go there; he will, I imagine, want a blow job. As we walk, I'm trying to decide what *I* want, what I will do; I picture kneeling in the damp grass—but we don't go to the park. Instead, he drives me back to my hotel, showing me, on the way, the sights—Coit Tower, where I went once with W. We lie on the bed in my room. He won't kiss. Tells me it's too intimate to do with someone he doesn't know— he doesn't want false intimacy. When he says this, I feel I don't either. I start touching him, he murmurs; I lick his neck, he murmurs, but also sort of moves away. I try to take his shirt off. "No," he says, "don't." He doesn't, I think, want his perfect body touched—or even *seen*. I trace his muscles through his muscle-T. When I go too far, he pushes my hand away. A game. And a struggle of wills; within that (as is always true), *my* struggle of wills. I can't help thinking his beauty shouldn't be wasted; it should be used before it fades. By him, the world, me. If it isn't used, then what's the use? I think. His skin is golden, the walls light blue; the curtains and the lamp- shade, ochre. Dennis Cooper, *The Princess Casamassima,* and a glass of water on the bedside table. The way we're *being together* feels pleasant, sad, odd. I ask him about bodybuilding. He tells me he does it for the pleasure of the obsession. In a way, he says, it's like his music. Usually, people spend hours in the gym so they can have endless sex. That's the way it works, at least in my imagination. But not for him. I don't believe his virginal attitude is fake. It may be for the best, I tell myself, that we just do what we're doing. But I want to *have* him. I can't help thinking, or feeling, that if we had sex, that would somehow make this experience *count*. I would know what we were doing here.

October, NYC

Seeing someone beautiful on the subway, I think, *I'd like to fuck your brains out*. Not knowing what I really mean by this; it's an automatic head sentence meaning: *You're beautiful.*

October

Tony's 25. He designs accessories; his hair's dyed blond. He is club-kid thin. We have "good sex." Tells me how he is going to conquer the world. He and his friends are going to have three lofts, one on top of the other. "I will *not* go to South Beach on the weekend," he says disdainfully. "I'll go to Spain—on the Concorde!" There are faint lines, delta-patterns, on his skin. "I don't like Flamingo East," he continues. "There are just *boys* there. I want to be the boy." We signal to each other with our breathing, like cartoon Indians sending smoke signals. I breathe. He breathes. I breathe in a different way. He responds. A game. He likes the band Massive Attack. "A good fuck"; after a while it becomes just sort of work, exercise, numbed. Later we eat blueberry yogurt.

November

Leaving my building, a cold day, dressed in my overcoat, my knit hat pulled down over my head, I hear one of my neighbors, a straight man, saying to his girlfriend, "Smurf." I turn around and stare. He says, "Well, you do—you do look like a smurf."

November, Saturday night

I run into Manuel at Uncle Charlie's. Equally embarrassing that I go to this bar and that once, five years ago (right after he'd moved to New York, from Yale, from Peru), I wanted to sleep with Manuel. Even though I now know and dislike him, I still want to. Slightly. But won't. The whole *point* of Uncle Charlie's, I think, holding my Rolling Rock and a smile, is that you're not supposed to run into anyone you know. We'd both rather be talking to someone else. I try not to stare too obviously at a boy in a leather jacket leaning against the bar. Manuel tells me that he had sex with a hustler recently. "Oh," I say, trying to be, if not polite, not rude, "tell me about it." He tells. Met guy in bar. Took home. Guy told him he was hustler, could do whatever M. wanted if he was willing to pay. "And," M. concludes, brushing back his black hair, (self-satisfied, cat-having-eaten-mouse-like), "I had a great time fucking him." Telling me this story is, for Manuel, a sort of a sex act in itself. Not consensual. I don't get and can't take this need to boast about having fucked someone. Standing in the crowded bar, I imagine replying, "Why are you telling me this?" Or: "I find it interesting that you're telling me this." Nothing, I think, is more American. More *American male*. But I remind myself, Manuel is not American. But then I'm not sure. Maybe he is.

November

A dermatologist's office. I wait for HIV results. Can't read the faces of the people leaving. Or the magazines. A bald muscular man on his way out asks the receptionist, "Are these free?" Condoms, I assume, in the glass bowl. On my own way out, I see instead small packets of sunscreen.

Saturday, 2 A.M.

I talk on the phone to a boy I met on AOL: GIVUJOY.

"Do you shave your dick and balls?" he asks.

"No."

"You are *so* not relationship material."

"That's great," I laugh. "That's going in my journal."

He plays with me. I lie on the couch, drinking orange juice and vodka, listening. "Do you want to come over?" he asks. "Are you coming over? I'll just be lying here ready for you all lubed up, oh yeah, with my firm ass ready for you and then you'll fuck me all night, yeah. My ass is so hot, even other bottoms want to fuck me. I really want it now…why don't you come over?"

I'm not sure how literal he is about being fucked all night long. I've never fucked all night long. I'm never sure whether to believe people when they tell me they *fucked all night long*. Figure of speech? Maybe there are lots of people who fuck all night. Maybe I'm sexually inadequate. I'm tired, I think, sipping my cocktail. I couldn't fuck him all night long. This could be humiliating; but maybe it's worth the risk. His voice and screen name are sexy. I can't decide what to do. I look out my window at the lights of Fourth Avenue.

"All right," I say a little cagily, "tell me where you live."

He gives me an address.

"OK, I'm coming over."

"That was the wrong address," he says.

"You shit," I say. "Why did you give me the wrong address?"

"If I thought you were *really* coming over I would have given you the right address."

"What's the right address? (I still don't know if I want to come. But I try to sound determined, *like a top*.)

"I'll tell you if you really want to come over."

"I really *did* want to come over."

"You know what I want," he says. "I want to cuddle. That's what I really want…."

January

The doctor.

1. He's slender and smooth, dark-eyed. We're resting after sex. His story: His cousin was his lover, seven years. Then it ended—he hasn't gotten over him. "I don't want to fall in love again," he tells me.

"It hurts too much." He just wants someone to have sex with. The way he dwells in his sadness isn't healthy, I think, but it draws me to him. We're lying on his bed in the half-light, with erections. Mine with a condom on it. And then we are lying in bed without erections. And then one with, the other without. The focus is on this, somewhat. But also on his story, his sadness. I'm afraid that if we're too intimate, if we talk too much, if it's more than *just sex,* he won't want to see me again. He tells me he isn't popular at the hospital; he gets angry about all the mistakes they make in the lab; people don't like him because of this.

2. I hold his toes while we fuck. A shape like a cloverleaf freeway. Spelunking, as if touch were sight. Reaching into a dark grab bag of gifts at a children's party. Or maybe playing pin the tail on the donkey. Do you remember what that felt like, wandering dazed on the patio in your own dark, blindfolded? The feeling of going over into another world in the middle of the day? The adults watching, while temporarily you crossed to the other side? I am gone from myself in that way. I'm in the haunted house, going down a dark corridor, unanchored, immersed, thrilled, feeling my way.

3. He is always polite when I call. But after a while he doesn't want to see me anymore.

February
On the subway, remembering as we pull into Union Square: Trying to fuck someone, I think, and having a hard time: It's like a child trying to put his foot into a shoe with difficulty, not able to get the angle right.

March
A boy who once rejected me on an AOL date enters the gym as I'm leaving, says hello. For months he's ignored me—or we've ignored each other. Now, I think, we're like enemy warriors who acknowledge each other as they pass during a truce on the streets

of some neutral city. Walking up Lafayette, I wonder if he hates me for being hostile toward him (because he rejected me). Maybe he's justified in this. I should have a better understanding of the rules.

May

I go out to Greenpoint. A boy on the street says to the ice-cream truck, "Can I have a cone, Mr. Softee?" I lick the shaft of Javier's dick. I play with it. He comes. He plays with the pool of come on his stomach. In his room, some of his collages are pinned to the wall. There's a pile of muscle magazines, a barbell, a TV, which is on so his roommates won't hear us. I don't come. No big attempt to make me come; I'm glad. I wonder whether he doesn't try to make me come because he doesn't care if I come or because he thinks I don't care whether I come—some people do care whether the other person comes, to some people it's very important, it's hard to know whether a person cares about that, how important it is. It gives me a kind of power, in this case, to not come. I'm *servicing* him, I tell myself. I guess because he's beautiful. I'm not obsessed, I think, by beauty—by his beauty—in the way I used to be. Prozac? Still, it seems somehow right that his beauty should be serviced. He isn't arrogantly beautiful. Maybe he doesn't know he's beautiful. Or maybe this knowledge is offset by other stuff he hates about himself. He smiles cutely a lot, and I'm not sure if I'm required to smile cutely back—I do, some, but not enough, I think, to satisfy him. I resent this. One of his pubic hairs is caught in my throat.

Gay Pride Day

I go to the "protein bar" with Javier. You can order a carrot ginger juice with designer protein. Or a carrot juice with creatine *and* designer protein. Or just creatine and water. There are several other types of proteins, but I'm bad with names. The sign on the door says: "You'll feel so good, you'll want to go out with yourself." The joke, I think, is obvious; the men here *are* going out with themselves. They're enormous. Someday, I tell myself, I want to write about men and size. I recognize someone who goes to my gym. So this is how he gets that way, I think. The smell of the place: halfway between food and gym. It's like eating in outer space. The men, I think, seem post-human. I wonder how Javier will respond if I say this. I order a carrot-apple with designer protein. I feel like an imposter and wonder whether this will become part of my regular life. I joke with Javier. He jokes back, which makes me like him. But the mood of the place doesn't invite sarcasm. We leave and walk to the Village. Javier's slightly more into the parade than I. We go to meet his friend Kevin, a cellist, J.'s only friend from The High School of Performing Arts. He's handing out flyers to all the black men who pass us on Grove Street. A sex party tonight at his apartment on Canal.

After we leave the parade, Javier and I go to a diner in Chelsea. He orders a Greek salad. I ask him how a sex party begins: What do you do when the first guest arrives? I'm really asking if he's been to one of Kevin's parties. He tells me he doesn't know; I should ask Kevin. Lots of energy kicking in from the protein shake. I want to go out with myself. Javier tells me how he once took "yohimbé rush." He was having a date and knew he was going to be the top. "I wanted to perform well," he says. I feel weird. I think about performance and eat my spinach pie. The hovering fantasy of *being a stud:* anxiety-provoking, heart-quickening, somewhat horrible to me but also pleasurable. The idea's frisson remains with me after we leave the diner. It's still there later, while we touch each other (intense pleasure!) in the movie theater and watch Disney's *Mulan.*

While we're having sex that night: the possibility, glimpsed, of sex without fear opens up like a meadow glimpsed through the woods on a passing train, and it's gone before too long.

September

The smiling bald man's face in an HIV-medication ad at the bus stop. Unremarkable now, I think. Just part of the landscape, but in the future, I tell myself, when you write your historical novel about the '90s, it's a detail you'll want to remember.

January

I fuck the Korean dancer. He's beautiful, looks a little like W. Says I have a sweet face. Impeachment looks like a sure thing. Hard to believe.

March, France

I go to the baths in Nice. An abandoned part of town. I find, after a long search, the right door. Fake plants are used to create a *grotto* effect. I wonder what people think about when they design bathhouses. Are they sincere and enthusiastic in their desire to make a space that "works?" How does this work? It's 10 P.M. in the fifth largest city in France, and there are four men here. Not what the *Spartacus Guide* suggested. I spend five minutes, then walk back down the Avenue de la République toward my hotel, past occasional tourists playing in the fountains (something you are, according to *Fodor's*, supposed to *do* in Nice). As I walk through the indigo half-cloudy night, I imagine a homosexual architecture school. First semester: design a bathhouse. I enter Vieux Nice. Thousands of straight teens own the streets, going from place to place, looking for a cool place among identical places (which exist for them—and me—to go between). French spring break, I guess; Fort Lauderdale with patisserie. You can buy sandwiches, sodas, or pastries. You can drink, be "entertained," I think, as I wander, depressed, through the swarm. I buy an Orangina and a small quiche. Maybe, I think, I should go back to my room and write postcards. I'm angry with myself for having chosen a cheap hotel. I walk instead to the pebbly beach, where I eat the quiche. Corsica is out there somewhere in the dark sea, I tell myself, trying to feel some *romance* or *power.* I compare my life to that of the straight French teens. I don't feel really homosexual. I do feel outnumbered. The waves appear in the dark, like men, and come to nothing on the beach. *Too poetic,* I tell myself. I try to think about *traveling alone.* I'm 37 years old, sitting on the shore of the Mediterranean.

Dan Perdios
My Ian Diary

January 18, 1994

I could never say the things I feel about you directly to you or to anyone else. Only here in my journal can I honestly admit these things. From the moment I saw you on Castro Street, I wanted you. At 6 feet 4 inches tall—a head above everyone else—you stood out among the many. When our eyes met I felt a thrill of energy. I was with friends, and it looked like you were, too. We both continued on our way, giving each other the turnaround look as we walked on.

Despite the throng of visitors for the Folsom Street Fair, I thought about you many times those next few days. I searched for you in every crowd. I beat off to the fantasy of you lying on top of me, of your arms wrapped around my body, of your cock deep inside me. I met lots of people that weekend: leather-clad bodybuilders; cute, cuddly bottoms; masters and slaves—but none of them had what I saw in you. You seemed to have disappeared; I imagined you had met some hot guy, the two of you stashed away in a steamy marathon. The weekend ended, and I kicked myself for not making the connection when I had the chance—another missed opportunity.

And then there you were in Guerneville the following week. I could barely believe my eyes when I looked around the bar and saw this big guy with a shaved head and long goatee. My heartbeat raced. I hesitated for a second to make sure it was you. Our eyes met, and you smiled. It's one thing to pass up an opportunity in San Francisco. I wasn't about to make the mistake twice. I walked right up to you and said, "What are you doing here?"

"What are you doing here?" you replied in a deep, low English accent.

"I live here."

"Lucky you. I'm just visiting for a few days."

"I can't believe you're here. Can I touch you to make sure you're real?"

"I'm quite real, and yes, you can touch me all you'd like."

I reached up and ran my hands through your goatee. Your hair was silky with a few gray hairs. You were so tall, I felt short beside you.

"May I touch you?"

Your words sent quivers across my body. "Oh yeah. You can touch me anytime you'd like."

You put your arm around my shoulder and pulled me into you close. I liked being near you. I liked our bodies touching.

"Let's leave. Come home with me."

"I'd like that," you said, and so we left.

Back at my place we devoured each other's lips and tongues. I played with your long goatee, and you liked that. You bit my neck and gave me a hickey, and I liked that. When we took off our shirts and looked at each other, we both sighed. You reached out and caressed my chest, and you groaned. I ran my fingers through the thick long black hair that covered your body.

You wasted no time before latching on to my nipples and squeezing them tight and tugging on them hard. I felt spasms of pain and joy. My cock was solid. Both your nipples were pierced, the left one double-pierced. On one shoulder was a tattoo of a dragon; on the other was a snake. Your body hair grew up through the ink, making the tattoo as natural as your skin, and that turned me on.

Suddenly, you reached down and put your arm between my legs and lifted me up into the air—me, who definitely likes to keep both feet firmly planted on the earth. I felt like a boy in daddy's arms. I giggled and blushed and kissed you and ran my hands over your shaved head. You turned me around and carried me to the couch, where you lay on top of me.

We kissed some more, and I reached down and felt your cock through your jeans. "Let me suck your dick," I whispered.

You slowly rose from the couch. I unbuckled your belt and unbuttoned your fly. Your cock popped out, all seven inches—and another piercing. I opened my mouth wide and took your cock with its P.A. all the way down my throat. I started to choke but found my composure. I wanted all of you down there. I wanted to swallow you whole.

Looking up at you aroused my spirits. When you looked down at me, I felt little. A bit intimidated. You seemed daunting. You looked like a Hell's Angel biker. You mumbled in a deep voice with a British accent. I couldn't understand half of what you were saying. But I know you completed sentences without saying fuck this or fuck that. You looked dangerous. Your size made you strong and powerful, yet you were kind and gentle and caring.

Your legs were like the redwoods surrounding my house. "I pedal a bicycle to work," you said. I sucked on your fat cock and felt the metal down my throat, while I ran my hands up and down your hairy legs. Even now, as I write this, I get hard. You sat back down on the couch, and we kissed some more and pulled on each other's nipples.

Then I lifted up one arm and pushed my nose right up into your pit, and it was ripe, beyond locker-room mustiness. I stuck my tongue out and tasted your raunch, and I almost shot my load. I licked your stench like a cat laps at a bowl of milk. I rubbed my face all around to get your odor on me.

You pushed me back and sucked on my armpits, raising both my arms high over my head and holding them there as you switched from one side to the other.

Then you pushed me to the ground and rammed your cock down my throat, and I sucked as fast and as deep as I could without chipping a tooth. This was when I noticed the tattoo around the shaft of your cock. In the shape of a star. "Wow. I like this, " I said and took your cock all the way down, inspecting your star at closer proximity. Each time I sucked I aimed deep for the star. I opened my mouth wider and wider. I wanted to reach and touch it with my lips. It drove me wild. I could feel my cock throbbing.

"Let's go to bed," I suggested, taking a breather.

"That's a good idea," you said.

We walked down the stairs to the bedroom below.

"On the bed," I said.

You followed the order. I lay on top of you, and again I felt like a little kid in daddy's arms. We kissed some more, and I wondered if you were feeling the same thing I was: the warm good feeling you get when you meet someone special. "You feel good. You know that?"

"You do, too."

"Will you fuck me?" I asked.

You rolled me over. "You got any condoms?"

"Behind you." I pointed to a box on the back of the bed. You grabbed a condom from the box and tore it open. I watched you place the opening over the P.A. and slide it on past the second piercing and down to the base. I grabbed some lube and greased up my hole. I worried a bit about the condom breaking from your piercing, but you seemed to know what you were doing, and I trusted you.

Your cock felt so big going in. I could see the piercing in my mind, and it turned me on. I wanted it further and further in. I wanted to feel it all the way up my ass. I wanted to feel it slam against my prostate. "It feels good." I whispered, pulling you close to me. I wanted the star around your cock to touch the skin of my ass.

You rose up and rocked back and forth, fucking me harder and harder. I grabbed hold of your nipples and yanked. You grimaced and fucked me faster. I ran my hands through the hair on your chest and traced the outline of the dragon and snake: with your body in motion, they seemed to come alive.

"I'm getting close."

I wiped the beads of sweat from your forehead. "Maybe we should take a break?"

You slowed down a bit, leaned forward, and kissed me; I held you tightly.

"Can I have a turn?"

We rolled over and switched positions. I put a condom on my cock. "There's something I want to do first."

You looked at me somewhat bemused. I lifted your legs, bent over, and spread your ass cheeks apart. I stuck my nose right down there and then my tongue as far as I could. It tasted sweaty and salty and even a bit shitty, and I liked it. It was enough to be nasty without being repulsive. My cock responded largely.

Then I pushed my cock inside you. I could tell you didn't often get fucked; your hole was tight, but you were willing and eager. I slid my dick in and out, and a big smile appeared on your face. "It's been so long," you said.

You pulled me down close to you and kissed me, grabbing my nipples. "I don't know how long I can hold out," I said. "I'm so close."

"Shoot all over my chest," you said, tugging hard on my nipples.

"Here I go." I pulled out and yanked off the condom and sent streaks of hot come across your chest and stomach. Then I crashed into your arms.

"Chew on my nipples."

I pinched one nipple and bit the other while you stroked your cock. Your breathing quickened, and you growled. "I'm close." I squeezed harder. "Oh yeah, I'm gonna shoot."

You shot gobs of jism across your chest, and some hit my face. I had never seen anyone come in such large quantities. I tasted your come: salty and sweaty. "Mmm. Nice."

We lay in each other's arms and napped.

That was the start of a wonderful three weeks together. Now you are back in London, back to your world; I'm back to mine. I treasure the memory of those weeks together and the friendship we've developed. I'll always think of you as my big Ian, and I'll always be your little Dan.

Mitch Cullin
Aguas de Marco

March 12, 2000

I suppose only love could bring me to L.A.—because I hate the city more than, well, Phoenix or Las Cruces (actually, I don't mind Las Cruces too much). And how weird to think that somewhere under all this smog someone is writing a screenplay based on my second novel; possibly even weirder that I have no desire to meet the writer or let the agent who put the deal together know that I have finally entered his world. I've driven nearly 500 miles, going where I swore I'd never go again—for love.

But this is Peter's L.A. (small coffeehouses, West Hollywood clubs, food-food-food, downtown warehouses)—not the same place I visited as a child and teenager, not that boring tourist stuff (well, unless being a tourist means us searching in vain for a road up to the Hollywood sign, hoping to piss on a few of those towering letters!). Tonight we stood in line at Pink's just to eat hot dogs, eventually pigging out as the sun set. Earlier we strolled along a Malibu beach, where I tried to get Peter to pose for some pictures: "No way, uh-uh!" I'm pretty sure I got a good one of him with his back turned, standing at the edge of the beach, the water moving toward him—also, he at least agreed to let me photograph our bare feet together (fingers crossed that it comes out!).

Anyway, Malibu was nice—got a beautiful blue seashell to take home with me tomorrow, a nice reminder of a very good day. We had tried driving to Malibu yesterday, but the coastal highway was closed (we found out a woman had tried killing herself by plunging her Volvo off the upper main road and down onto the coastal road— reliable ol' Volvo didn't help her attempt, she should've done it in a Yugo instead), then there was a shooting on the Santa Monica pier—

another California drama that stopped all traffic. At least we made it to Malibu this afternoon—then Pink's, then a long walk past the shops on Melrose.

How can I sum up my feelings about today with Peter? Let's see... hmm...how about...pure bossa nova...that's it! Pure bossa nova with Peter driving, me beside him, my hand in his free hand—even as he weaves around traffic, zooming to stops, turning here and there. Holding hands even as we get lost in Santa Monica. A red light means a kiss. I can kiss him when we're at a red. We've kissed so much, in fact, our lips are chapped; we almost look like circus clowns, or—as Peter's friend Alex has kidded—like Naomi Campbell wannabes. And all the while it's bossa nova, coming from a mixed tape that has been the soundtrack to our sight-seeing—Peter's soundtrack when he's in L.A. without me, I think, because he knows the words, sings them under his breath perfectly while driving. Ask me how I feel about today—I say, "Samba, baby, samba!"

Gassa nova too—but in a good way! We started out at the Farmer's Market, great place for a Sunday breakfast (in our case, breakfast/lunch because we slept in again) and people-watching: elderly couples, rough Hispanic teenagers, trendy ponytails and cell phones and parents pushing strollers. I had a knish, in honor of The Beatles who had also tried knishes there. We sampled some hot sauce too, which nearly killed us! We ended up scrambling around the Farmer's Market looking for water.

Then, while we were waiting for our food, Peter kissed me. See, this is what's incredible—I hate public displays of affection, cringe at them. And when I see two guys doing it, I usually find myself thinking, *You're just trying to shock the easily shocked straights.* Still, with Peter it seems incredibly natural and right, and I delight in it. In fact, I must hold his hand as we stroll around the Farmer's Market; I must kiss him at Cantor's or when walking through Chinatown or studying the interior of Union Station, I can't help myself—and I suspect he feels exactly the same way.

Anyway, the kiss at Farmer's Market was classic: No sooner had our lips parted when I noticed Larry, an old friend of my father's, walking past us (a man I knew from my childhood in Santa Fe, whom I had once visited in L.A. 14 years earlier). So there was Larry, and there were Peter and I kissing. All the same, he didn't notice me—and I made no effort to reintroduce myself, though perhaps I should have. I think he would have liked to see me again; he probably would have been glad to shake my boyfriend's hand too. Feel kinda bad about not saying hi...

Now we're back at the Livingstone Hotel, which is great. The room has a late '40s quality to it, the wallpaper is peeling near the ceiling. Last night, after returning from dancing at Rage and drinking apple martinis at the Abbey, we snooped along the dim hallways—but no signs of life could be heard coming from behind the other doors; no other guests were walking around. Kinda spooky: In the two days that we've been here, I haven't seen another soul, aside from the elderly desk clerk and a guy who smokes his pipe in the lobby every afternoon. Still, it's nice feeling like the hotel is ours. I mean, we can make as much racket as we want; we can laugh and moan and roll about without worrying too much that we're disturbing someone—and I don't think the fedora-wearing ghosts passing through the walls mind us at all, because we're very respectful of this wonderfully decaying place, and they're probably grateful for our appreciation.

This morning, while Peter was showering, I sat out on the balcony (where the wide red-brick ledge made an idle place to sit) and spotted a mockingbird in a nearby tree. OK, I can't say if it really was a mockingbird, as I don't know birds very well—but it did mock me. I'd make a tweeting noise, then it'd make a tweeting noise. The more I tweeted, the more it tweeted—until finally it jumped from the tree and landed within two feet of me. When I tried scooting closer, it turned and flew. Oh well.

Then it was my turn to shower, and afterward I saw Peter sitting on the balcony ledge, quietly enjoying the sunlight. He didn't see me watching him, because I was inside dressing and could see his reflection in the window. But how contained he looked to me, so peaceful and reposed—hands folded in his lap, legs stretched out along the ledge. And if I didn't already realize how much I love him, I would have known right then. OK, I know I go on and on and on about him— our lovemaking, his sense of humor, the whole separated-at-birth joke we keep imagining is true (you know, ying/yang, different sides of the same coin, Irish boy from New Mexico/Asian boy from California, writer/painter). But the fact is I am in L.A.—no one else could have brought me here except him. Need I say more? Well, how about this, a Rumi rumination: *Gamble everything for love, if you are a true human being. If not, leave this gathering.*

All right, let me finish this up here, because soon he's coming to bed, and I want to be ready for him—plus, tomorrow I head back to Tucson, so I need to hold him for as long as I can (running my hands along his shoulders and spine, my chest against his chest, my tongue pushing inside his mouth). And if he asks me to stay another day, I will. I'll do whatever he wants; my calling is very specific. Needless to say, I'll fill you in later.

Clifford Chase
Rebound

Sept. 11, 1992

Assuming Glenn and I really are breaking up, and not just taking a break, how does one find a boyfriend? I thought I was in love. Four years with him.

Sept. 14

Half a boner thinking of Glenn. Grind it into the mattress.

Oct. 10

Went to a party last night with Robert. Note: The boy I was most attracted to, I hardly talked to. There was this other guy, from Tennessee, I think: Keith, who was really cute but maybe a little dull. Bulky shoulders and these sleepy blue eyes that conveyed a sexy, insinuating stupidity.

What makes another person interesting?

Oct. 12

George invited me to a Gay Games mailing party after work, so I stayed late to help. I figured I'm single, try something new. We stuffed and licked envelopes for two hours. The boys were sort of cute, very nice, and not the least bit interesting. There was this cute black guy there, about Glenn's size and build. I said stupidly, "You look familiar to me." He smiled. His name is Barry.

Oct. 13

George called this morning and said Barry wants to go out with me. Why not? He seemed to have a good sense of humor. Plus a nice butt.

Oct. 26

Much sniffling and sneezing. Keith, the sexy Tennesseean, called last night. I liked his voice. I like a manly voice, with a little fagginess mixed in to reassure me. I said I'd call him when I was over this cold.

Oct. 28

This guy Barry and I are going out Halloween night. More or less a blind date. It seems a mistake, but what else would I do for Halloween? I'm seeing Glenn around 1 o'clock the same day. Hopefully, I can go to the pool and swim off whatever bad vibes there are. I sense this is a "final" meeting of some kind.

Robert said: "Be forewarned. I think Glenn shaved his head." The news depressed me: Glenn's fabulous new life without me.

Oct. 31

I'm sick *again*. Now I have to cancel this date with Barry.

Glenn's head was indeed shaved. He looked a little like Zippy, quite honestly. We chatted, ate, then began the final round. I arranged my plates symmetrically. He said, "Well, I'm optimistic about our being friends." I agreed, adding, "I'm glad you feel that way." Long pause. He cleaned up his spilled sugar, gathered the paper packet into his cup.

Nov. 7

Will I ever figure out sex? I think of myself as such a fag now, but if I add it up, I actually have more experience with women. I came out so late, and then there was Glenn. Ironically, I think I was a better hetero lover; I seemed to have better sex with girls. Maybe I'm too romantic to be a fag.

Still groggy. The doctor says I have postviral fatigue.... Keith called. I felt open to him. I definitely wasn't doing all the work. Something really sweet and sexy about him, something crooning about his croaky drawl. The things he told me about himself were interesting to me. His mother was a beauty queen, his father a college jock who made him play football. Thus turning him into the fucked-up, sexy faggot athlete he is today.

Nov. 14

I'm cat-sitting at Pascal's in the East Village. Black and slinky, Kato just came and looked at me and walked away. I guess that's all he's ready for.

Nov. 19

Just back from my first date with Keith. He's awfully cute, and there's some sort of connection between us, but also certain warning signs: (1) Each time I've talked to him, he's mentioned going out drinking and having a hangover. (2) When I said I've only slept with four men, he recommended Club 82 on E. 4th St. "You can go get a blow job. It's safe." I thought, *But I want a blow job from you.* (3) He mentioned that his last boyfriend was violent. (4) He seems to revere a sexcapades sort of gay life that I've just never been able to relate to: Fondly, he recalled an orgy on a boat when he was in college. (5) I'm not sure he's attracted to me. Maybe I'm too vanilla.

Nov. 22

Another date, this time with Barry. I'm really attracted to him. We went to his apartment after I met him at work, and he changed clothes in the bedroom with the door open. He has a beautiful body. (Weights and handball five nights a week.) Glimpse of his full, dark ass in white briefs as he disappeared into the closet. My own shorts were wet when I stood up. We went to dinner. The restaurant was hot, and he stripped to his T-shirt, and I thought, *Wow, biceps.* His skin is very dark, darker than Glenn's, but his face isn't as handsome. Very rounded features, but cute and very masculine. An intense gap between his teeth.

He's very much a heart-on-his-sleeve kind of guy, though also kind of immature. He said so himself, and then I noticed it: We were eating at Bombay, and he started speaking in an "Indian" accent. He also seems like one of those happy-go-lucky people who actually are really negative.

I want to have sex with him anyway.

Dec. 13

So what if Barry isn't "it"? I took him home last night.

He saw Glenn's drawing in the kitchen. "Oh, that's right—you said he's an artist," said Barry. "Is he any good?"

"Yeah. Actually, he's kind of famous." I wished I hadn't said that—it's rude to Barry. But it's how I feel. I have enormous respect for Glenn, and I miss him. I saw the picture of him hanging above my desk, and how I missed his face.

And yet the sex with Barry wasn't bad. He has the most beautiful, smooth, glowing, almost indigo-dark skin, even-toned and hairless. He's quite muscular. Pretty short but really built, very solid. Hot. Smallish dick, but I liked holding all of it in the palm of my hand. He was very relaxed about sex. We wrestled around, stopping to talk, wrestling some more, different levels of intensity, then more talk. He can go from one to the other quite effortlessly. This morning we made out some more. I lost steam, we talked a bit, then he said he wanted to come and began to jack off. "Am I being a pig?" he asked. I said, "Not at all." I found his directness refreshing. I guess I felt OK about not going further. I thought, *Well, I'm going as far as I want.* But once he came, I wanted to. So I jacked off too, with him kissing me. I had some trouble focusing but eventually did, thinking of him for some reason at the moment of the crest, thinking of the white stubble under his chin where the hair would grow out gray.

Dec. 19

Ran into Keith on the street; we made plans for a possible dinner Monday in the neighborhood. What a hard-on he gave me. I kissed him goodbye.

"Can we kiss in Brooklyn?" I asked.

"I guess so," he replied.

Jan. 1, 1993

In San Jose at my parents' house, remembering a stray snippet of a moment with Glenn: "Those jeans give you a sexy butt," he said.

"They're baggy. You can't see my butt."

"I can imagine it."

Then wondering why he stopped feeling that way.

* *

In the park, the roving eyes of a guy who was just doing pull-ups flash upon me and away as my sister and I walk by. Was I cruised or did our eyes only accidentally meet? He was tall with tanned, bulging, long thighs—maybe 21. I imagine him thinking, *Who is that slender and apparently young and possibly cool person here in my old neighborhood?* He's home from college, and what if his sexy running and pull-ups are just a way of coming out?

I also note there's some kind of halfway house for delinquent boys on the next corner. I saw a black teen going into the house in the rain this morning. Something about the detail of the rain, his being out in front of his group home—he came to life for an instant in my mind.

At Burlington Coat Factory, looking at sheets, I saw a set of zebra-striped material. Alone, I made that Eartha Kitt kitty-growl to myself. If one is campy in an empty aisle at the mall in San Jose, does one make a sound?

Jan. 2

Brooklyn seems empty right now. Odd to get home on a Saturday night—who can you call? No mail except bills. I've been snacking ever since I got home, and watching TV and beating off. Tears in my eyes through the whole ridiculous movie on the plane—*Last of the Mohicans*. Then I went to the lavatory and cried outright. By the time I got out, there was a line down the aisle. Someone had even jiggled the knob, which made me mad, so I concocted retorts in case anyone said I had taken too long: "Maybe I shouldn't have flushed, so you could see all the work I've been doing in there."

Feeling slightly erased after several days with my parents. As I served the turkey, Dad asked for dark meat. He said, "I guess I'm the only nigger."

Jan. 8

Wednesday night with Barry was a disaster. He was weirdly distant, affectionate only at moments. After television, the cuddling was constantly interrupted by phone calls. "I'm sorry," he said, "I'm really out of it. I must be really boring." We lay around for two hours or more. "You've had a stressful couple of weeks," I offered, but my feelings were hurt. As he lay with his eyes closed, he said, "Did you ever wish you could disconnect all that shit you're thinking from the other part of your brain, the part that breathes and farts?" (I thought, well, I could do without the farts...)

I said, "Does what's on your mind have to do with me?"

"Yes, that's part of it."

A side note: Thinking he was Glenn, I had withheld this question for *two hours,* believing it would be pushing him too much even to ask. But he, not being Glenn (or my mother), simply answered. Then he said he didn't want to talk about it right now, which he repeated six times, and six times I said OK. Either he thought *I* was someone else, or he was giving me six chances to coax him into talking about it.

Then he started really flipping out, making these fake whimpering noises and exclaiming, "I wish I could just shut up!...I have all this shit going on in my head—what I have to do tomorrow, the next day—and I say I'm too busy, when really I'm just lonely and trying to fill up my life...see? I can't stop babbling." He hit himself with the pillow. "I'm freaking out." And that fake crying sound, which I thought at any moment might become real.

By this time it was getting late, and I was sleepy, and either because of that or in spite of it, I pretended to myself that nothing out of the ordinary had just happened. We were quiet for a while.

"There. Three minutes," he said. He was calmer.

"Could I stay over?" I asked.

"No," he said, laughing. I thought he was kidding.

"Really?"

"Yes, really."

I was sort of pissed. It would take me an hour to get home, and I was tired *now.* "Well. I'd better get going," I said. I lay there a respectable moment, trying not to be too abrupt. As I rose and put my watch on, he began to apologize. At least he was sorry. "It's OK," I lied. I kissed him. "Take your space. Don't worry about it."

He said, "It's just that I don't always do enough for myself."

"Don't worry about it."

I took a cab home. But as I lay in my own bed, tossing and turning, I was pissed. This morning I thought, *There are too many twists and turns on this road.* Last night he said, "You'll get bored and dump me in the recycling trash bin where I belong."

Well, it's true, he *is* a stopgap...

Jan. 20

Glenn: "So, what are you doing for your birthday?"

Cliff: "I'm having a party, I guess. I can't really deal with having you there."

Glenn: "OK."

I'd been thinking of telling him about my father's nigger comment. Decided against it.

Jan. 22

Hilarious that I'm supposed to write a gay bar guide, since I hate bars, especially gay bars. Went to two tonight. The first was an over-30 Christopher Street crowd. A guy about 60 as I squeezed past: "Don't grind when you go by!" Two go-go dancers, a blond and a brunette, both pretty sleazy, especially the brunette, who was just a little overweight.

I cabbed it to Boy Bar, which has reopened. My fortune cookie yesterday said, "Don't mistake a temptation for opportunity." The temptation in this case wasn't sex but self-hatred, the kind where you stand around and no one will look at you.

I asked the bartender who did the videos. "Me!" he said. A big goofy Mark Morris kinda guy, his shorts pulled halfway down to reveal the tattoo on his hefty ass. His videos really are good.

I stayed about 45 minutes. He refilled my beer, which only made me drunk, not brave. I was there too early, anyway.

Jan. 23

I saw that foxy neighborhood boy again, the tall dark one who dresses very much on the left. He wore a purple shirt and tie tonight, ultrahip in a goofy sort of way—dapper. I always see him at art openings.

Too bad about Barry. I think about him sometimes.

Jan. 31

I'm glad I threw my own birthday party. Ralph brought a huge cake with 35 candles, and he turned off the lights before carrying it in from the kitchen. Everyone jammed into my apartment, singing to me. A lot of love in the room.

"What are your wishes?" asked Pascal.

"Oh, I have lots of wishes," I said airily. Of course, what I really wished for at every wishing opportunity was a boyfriend.

Later George said, "I can't imagine what kind of boy would be right for you."

I'm not sure either.

Feb. 6

Snowing out. Jimmy Scott singing "All the Way." The CD given to me by Glenn.

Feeling very sad lately. "Have you ever seen me this way?" I asked Noelle (my therapist) yesterday.

"No," she said. "I wouldn't say you're depressed, exactly. You seem to be drifting."

What's changing in me, and what isn't?

Feb. 10

Blind date in a half-hour. Today at lunchtime Pascal and I browsed in the tacky furniture store on Madison. "This more and more looks like a gay brothel," he said in his clipped Swiss accent.

A bed with a leopard quilt—I said it was the perfect bedspread for my blind date tonight.

"Are you sex-starved?" asked P.

"Ever since Barry freaked out on me, yes."

* *

Ben [the blind date] was just OK. Short. Not really handsome—gaunt face, big nose—yet possibly sexy. Or maybe once he was sexy, when he was younger, so maybe he still thinks he is, which would mean that he might still be.

He's a writer, and I wonder what it would be like to date another writer. I can't tell yet how smart he is. We parted after two drinks, but maybe we'll get together again.

Feb. 19

Went to a dance concert with Ben, against my better judgment (I was sniffling and sort of out of it—allergies, I think). He looked cuter. I'm still not sure I want to get involved with him. He chain-smokes, and it turns out he's also sort of a pot head. We disagreed about the performance. I found it very General Foods International Coffees—something Anna Maria Alberghetti would enjoy. He found it "beautiful." I think I sort of convinced him otherwise, or did I simply ruin it for him? It made me miss Glenn, who seems so much smarter and more interesting.... Even so, it's calming to be "dating." It contributes to that "I'm just fine" feeling.

Feb. 21

In my dream last night I came upon a handsome workman who'd fallen unconscious. The locale was some cross between Santa Cruz [where I went to college], Beirut, and Jerusalem. The once-peaceful collectives outside the city walls were now bombed out. The big guy woke, groggy, unable to move. I asked what had happened, but he wasn't sure. I thought, *I hope he's gay so that after I save him we can be lovers.*

I was attracted to this guy Sam at George's party last night. I have a little hard-on. He wasn't so handsome, but he had a hairy chest, wrists hairy as paws, blue eyes above a 5 o'clock shadow.

* *

George just told me he's straight. So much for that.

Otherwise there's Ben. I'm undecided. Then there are neighborhood crushes, and how do I meet them? This very cute, very short little fellow in horn rims who lives on North 7th Street here in Brooklyn. Looks sorta like a sexy Muppet. I borrowed his newspaper at L Café one day. Is he gay?

Then there's this tall blond guy at the pool, with a kind of nerdy face, glasses, and perfect, lean shoulders, that slightly wide kind of hips, all nearly hairless. (I prefer body hair, but anyway.)

Feb. 28

Disappointing date with Ben last night. He's really sweet and smart, but I don't seem to be attracted to him. I suppose it's possible to be only kind of attracted to someone. He *is* kind of cute—nice jaw, nicely thinning hair, pretty blue eyes—except they look so baggy and tired.

Sad about Ben, because I really do like him. Physical attraction, friendship—it's a mystery to me, how they do or don't work together, which to look for, whether to favor one over the other.... I really thought I was into having an affair with Ben, but then when he actually showed up, he just looked so short and nebbishy, hunched in his cap and coat.

March 6

Went to The Bar last night and struck out. Dinner tonight with Ben. Well, maybe I'll be pleasantly surprised. Maybe his cock is some kind of mesmerizing cobra.

March 7

Made out with Ben last night. Another mixed bag. He was passionate and a little too rough—the nipple-pinching "Oh, yeah!" school—which I wasn't crazy about, but it didn't turn me off either. He had a surprisingly cute little body, pretty hairy even on his back, which I kind of like. He's tiny, but he's surprisingly fit. As I first put my hands up his shirt and felt his firm back, the few stray hairs there, I thought, *Hmm, this could be better than I expected.* He looked cute with his shirt off.

Earlier he showed me a picture of himself in college. I was right: He used to be much more handsome. He hasn't aged so well. It helped me delineate those features that are still cute—the blondness in his eyebrows, very nice jaw and mouth, nice cheekbones, very blue eyes.

We made out for maybe 45 minutes, and then we were both ready to stop. At one point I took his cock out of his shorts, but then I put it back again.

Am I a prude or just an old-fashioned girl?

March 8

Connecting with Ben made me miss Glenn again.

March 13

A huge storm, snow somehow combined with thunder and lightning.

I had a really nice time with Ben last night. You know, he's OK. We made out off and on for a long while, talking in between. Finally, the safe-sex conversation came, putting a damper on everything somehow. Maybe we were both ready to stop anyway. I'm still not sure what's going to happen with him. We may not ever go all the way, whatever all the way is. But I'm liking the way he makes love. I haven't had such good sex in a very long time.

"You're very intense," I said.

"Do you mean I'm too intense?"

"It's a compliment." At least I think it is.

Outside, the wind is so strong it's snowing sideways.

March 20

Ben and I went to his parent's house on the Island for his birthday. A little too soon to be meeting the family. His brother-in-law said, "You gotta get him to quit smoking." Hey, I just met the guy.

Back in the city, he asked me to sleep over—his birthday request. It seemed manipulative, but I complied anyway—immediately regretted it. Me, him, his Chihuahua, a cat and a stray kitten, all in his tiny studio apartment. An old torn blanket on the bed, the litter box not two feet away. We made out again, he was really intense again, and we stopped in the middle again.

I couldn't sleep—the kitten running around the apartment all night.

March 27

Of course, I couldn't not go to Glenn's opening—his first solo show, after all—but it left me feeling defensive and sorry for myself.... I noticed that he had gone and bought for himself the very $250 shoes he had given to me for my 34th birthday, and I knew he bought them because he isn't my boyfriend anymore, so it doesn't matter if we own the same shoes.

His friend Kate from San Francisco said, "I was really sad to see you guys break up."

I replied, "We were sad too."

March 28

I was going to go with Ben to Provincetown this weekend, but this morning I called him and canceled. Strong feelings of regret. But I've also been feeling very hemmed in by him.

March 29

I dreamed my old dog Sam came down the hall wearing the most desperate and sick expression. "Sam! Sam! What's the matter?" I said, afraid he'd just scoot by me in his animal panic and despair, running from his illness. But he stopped and looked at me sadly, and I began petting him. "What is it?" I crooned. "What's the matter?"

Maybe I *should* go to Provincetown...

I suppose it's possible that I like a lot of things about Ben but definitely don't like others. When he called yesterday, he got cut off twice because the kitten had chewed through the cord.

April 2

...I don't know, I guess life will wash things onward, part of me lagging, part of me swimming forward, and maybe everything will suddenly seem in sync again, which is I guess what being in love feels like.

I dreamed about that blond guy at the pool. He owned a thrift shop, where I searched for every cool thing so I could get to know his tastes and show off my good eye. He knelt beside me just as I opened a tiny drawer that was filled to its tiny brim with an amber, rectangular jewel. "Beautiful, huh?" I said. He smiled.

Eric Brandt
Penis Noir

Saturday morning, April 26, 1997, 3:30 A.M.

Dear Diary:

OH MY GOD! You won't believe what happened to me tonight! (Oh, all right, so you've been expecting something like this all along.) Remember my good friend George? We went on one date, had bad sex, and then he dumped me? Well, it was gorgeous today—a California day, all warm and sunny. I couldn't seem to get a lick of work done, so I decided to let bygones be bygones and called George and asked him if he wanted to go out for a drink at one of the two bars in the Castro that have sunny balconies.

We meet at the Metro, but the drinks taste sour, and the sun has slipped behind a building and left us in the shade. So off we go to the Café, the girls-and-boys place with an outdoor patio. We head to the back bar, but there is no bartender stationed there, so I say, "There's no one back here!" To which a very cute, flirtatious Amerasian with two beepers on his belt replies, "What about me?!" I explain that while he seems very nice, what we really need is a bartender, so we go to the front bar and get our drinks. We try the patio, but all the sunny spots are taken; we decide to move to the balcony. As we pass, the Amerasian boy with the two beepers says something else that is flirtatious, and I invite him to join us on the balcony, but he's playing pool with his friend.

We sit down on the balcony, and George tells me to go. I ask, "You want me to go? Now?" Mistakenly, I think he wants me to beat it so he can either seduce the Amerasian or some other boy he sees, so I disappear and play pool with a lesbian who can't find anyone else to beat. Throughout my game of pool, I continue making periodic eye contact with the Amerasian, trying to gauge whether he's going to talk to George or to me. I strain to see if George is talking to someone else, but George seems to be concentrating on the view from the balcony.

The lesbian finally finishes me off, and I start back toward the balcony. On the way I pass the Amerasian, who says something else flirtatious, so I introduce myself just as George steps back in from the balcony. Seems that when George told me to "go," he wasn't trying to get rid of me, but trying to encourage me to go talk to Two Beepers. So now George and I are talking to the Amerasian, whose name is Lawrence (which he insists on our pronouncing as "Laurent"—you know, like Yves Saint Laurent). George asks about the two beepers, and Laurent says, "One's for work, the other for pleasure; one beeps, the other vibrates— guess which one is which!" Laurent is now playing pool, and he tells me that his opponent is kicking his ass, and I ask if he likes that. The conversation continues at this high level of sophistication, till George and I are ready for Chinese food and invite Laurent along.

At the restaurant we are seated with Laurent across from me and George next to him. It's a good thing that the place has long tablecloths, because while we are eating Chinese, Laurent places his foot in my crotch and his hand up George's shorts. The meal was delicious!

Standing on the street after dinner, Laurent, ever the cool one, suggests we go someplace to watch a video and smooch. George worries that it might be complicated because he has a roommate. So we troop off to my place, but not before stopping at a liquor store because Laurent *must* have more wine. While Laurent smokes at the curb, George hurriedly tries to pick out a wine; I stand at the counter, ready to pay.

"Red or white?" George asks, at a loss.

"Red or white?" I call out to Laurent.

"Red!" he answers, blowing smoke.

"Merlot or Pinot Noir?" George asks.

"Merlot or Pinot Noir?" I repeat.

"Penis Noir! Penis Noir!" Laurent gleefully calls back as I blush before the expressionless cashier.

* *

Watching a video was a silly idea anyway, so we are chatting and smooching without ever turning the TV on. Suddenly, George and I are helping Laurent off with his shirt, and then George has removed his, followed in quick succession by a flurry of pants and designer briefs, and then they are both naked and argue that I should be too. I had whispered to George earlier that whatever else happens, I get to eat Laurent's ass. I'm doing just that, and George is alternating between blowing him and kissing him, and then as I take a minute from his asshole to nibble on his thigh, I notice a puddle of come there. (Did I mention that Laurent was 25 years old? His mother's Vietnamese, and his father's American of Dutch descent. He lives with his boyfriend in Mountain View, a suburban town, in an "open relationship"—as long as he has more sex with his boyfriend than any one other person, they are content. He claims to have been a trainer before he started working for Charles Schwab, and by the looks of his tight little body, I believe him—the boy has a butt of steel!)

Things roll along: I get a blow job from Laurent while George is sucking my right nipple and then kissing me, wondering in an aside whether I'll talk to him in the morning. I say, "Yes, just keep sucking my tit," and then we fall into a daisy chain, and then I am really sticking my tongue as far as humanly possible up Laurent's ass when George asks if I have any lube and condoms. I pad off to fetch the same, and return to hear George telling Laurent he wants Laurent to fuck him, which surprises me a bit since all indications suggest Laurent would far rather *get* fucked, but George rolls a condom onto Laurent's enthusiastic dick and attempts to sit on it while I go back and forth between Laurent's talented mouth and George's dick.

Then they are finished (whether any penetration occurred remains a mystery) and lying together on the floor. (Did I mention that this is all happening on top of the oriental rug that my parents bought when I was 3?—I paused for a moment to reflect on whether my mother might be rolling over in her grave.) As I was saying, George and Laurent are lying together on the floor. I lie next to Laurent so that he is in the middle. I'm still frisky, so I start kissing both of their nipples and work my way down their bodies until I get to their feet. I pull one sock off each; I've decided I'm in the mood for a little shrimping! They seem to quite enjoy this, one giggling while the other moans, back and forth, back and forth.

Things heat up again: Laurent is going down on George and once again offering up his muscular ass for me to enjoy. I can tell his rosebud is now in full bloom, so I rub—no, actually, I am *slapping*—my dick against his warm, moist portal. I decide that though I'd like to do it, because of all the alcohol and recent sex, I'm probably not up to finding the condom, lubing up, and staying hard enough to penetrate him, so instead I push two fingers up his butt (beautifully muscled, you will recall) while I pinch his nipples and lick his neck. So, if you can picture this, George is on his back with his legs spread, Laurent is on his knees facing George between George's legs, masturbating himself over George's crotch, while I am behind Laurent, two fingers up his butt, pinching his right nipple and kissing him over his right shoulder. Of course he comes (he claims it's the fourth time since we started all of this), and he is determined to get me off, so he turns around to kiss me full-on, yanking my dick until I take over and shoot all over his smooth tummy.

Then I get a blanket to cover us where we lie, sandwiching young Laurent between us. We chat for a while, and then George decides to get dressed and leave. Laurent's beeper—the vibrating one—has gone off several times during sex, but he doesn't bother to answer it. Pleasure seems to be covered for now.

He's sleeping in my bed as I write this, and I have to say that it is quite an experience to nestle my crotch up to his muscular little butt. I better return now before he misses me.

Anthony Ehlers
Oblivion and Maybe Some Dancing

5 January 1994, Johannesburg

Midweek cruising. We go to the Cha Cha Palace, as Nicholas calls Champions. Busy for a weeknight—lots of good-looking boys and chic lesbians in black. It's chilly out, and we don't dance. I order a gin and tonic. After a drink or two, we decide to split to catch the strip at Gotham.

Gotham, a little Gothic house of sexual horrors, stuck in between the crumbling buildings of Hillbrow. The homeless sleep in the gutters, and children in torn clothes run around with dilated pupils and shrunken bodies. It's mercifully black inside so we can't see the rot of decay or the people making out, but the staircase is lit with black votive candles on each side of the low steps. Even the air smells depraved. I like it.

Batman Bar: smells like alcohol and poppers and, faintly, old semen and sweat. The atmosphere is quiet and moody and edgy with sexual tension. Next door is Robin's Corner with a bit funkier, younger crowd. A blue argon light rings the bar counter—it looks eerie, especially in the smoke.

The bartender wears black jeans and a silver-studded belt, no shirt; his stomach muscles remind you of the splendid things you can do with the human body if you put in time and assiduous effort. The festive season's decos are still up—Nicky declares the place is a firetrap and shudders.

On the stage a bald-headed black man is sprinkling powder on a raised dais in preparation for the strip: a "cowboy joyboy" (yawn). A stoned boy (quite cute) dances alone on the floor in languid steps. He's obviously moving to his own music, out of sync with the energetic Janet Jackson remix. We take a slash in the pissy unlit toilet that hasn't been flushed since New Year's night. Nick puts money in the condom machine: it swallows the coin noisily, but no rubber is forthcoming. He smacks the machine. Nothing. I laugh. Safe sex in the '90s is not always as easy as it looks. Sometimes I think it would be easier to just fall in love.

Nick is steadily getting drunk and grows distant from me, from everything. I hold on to my drink; it leaves cold, wet streaks against my palm. My hands are cold, numb. On the TV in the corner, soundless porn plays: complicated hard-core sex shot from impossible angles; finally, it numbs the brain. I feel unsettled, restless, excited. There is a burning heart somewhere in the middle of this icy sexual complacency.

I can't wait for the show, so I proceed to a dark corner to idle around with intent. There is something about being in the dark with strangers that thrills me; lust crackles in my body like the sound of new leather. Shadowy bodies are slumped against the wall. Inviting smiles, cold eyes. A cigarette tip ignites against the dark. Restless hands longing for a stranger's touch. Nicholas and I always do the sex-club circuit. Tonight Gotham, on another night it might be Zoo. The Balcony. Jeb's. Cosmos for a Saturday JO party. Another shadowy figure appears, his white shirt glowing ghostly in this smoky dark light.

Closer now…

My heart starts doing its crazy dance. I start to play with myself through my jeans. His eyes glitter darkly; his hand rubs his crotch lazily. He is older, late 30s, but he has a nice, solid body. Tall. I pull out my cock, semi-erect. He toys with his to get it ready. Now he is standing in front of me. I close my eyes and feel his hand on me—warmth curls around my shaft. A rough kiss, his rude tongue invading my mouth. Groping, my hands probe his fleshy, hairy ass. His mouth tastes of beer and cigarettes. I coax his head down down—there!—he swallows my cock easily.

Now my turn, on my haunches for him, sucking his short, stubby, and incredibly engorged cock. I'm aware only of my breath rushing through my nostrils, the smell of him, the taste of this foreign cock between my lips. He is whispering something I can't hear. Maybe it's not him; maybe it's me.

The strip show has started. I can hear whistling and clapping, and the erotic thumping bass rattles the floor. I feel the vibrations in this man's hairy, tense scrotum. We swap positions again. Two other silhouettes, watching us, watching. I lean against the rough concrete wall, cock my leg, and let the man suck me while I smile and stare at the two newcomers. I hold the back of his neck, feeling the silky hair shaved closely on his nape, silently asking for more. He sucks me for a long time, jerking off while I'm buried to the hilt in his throat. I feel the hot, thick come hitting the hairs of my bare leg, and a close, thrilling erotic charge squeezes my windpipe shut. He moves off me, and another mouth, a stranger's lips, engulf my cock. Cool fingers coddle my balls before slipping furtively to the crack of my ass. His friend starts to play with my nipples, pinching them through my thin T-shirt. I invite the twisting pain—it's about the only thing that feels real. I reach awkwardly to stroke his cock through his jeans. He unzips, and I haul out a nice long cock, thankfully cut: dry and smooth and warm; my thumb rubs the first slick beads of his precome on the fat head.

I know I'm about to ejaculate, but I can't feel the proper triggers, the warning sensation I normally feel when I'm jerking off on my own. While being sucked off by this stranger, it's as if I'm detached from my own sexual experience and my body has entered some sort of sexual séance. I see rather than feel the come fly out of me: a white arc into the smoky, seedy air, narrowly missing the man's face. Grave, dark eyes have gathered around me, each moving in to feed, to taste, to devour. I am ready for them.

Wash scrub rinse away the stickiness and shame from my hands and face in a brown, scarred basin. The water pressure is weak; the water is tepid. I can't look myself in the eye in the cracked mirror. Near me a man drops to his knees and starts to suck on an enormous purplish cock shoved through a glory hole. His own erection protrudes obscenely from his opened fly. My ears are ringing with the loud disco: Donna Summer (*"I feel love/I feel love/I feel love"*). I need a cigarette. Badly.

141

God, Nicholas is such a total exhibitionist! Sitting at the bar without the benefit of his jeans, his head thrown forward, his long fringe an untidy dark shawl hiding his face, he is solidly pumping his cock for all to see. What do I feel? Disgust? Envy? I don't know—some thick emotion in between. When he throws his head back, I glimpse the bottle of poppers under his nose.

An old man in a shabby suit hangs over Nicholas's shoulder to get a better view of his dick. Let's face it, Nick is very well-hung! Otherwise his self-gratification goes largely unnoticed. Nicholas likes to do things for an audience. Once he did a stunt on the pool table with four other guys—people *still* talk about that.

11 October 1996

Rain has given way to a drizzle. Champions is dying, having had its trashy moment of fame about three years ago. Sad but true. The bar is quiet, and we dance while we wait for Chance (Nicky's new flame) to arrive. Nicholas gets too hot, so we sit outside. He points out some guy who went to school with us. We walk around to get a better look, to see if I recognize him. I don't. Just a whole lot of trashy sorts milling about on the damp lawn. Chance arrives late, his eyes as glazed as doughnuts from too much coke. He and Nick kiss, and he passes some grass from Malawi around.

We are some of the last to leave, the place fast preparing to close. It's just our little trio, a bigger drunker group and two or three people too stoned to move. The staff look bored, and the stocky little bouncer smilingly tells us to "Fuck off home." A guy is sitting and leisurely picking his nose. The atmosphere is like the dregs of a wedding reception—everyone is slow and breathless and spent.

As we file out, I notice that with the drunk group is none other than the notorious Lucien. Lucien—mmmm. In white jeans and top, leaning against the banister. Even though he is patently stoned, he is shockingly good-looking—sleek jet-black hair, dark skin, perfect bone structure, sensual lips and that sexy crooked tooth in the front.

"Bye," he says with serious eyes. I say "Bye"—insert dramatic pause—"Lucien," and carry on walking. This beautiful but very drunk woman with him rushes up to me and flings her arms around me, "You're a very cute boy!"

Somebody behind me is saying something like, "Yes, he is, isn't he? I think I should take him home."

Lucien interrupts. "How do you know me? Do I know you?"

I tell him I know him; he's a dancer. He looks intrigued. He says, "Hello, beautiful." I take it he doesn't know my name.

The drunk girl says they're going to "the graveyard"—which used to be Gotham and has since been renamed 58. It's still exceedingly dirty and shameful and lots of fun. I know Chance wants to go, so we badger Nicky into stopping for one drink—"Just one drink, that's all, promise." We arrive in the drizzly street moments before the battered yellow taxi pulls up—and Lucien & Co. pile out, laughing and spilling drunkenly into the street; beggar children clamber around Nicholas for cigarettes and loose change.

Lucien and I climb the dark painted stairs lit with candles, and it makes me think we are entering a haunted house. Our arms are around each other's waists. I tell him I saw him here a while back.

"Oh, yes, I was kind of in a bad mood."

I ask him if he is in a bad mood tonight.

Slowly, "No."

We kiss on the staircase. No, strike that. We attack each other—tongue, mouths, faces, fused and lashing. Bodies crushed against each other. We're precariously balanced on the steps, as we kiss and claw at each other's buttocks and backs. We're locked. I'm drunk on the taste of him, his lips, his tongue, his saliva burning me up. Suddenly, things go too wild, and he pushes me back. I think—I feel—what I believe is a wall behind me. It's not. It's a loose pillar. A loose free-standing gaudily painted pillar that is shoved backward with the force of our bodies, toppling over to smash the multipaned stained-glass window leading to a narrow balcony. I almost fall, but he pulls me back, and laughing over the sound of shattering glass, we race off into the dark recesses to hide.

We dance. If a snake had a pelvis and a long, all-knowing grin, it would look exactly like Lucien. We dance and what we do on the minuscule dance floor is more shocking than any sexual act. When I scoot my rump across his crotch, I feel the hot lump there—it thrills me. ("Cockteaser!")

We stop only to buy drinks. Lucien's drunk woman friend drops her naked breasts on the bar counter and shouts at no one in particular: "Look at these! Aren't these beautiful tits?" Chance and Nicholas are drinking fast, smoking slowly, and kissing whenever they remember they are supposed to be in love.

I must be glowing with guilt. Lucien wants me to go home with him, but I don't want to. Too drunk. I would never get it up now. Anyway, it's great just feeling desired. Sometimes I feel like a sexual cipher—empty, hungry, self-destructive—but tonight I know I don't want sex. Only oblivion and maybe some dancing.

12 October 1996

Wake up with a bruise in the small of my back and don't know how it got there.

31 March 2000

Last Friday of the month. Payday! What did that magazine say about alcohol and drugs? "Many individuals can't maintain their decisions to stick to healthy behavior after getting high." Yes, well. (Clear my throat.)

We start out at Stardust—the Palace. We are so bored, we just drink and smoke ourselves to death. Then Nicholas and I go to Champions, ostensibly to sober up—but he starts ordering shooter after shooter, which rips the lining off my stomach.

I (literally) run into a bewildered Kian, an Irish-American who is stuck in the city for the night due to a mix-up with the airline. Not cute, but nice curly hair and bright intelligent eyes. He wants to go to the Heartland. So we all traipse over there, Kian bouncing in the back of Nick's BMW.

New Moon. Downstairs is the pool area and bar, a dance floor. Upstairs a maze of dark muggy warrens leading off from a bar where endless porn is shown. Nicky finds a blond boy with tattoos and a cheeky grin to speak to at the bar. Kian and I saunter off. A bit of groping in the dopeheads' corner, and I'm inviting my little Irish charmer upstairs to "watch XXX videos." On the screen a blond porn stud wearing only a T-shirt that reads BAD FUN balances a Budweiser along the length of a monster cock. We ask where we can buy some poppers.

I drag Kian into the dark room. It's dim and hot and crowded; the place is writhing with bodies.

"Stay close," I warn Kian, and he grips my hand tightly.

I can't see the walls, black-black—everything is like a dream. From the muddy dimness, darker shapes break away, forming looming silhouettes, coming closer. People bumping into me—by accident? I don't know. I get bumped harder. Kian's hand slips out of mine. I hear whispering. I'm cornered against a wall. Hands unzipping me, touching me, peeling my shirt back from my shoulders.

I am no longer in control. Things are moving fast, too fast—it's all crazy. I'm being offered poppers. The drug explodes in my chest, making me hot and panicky. Not for long. Soon I'm laughing, drunk, falling to my knees and attacking a belt buckle, unzipping.... I hear echoing from the dance floor downstairs this strange repetitive dance music (*"I want to fuck you/I want to fuck you/I want to fuck you"*). I'm giving blow jobs to three different faceless people. One I hope is Kian, but who the fuck can be sure?

I look up. By now my eyes have adjusted to the dark. Nicholas is standing against the wall, drink in hand, watching me. A gloomy shaft of light from the bar makes him stand out in the darkness. He is staring at me with an inscrutable face—vague, emotionless, cold. Somehow him being here, so close, disturbs me.

When I look again, he's gone.

At one point, I have two dicks in my mouth simultaneously. I reach out blindly, half-mad, for an enormous cock waving in front of me, very long with a huge, almost perfectly round head. I have such an intense, single-minded craving to have that cock in my mouth, but the man mildly pushes my grasping hand and greedy head away, carefully zipping his turgid penis back into his pants.

Time fractures, confuses. Kian is gone. *Where?* Who cares? My mind is so apart from everything that is happening. I'm laughing, mentally concentrating on doing two things at once—like jacking off my own dick while sucking someone's cock. Now the darkness becomes suffocating. I find a tiny window along the wall in the dark room and open it: a tiny patch of sky opens above crumbling buildings and the bright knot of lights of the petrol station. I can see a few stars in the deep-blue night sky. The air is cool and clean.

Afterward I feel so detached and sore and bruised and, fuck, I think I'm going crazy—I don't know if I want to kill someone or hunt down somebody else to have sex with. I recall the look of a rabid dog in my gran's street when I was a kid—a sort of crazed, lonely, sick look. I imagine I have the same look. Sexually, I'm spent but still, still, still consumed with some dark hunger; it's as if I'm trying to stuff myself full of this surreal sexual contact.

I'm angry at myself—not from a moral point of view—I don't have any guilty or "dirty" feelings about doing something so very unholy—but I am disturbed by the intensity of my abandon. *Well,* I ask myself, *what did you expect, going into a dark room with a total stranger loaded with lethal shooters and six months of suppressed celibacy looking for an outlet?* All that hidden, sexual loneliness is bound to come rushing out like lava from a volcano.

Outside, the cold air hits me with a sobering slap. I wander around looking for Nicholas with come drying on my cheek and come making my shirt stick to my body, the smell of cock and amyl nitrate in my nose, cloying, a terrible intimate smell. As it turns out, I have to drive the fucking Beemer home on my own as Nicholas drove that tattooed blond drunk boy home in his car. Sometimes I wonder if Nicky and I realize we are not 22 anymore? I arrive home at 4 in the morning and take a long hot shower and suck an antiseptic throat lozenge. I creep between clean sheets with a warm body and damp hair. Sleep would be ephemeral and thin.

Tom Ace
Last One to the Car

Lone Pine, California, February 2000

Two nights ago, I was walking on a quiet residential street near Doheny Drive in Los Angeles at around 10 P.M. on my way to a concert up on the Sunset Strip. Four guys, in their 20s or so, came running after me from behind; the one in front said, "Gimme your money, motherfucker." I outran them and got away. *Fuck,* I thought, *I lived in L.A. from '81 to '83, and nothing like this ever happened to me. Have things changed that much since I left?* Pissed me off, but at least it was nice to know my 40-year-old legs still kick ass. Then I remembered a time about 16 years ago in Colorado, when being able to run fast had come in handy indeed. That time it wasn't muggers I was outrunning; it was a 21-year-old named Eric.

Eric was an undergrad—a business major, I think—whom I'd met on the sidewalk outside the dirty bookstore in Boulder. Too bad I never met any other boys on the sidewalk outside, what with how gross the inside of the store was. We went back to my apartment and enjoyed the first of about a dozen fucks we would have over the next few months. He said he was bi, I think, or at least had had his share of straight sex. He didn't talk a lot, didn't have much of a sense of humor. Hanging out with him wasn't painfully boring, but I wouldn't have bothered if it weren't for his boyish face, lean hard body, and fine dick (not listed in order of importance). He was butch, but not excessively so, and cultivated a simple, unadorned style. He favored blue jeans, athletic shorts, T-shirts, sweatshirts, and definitely no designer underwear: the look imprinted on my sexual taste from countless frustrating episodes of secretly lusting after straight friends as a teenager.

Eric said he'd been in a frat the previous year, but was now living with a roommate who didn't know he was bi (or whatever he was). He didn't have any frat house sex stories to tell me, but he did mention that his roommate would get on top of him and mock-fuck him when Eric was lying prone on his bed studying. All in good clean straight-boy fun, of course. I told him that if I had a roommate who did that, he'd better be prepared to deliver the goods.

Eric was sexually aggressive in a selfish straightish-top way; lots of fun if you like that and probably horrible if you don't. Our sessions became fairly routine: I'd suck his dick, he'd go to fuck me, I'd stop him and hand him some lube (he'd never ask for it), and then he'd fuck me about as hard as he could. I can't keep from coming if a guy has a big dick and fucks hard, so our sessions were characterized more by intensity than by duration.

He didn't make much noise during sex, verbal or otherwise, but occasionally he spoke up. Once, while we were doing it doggy-style, he told me "You've got the best ass in town." I actually disagreed with that assessment, but I didn't think there was any point in contradicting him. He once told me he liked having sex with me because "chicks" would "freak out" if he fucked them that hard. It was nice to know I was good for something.

Much as I like getting fucked, I wanted a little variety from time to time, and Eric had a very desirable ass. Problem was, I couldn't fuck him without first enduring a stream of whiny "I-don't-wannas." If I persisted, I prevailed, and things smoothed out after we got over the initial hump. More than smoothed out, actually; he'd make like he was just discovering the nerve endings in his rear end, and say that we really ought to do this more often. But somehow those realizations would disappear by the next time he came over, and the "I-don't-wannas" would return in full force. Curious boy.

One fine summer afternoon, we went for a hike in the hills just outside of town. Taking a short hike is the Boulder equivalent of having a drink or two; you're not allowed to live in the town if you don't like the outdoors. We hadn't discussed any agenda in advance, but we both knew that the outing was to be followed by going home and fucking. After we'd had enough and were walking back, he turned to me abruptly and announced a deal: "Last one to the car gets fucked." Without waiting for me to agree, he ran off with a good head start—but he didn't know that I could outsprint most anyone. I beat him to the car. He admitted that I'd won fair and square (not mentioning how unfair it would've been if he'd won with a head start). I could see the wheels turning in his head as he tried in vain to think up a way to undo what had happened, all the while making a cute futile effort to hide just how pissed off he was. He wanted my ass, plain and simple, and went into full-on calculation mode to find a means to that end. Meanwhile, I was withholding my glee at having beat him at his own game, and loving how I didn't have to calculate and wangle because I was holding the winning hand.

On the way home I savored the thought of getting my dick into his fine straightish-boy ass, a special kind of anticipation made possible by the contest: Eric's gift to me, if unintended. Back at my place, he made one last attempt to see if I'd be willing to forfeit what I'd won. Not a chance, I told him, and his ass was duly penetrated— although this time, I didn't hear any of his usual "Gee, this feels great—let's do it more often, heh-heh." I made sure he got a good, solid fucking, if not quite as hard as the ones he liked to deliver to me. I have some sense of mercy.

Next time he came over there was no mention of his previous defeat. I reckoned it would be the usual suck-his-dick-and-get-fucked routine, but Eric added a new twist. I was on my knees blowing him, having a great time at it—when he pulled his dick out of my mouth, turned around, reached back, and pulled my face into his ass, not saying a word in usual Eric style. Most guys wait for some indication that you want to rim them before putting their ass to your face; Eric was one of only a handful I've encountered who didn't. I can't help but think it was his way of getting even with me for what had happened the last time. I breathed nice and deep; he had a fine ass scent, but I'd recently decided to stop rimming for health reasons and kept my tongue in my mouth. After a while he gave up on waiting for me to lick him, took me to the bed, and proceeded to fuck me as usual. I explained afterward why I hadn't licked his ass, and he understood just fine and said it wasn't something he'd ever do.

Not long after this, Eric stopped seeing me. He told me all we ever did was have sex. I thought, *Yeah, that's because you're a boring person, Eric. That's why we've been fuck buddies and not boyfriends.* At the time, I couldn't imagine giving up on hot sex for some silly reason like having nothing in common. Given access to the hottest dick in town, I'd have preferred to milk it for more than just a dozen go-rounds.

Dear Eric: Wherever you are now, are you still getting so much good ass or (even if you can't fuck it quite as hard) pussy that you're turning it down? Are you still bi? I loved the fucks you gave me, but what sticks in my mind is your little contest, your attempt to squirm out of having lost, and finally, the way you gave it up like a man. Some butts I've had offered to me, others I've charmed my way into, and others I've paid for—but yours is the only ass I've ever won.

Clint Catalyst
A Love Like Ours Is Dangerous

April 10, 2000

    I've been thinking about that speed-addled stint back in '95—the two-month "vacation" (talk about using a term *loosely!*) in which Spencer & I blazed cross-country via Amtrak train & intervals of riding the silver pooch (I can't bring myself to say the *G* word) bcz we were such methamphetamaniacs, so psyched-up & psychotic & paranoid beyond belief that we thought "They" were after us. They being the Mafia or some Kill-a-Queer-for-Christ extremist group or relatives of his who were allegedly hot on our trail bcz it was my fault he's gay, for making him gay. That speed-addled stint, which melted over 10 grand worth of plastic back when I still had credit cards that worked & just about tossed boneyard topsoil on our parents' heads, the stint that took us all the way to Salem, Mass., like some chemically dependent honeymoon, which yielded nothing much but killer sex & a 120-pg sketchbook I filled with doodles & letters/journal-entry type stuff addressed to him. Although I've yet to show Spence that journal, here I am now, pecking away at my laptop keyboard, writing a letter/journal-type entry thing to me, to myself, simply bcz of how goober I feel for reminiscing, for wanting to feel his goober.

    If I had any shame, I'd be blushing about now. Instead, it's a hot L.A. summer afternoon in the middle of spring, the sky a mottled *Hustler* pink, & I'm all hot & bothered thinking about Spencer. I'm also bothered by my neighbors, blasting their waily lesbian folk music that's working my nerves like chirpy Chipmunk sing-alongs. Or dorksquad Backstreet boy bands. It's difficult to have shame when surrounded by assholes, don't ya think? What an arrogant statement. But seriously, though, show me a guy who's humble when pissed off

& I'll show you a guy who has a Valium 'scrip. That or a lobotomy in his background.

Speaking of lobotomies, I rented a Jeff Stryker porn earlier today. Yep, an "erotic thriller," heh-heh-heh. Somehow I went from running an errand to pick up my laundry to scanning the shelves at Video Active. Anal-ways, the video was pretty much the Suck-My-Fuckin'-Dick-Dude/Yeah-You-Know-You-Want-It standard, but what set me off was the fact that I kept getting interrupted while watching it. *Ahem.* Watching it with one hand, that is—but that's a given. Who watches Jeff Stryker for a great thespian moment? Anyway, here I was, holed up in my room stuck to the bedspread with the windows sealed & the blinds shut, the telephone incessantly ringing (& me too lubed up & lazy to move from my bed & turn off the ringer), my roommate knocking on my door to remind me that it's my turn to vacuum the stairway, her cat meowing from the balcony like a wounded wildebeest, the downstairs neighbors arguing in Spanish, all exclamation points & thuds from things being thrown, & all the while the people in the back unit with their Lilith Fair-esque acoustic tunes blaring, just like they're blaring right now.

I felt, at the very least, annoyed by all the outside involvement in my afternoon isolationist masturbatory act. It seemed so Can't-I-Just-Have-Five-Minutes. So Audience Participation. So public. Which sparked a few synapses, fused some memories of public sex w/ Spencer. Ah, that "brainstorming" thang…tricky, tricky business. In the end, memories of Spencer (& me w/ Spencer) were what my mind was screening—rather than the screened image of Mr. Stryker, all salon-tanned & greased up, pumping his pelvis on my TV—that did the trick.

This incident led me stumbling onto thoughts of Spencer, & I got out that old journal, got excited, & got my rocks off again. Unlined white paper, navy ink in my difficult handwriting: *We can't tell anyone. We can't tell anyone anything. A love like ours is dangerous.* I love the sound of those words; they're so adolescent & erotic, like *My parents are out of town for the weekend & It only hurts at first.*

The thing that turns me on about sex in public is that it's a generally unremarkable act under remarkable circumstances. There's nothing revolutionary about fucking to conceive, also nothing earth-shattering about fucking to come. But fucking while trying to keep from being caught—especially *butt*-fucking while trying to keep from being caught—feels like a terrorist act. At any moment the whole thing could explode, go up in cinders. At any moment an everyday occurrence is interrupted by something sacred & profane. At any moment something could go wrong that'd blow the moment.

So there we were, in the middle of a train cabin rattling toward Boston. We'd boarded in St. Paul, & after countless hours of passing Spencer's Walkman back & forth between us to pass the time with mixed tapes, we were getting restless. Hours in transit are *so* draining. I'm about as patient as a cranky 2-year-old, & the novelty of the window scenery—quaint New England homes & autumn trees a smear of orange, of red & yellow leaves—had worn off.

Spence was reading *Love in Vein,* the Poppy Z. Brite vampire anthology, & I needed something to get my blood rushing. The sight of his pale slender fingers as they turned crisp pages, the bleach-blond stalks of his Aqua Net bangs: That did it. I felt like a predator. I wanted to, needed to devour him. Right then & there.

I wasn't aiming for homosexual Harlequin material. Nobody's ever given me flowers, & if he did, I'd think the gesture was a goddamned lie. Awkward fumbling beneath my wool overcoat & the brisk circus wet-seal act: Now that's what I call real, that's what was real. His touch laced with fear was kinetic, exciting; the prospect of being caught was what made it more than just another romp in the hay.

That & the arsenal of rotten odors chugging out of the chubby lady an arm's length over from us, separated from our scene by the two or so feet of the walkway/aisle. A mixture of sweat & a vile sugary stench in which she was marinating—& which a bloody brown Rorschach blotch on the seat of her synthetic green trousers soon revealed was from *that* special time of the month. Raunchy, but I love imperfections. Regarding the nature of this moment, there was no room for humanity, only its marketable parts: pleasant conversations, a rigid posturing. Yet there she was, bleeding with sincerity &

oblivion & bad breeding, & there we were, lost in a sexual bliss of our own strange, collaborative design. Two scrawny faggots in a frenzy, half-hidden but in broad daylight. Our heads jerked, eyelids fluttered. Wrists bent; fists tugged, slick with spit.

When I came, my eyes narrowed to slits, & a gorgeous avalanche-like commotion of stuff came crashing through, gold & piercing light & what felt like everything, though I didn't really see anything. No concrete images. Nothing I could hold on to.

When I caught my breath & opened my eyes again, I thanked Almighty we hadn't been; we weren't. Caught by the train conductor, that is. I wonder what I would've said... "Oh, excuse me sir, just playing a little game of Hide the Hot Dog to pass the time?"

Since I haven't written an entry in appx two mths, it's probably apropos that I mention my birthday, a mere two days ago. I turned a whopping 29 yrs of old, which pushes me so close to the big numero 3-0, I can hardly handle it. Once I abandon my role as a roving 20-nothing, what's next? I've already kicked drugs, abandoned alcohol. I even did the whole midlife crisis bit at 27 when I finished grad school & it dawned on me I didn't have the foggiest who or what I wanted or wanted to do. At 30, will I be forced to abandon my romantic notions of being an Avant-Guardian (yep, that spelling's intentional, Ms. Bee) & trade it all in for a suit, tie, & employment as a teacher? The whole "What do you do?" query for me as a whopping triple-decker is terrifying. Gone will be the days of my misspent youth. Imminent will be my duty to fill in the blank. I...collect checks? Sue & bruise easily? Spend my days soul-searching? Invent a cliché? Ride to live & live to ride & have more fun as a blond?

Oh, enough of all that. More of the reckless "good ol' days" stuff. Spence, me, & the back row of a Greyhound (there, I said it!) bus. We were somewhere in Colorado, en route to Los Angeles, where our next master plan consisted of scoring more crystal from Tara & tearing it up at Disneyland. It was late, a view of snow glistening by moonlight in the early A.M., & some queen an aisle up & over latched himself onto us like a Prada backpack. He offered us pot, said he had a 'scrip bcz he was positive.

The grass put me in a stupid, horny haze. Somehow our mono-syllabic attempts at chatting the old queen up progressed to jacking each other off beneath my jacket & playing alternate rounds of "blow job–bobbing for apples." Occasional obligatory small talk with the O.Q. while Spence & I (secretly) sucked each other off. It was almost too hot for me to handle. My right cheek rubbed against the uncomfortable material of seat when I went down/as he leaned into me, the industrial fiber like woven sandpaper with a harsh under-odor of dust & sweaty ass cracks, a blend of the years & of rarely laundered garments. My left cheek was smashed against the frostbitten window when he went down on me, slapping the glass with bumps, & the bus lurching forward, weaving precariously, the driver shifting gears. As to what transpired amidst this particular stretch of our story, let's see: White-trash denizens up & down the aisle during our sexcapades, mullet-headed acid-washed denim small-town monsters sliding by our huddled forms & fanning the restroom door, the miasma of human remains wafting. All of this in Colorado, a blatantly homophobic state where Prop or Amendment 2 or whatever had recently passed, & the likes of us could've been lynched. So trashy, so tragic. Right down to his dried come, which stuck my T-shirt to my chest, & I was stuck wearing it for another day, no change of clothes due to a checked suitcase. Gotta love it.

The Amtrak scene, our gig on the bus: What I cherish most is the sheer intoxication of our moment(s), the outside world eclipsed by the immediacy of our task at hand. Sometimes when it's late at night & I'm sprawled out in bed, I lose myself in that illusory realm again. I drift into a time when it was Spencer & me & a "Fuck you!" to the outside world, when we were young & drunk on love & hubris cocktails, when life was pleasure & we were going to live forever. It was the only thing that made sense; he was the only thing that made sense to me at the time.

When I think about Spencer today, when I think about being with Spencer, it's like a comet passing. A white-hot blaze burning in the wide-open black of logic & reason. Never mind if our love was lust & our lust was fueled by drugs. Never mind if he's 2,000 miles away

& I'm 2,000 times more demanding of whom & what it is I want & won't (probably ever) have. It's what *was*. It's what I've had & what makes me who I am. I can feel it in the words of that journal's page: something incendiary, exciting. I can feel it in the syntax of the now, a language not just on this page but that imprints itself on the blanched surface of my memories—before it withers & fades beneath the something new of tomorrow.

Kevin Dax
My Second Croat Cock

Saturday, 19 August 2000

Up very early, awakened by strong morning sun in my cheapo
Zagreb hotel room, and up against an early checkout time anyway.
Shopped for breakfast, took coffee at my now-usual sidewalk café.
Took bags directly to the bus station *garderoba,* then on foot for all of
the lower city again: the pretty National Theater (dark today, in
mourning for the untimely death of a beloved diva), a nice belle
epoque bar nearby, then up to the old city for the open market. Tried
to see the Dürer in the cathedral sacristy (closed), then down to the
Strossmeyer museum: nice art collection, but ill-lit and too hot.

The heat wave continues. I phoned Sasha. He wasn't able to see me
off, so I ate a sandwich alone and waited for the bus to the coast. The
country outside Zagreb begins flat and unremarkable but becomes
forested and mountainous. Pretty, but I was deep in the fourth Harry
Potter book and content to settle in for a long ride. An hour or so into
the trip we stopped, and everyone got off to visit the toilet and bar of
a mountain restaurant. Air distinctly cooler, sunlight still brilliant. I
got back on the bus early and idly watched people retake their seats.
Almost unconsciously, I noticed one possibly studly young guy in dark
wraparound glasses. Realized he had been sitting opposite me on the
bus the whole time.

I still really wasn't paying much attention. He was too straight to
even consider cruising, and I was enjoying my book. Did notice his
face, though, when he took his shades off briefly. His dark glasses
hid a big, fresh, swollen black eye—lots of red in the white of the eye,
blue and purple above and below. After half an hour or so, I realized
that something was happening on his side of the aisle. The bus was
half full, with people behind us and in front. He had his two seats

to himself, just as I had my window seat and spare to myself. Looking out the window and listening to a Walkman, he was squeezing his dick through his long, loose shorts. Yikes. That got my attention. Twenty minutes of torture: staring at him, then trying not to stare. I took stock finally of his looks: dark blond scruffy-nice haircut, early 20s maybe, well-proportioned, handsome square-jawed face, medium height, tight tanned body, judging from his forearms and lower legs. He wore the international young-guy uniform: loose T-shirt and American-style baggy shorts. So he was thinking about his girlfriend maybe, or was just one of those European guys who feel themselves up in public all the time. For a long while I was mortified but rapt, anticipating the humiliation of being caught watching but unable not to look. I knew too that the woman in the seat behind him would sense, if she was at all alert, that my attention was fixed on my neighbor. I couldn't bring myself to check over my shoulder, and I couldn't stop looking at his lap, where the outline of an erection was clear under the folds of his shorts and in his lazily moving hand.

At a certain point it seemed certain that he knew I was watching, that in fact his slow-motion jacking and backhanded pulling were all for my benefit. This was a different kind of torture: an hour or two more on the road with a hard cock across the aisle. I readjusted my body to face him as fully as possible and propped my head on my right arm, shielding my face with an open hand, so I could stare without turning my head. Hopefully, from behind I would appear to be dozing. Now he was driving me nuts. He pulled his cock up and along his thigh, just out of sight under the hem. He dipped a finger under the edge of the cloth, tapped the head of his invisible dick, and then pulled out his hand to rub his precome between his thumb and fingers. Then he began, occasionally, casually, to flash the head of his dick at me, then much of the shaft: It was a big one, slender, with the same gold coloring as the rest of him, but red in the fat, pointed head. Unsheathed, the edge of the foreskin drew a nice curve starting from below the piss slit. And all this time he rarely and only obliquely made eye contact.

After hours of this pleasurable teasing, we arrived in Rijeka. Everyone got off. My ferry wasn't leaving for several hours. I ran to the left-lugggage office and deposited my bags, locking all my valuables in them first, keeping only some money. I hurried back into the crowded street to look for him, worried that I'd lost him. But there he was, smoking in front of the train schedule posters. I went up and asked in English, in my politely friendly way, "Can I suck your dick?"

"What?"

"I would like to suck your cock."

"OK." He exhaled some smoke, smiled slightly, and said something more that I couldn't make out. I asked him to repeat himself. He said he would miss his bus home to Pula. He wanted 400 Marks (perhaps $200). I smiled, shook my head, and said I was sure he was worth it but there was no way I could do that. As I walked away I began to laugh silently at myself and at life. But then he reappeared out of the crowd in front of me and said, "How about 100 Kuna?" ($8).

As we wandered the side streets of the town looking for a spot with enough privacy for a blow job, we talked. His English was good, his manner taciturn-butch but not surly. He's 26, a university student in horticulture. He boxes, which is where he got the shiner. Marko said that he didn't need sex every day but with certain girlfriends he could fuck six times a day. I asked him how he knew I would be interested in his dick, and he said, "Something in the eyes." I asked him how many men he'd let suck him, and he said, "Some." He said he liked the possibility of being seen by passersby when having sex—he liked the element of risk. I thought that maybe, after all, there is a God.

We found a street that felt suburban and deserted. Behind a kind of freestanding cement shack near a cluster of houses, we would be out of sight, barely. I hoped that the housewife next door wouldn't choose now to step out her back door. As I fell to my knees, he said, "In this situation I come fast."

I responded, "In that case I want you to come in my mouth."

"What?" But by then I already had the elastic waist of his shorts pulled down several inches, then his dark boxers too. My hands were up and down the back of his thighs and on his firm, fleshy butt. I had only a split second to take in the light-brown hair fanning out from the base of his cock, the fade from tanned stomach down to pale hips, and his drooping uncut (of course) cock. I clamped my mouth on him fast, enjoyed feeling him quickly grow hard. Erect, his cock had a nice upward curve, but I was still able to get him all the way down my throat. Not the time or place for lackadaisical sucking, so I built up a fast rhythm immediately, banging my nose against his stomach and pulling back with full suction. At first he stood straight, unmoving, but then he began contracting his butt and pushing his body into my receptive face. I was too focused even to suck on his nice big balls, which swung in the heat, much less get my tongue up his blond butt. But my hands kept busy with his unshaven balls and his crack while I continued to Hoover him. I moved my hands up his flat stomach to his swelling chest, pinching his nipples and brushing the light patch of hair on his breastbone. True to his word, he was getting close fast. He made warning moans and then uttered something urgent—but I wasn't going anywhere. He shuddered and shot what seemed like a big wad deep down my throat, the base of his dick pulsing against my lips.

Like a nice sex tourist from the planet Millionaire, I gave him 250 Kuna, 2½ times the money he asked, and asked him if he wanted to have a beer. We returned to the main pedestrian street, mostly 19th-century Italian in style. We talked quite a bit more. He wanted to know about America and my profession. I asked him about Croatian politics and what life was like for people now, what life was like for him. I was pleasantly distracted by the bright ugliness of his black eye in his otherwise classically handsome face. He kept his dark glasses on most of the time—so as not to scare people, he explained. He asked me about my wanting to eat come, and I gave him my usual spiel: that it is entirely safe for him, the sucked, and most likely safe for me, the sucker. I didn't tell him that I really don't care anymore how safe it is or isn't. If a guy is hot and I'm lucky enough to suck him, then I want to suck him off properly and get his load. After a good while he asked me, "Do you want to go again?"

Delighted, I said, "Yes! But you know I've spent all the money with me on our beers."

"Not for money this time."

We searched different alleys. There was some suspense about whether we would find another hiding place. There are nooks and crannies in every old town in Europe, but nowhere with real privacy. In a dilapidated quarter near Rijeka's sad, ruined Roman Imperial arch, we went up a stone spiral staircase with open unglazed windows set in the curving wall and an apartment door on each small landing. Marko leaned back against the window opening. Anyone passing below could have glanced up and seen him, the back of his shirt and his head just 15 feet away. The woman of the house, once again, could have spied us from her peephole or if she stepped out her door. A dog barked nearby, sensing our presence. I knelt near a broom and a mop. He whispered, "Now you will want to eat my come again." He smelled and tasted as good and sweaty as before. He got hard just as quickly. I was as determined to get him off as the first time, but I wanted to go a little slower and easier, as now we were buddies, and I didn't want it to be over. But I did want him to come, and I worked on slurping and sucking his next load out of him, making my mouth and throat a snug meat-tube for his bursting cock. This time he held the back of my head with both hands, domineering but friendly, as he jammed into me again and again. When he came, he pulled out halfway, forced my mouth wide open with a hand on my chin, and came all over my tongue and lips. With the head of his dick, he pushed the still-spurting come around my mouth and then pushed in to the hilt to fuck my face for a last few strokes.

I stood up, he pulled up his pants, and we walked down the staircase and out into the quiet street. I accompanied him to the bus station, and we talked again. He smoked again. Neither of us suggested maintaining contact or exchanging information. I cursed myself for locking up my camera. He probably would have permitted me a snapshot of him, cigarette in hand, black eye hidden behind his sci-fi sunglasses, in that sun-filled Istrian piazza where we shook hands to say goodbye.

David Leddick
I Don't Even Remember When I Was a Virgin

Paris, January 15, 1994

Jet-lagged, I just awoke and thought, "I'd rather be alive at this moment than at any other time."

Sunday, January 16, 1994

I discussed the Michael Jackson scandal with my brother-in-law and told him, "Thirteen isn't so young. I don't even remember when I was a virgin." Shocked, he called out to my sister, who was reading in the next room, "Joan, did you hear that? Is that so?" And she replied without losing a beat, "Oh, David has always managed to amuse himself, whatever the circumstances."

In a so-so book of erotic drawings by Eduard MacAvoy (French despite the name), a passage he wrote translates as: "Form in itself carries its own beauty, spirituality, divinity. There is no need to know the soul that lies within a beautiful body lying next to yours. The body has its own language, untranslatable and sure. It has its own separate soul."

The way people behave making love is so often nothing at all like their verbal personality. Our culture says it is wrong or superficial to only love the body. But I think it does have its own existence, quite separate from the mind it is dragging around with it. And you can love it and endure the much less satisfying mind it contains.

Sunday night, January 23, 1994

When I think of lost loves, the phrase passes through my mind: "Time dragged them out of my arms."

When I leave New York to go to the airport, I pass through those dreary Queens suburbs of square houses built close to the walls that enclose the highways below, curtains blowing from upstairs windows. I imagine linoleum on bedroom floors, iron bedsteads with thin mattresses and worn bedspreads. I think of retreating there to lose myself in the hidden dramatic sexual lives that could be taking place in those houses.

Monday, January 31, 1994

The saddest part of seeing Adam Saturday afternoon wasn't that he was paying a duty call, slightly bored, and that I was slightly bored too. The magic I had endowed him with is virtually gone, and now he's just a young guy with some nice qualities whom I would never have known or tried to know if I hadn't fallen in love with him. My love for him *was* our child, and it has left home.

Saturday, February 26, 1994

Felix is dead. He must have died even before I left on safari, when no one was answering the phone those several times I called Houston. Thinking of him I remembered how he once told me, when I said I was getting too old to hope to have a new lover, "No, you are like a great classic car. Some people will always want to drive you." He said as I left Houston the last time, "There are many definitions of love, I realize, and people use the word to communicate many things, but I really do love you." I knew that, but something always stood in the way of my responding.

Tuesday, March 8, 1994

Memories return. Memories so much a part of mind that I forget to single them out to remember specifically. As when my lover Warren slept with Antony Tudor, the choreographer, to further his career supposedly, though how he thought that might happen I can't imagine. More likely because someone famous wanted to sleep with him.

I remember saying, "How could you? He's so old!" Antony Tudor was probably in his middle 50s then. And Warren said, "Well, his body wasn't any worse than Vern Fry's." A friend of ours, soft and decrepit as a white slug, though about our age. Actually a lot older but we just didn't realize it most likely. And that was the reason. Tudor's body wasn't any worse than the worst body of one of our contemporaries. Poor Warren, like so many I've seen since. So ready to do anything to get ahead with no clear idea of where they want to get ahead to.

Sunday, March 13, 1994

I went to London this past week to see the exhibit of "The World of the Ancients" at the National Academy. There was a tiny bronze of Alexander the Great that I had never seen before. Lithe and very long-legged for that or any classical period. And a foot-high bronze of Ajax contemplating, very beautifully done with the nipples in some shiny metal, perhaps gold. A very sensual piece. This feeling for naked beauty changes little through the centuries.

Miami Beach, Sunday, March 27, 1994

Tonight as I rode home on my bicycle from the Rothchild's, the night was everything the tropics should be. A blazing moon overhead in an indigo sky. The trade winds blowing the palm trees to make shifting slats of black and light from the streetlamps across the smooth macadam under my wheels. It was almost dreamlike to drift through the night down Flamingo Drive between the rows of wedding-cake houses hiding gangsters behind their iron fences and brick walls.

Paris, Monday, April 17, 1994

I saw Rupert Everett at the gym this evening. His face is somewhat worn, but his is the body I'd like to have. As tall as I am, my shoulders are squarer, but he has more defined biceps and good pectorals. And a nice thin torso and a narrow waist, which I have never had. His legs were covered in sweatpants, so one can't compare. Probably not as good as mine, which are my best feature.

He was completely ignored by the French, who most likely didn't recognize him but wouldn't flicker an eye if they did. In Hollywood a film star wandering around a gym would have everyone agog.

Monday, April 25, 1994

Can love be right over the horizon? And how would I fit it in? Read about someone today who wanted to get a larger apartment because where there is a place for someone...it inevitably gets filled. I should think about this.

Wednesday, May 4, 1994

In the night I thought of several things Howard Hussey said to me. "You are like a recent divorcee. You've seen a lot, but you're ready for more." This must have been in the early 1970s when I was first back in New York from Paris, just getting over Frank Andrea.

He also said, "Every time you leave people you give the impression you're going somewhere more interesting and more glamorous." Is it vain to record things other people say about you? Sort of like having your own photograph up around the house. Except that this is in the depths of my journal.

Sunday evening, May 15, 1994

One of those summer Sunday evenings in a big city when the neighbors are playing jazz, your cat is growing old, and all you ever cared about was love and now you have to face it, as the soft air blows through the lonely evening and the jazz plays, it's all too late for that. As my mother used to say, "This is one of those evenings when I'd marry the garbage man."

Thursday, May 19, 1994

An interesting quote from a magazine I read on flights to Düsseldorf and London. A woman called Mihri Fenwick on Coco Chanel: "There was nothing human about her. But if she wanted to, she could act the part of a human being marvelously well."

Miami Beach, Friday evening, June 17, 1994

I arrived yesterday. When I passed through New York, I saw

David Hook from the London office for dinner. We talked about families, and I told him how disappointed I was in some of my nephews and nieces. This man, who scarcely knows me and doesn't make a very sensitive self-presentation said, "They are not your family; they are your relatives."

When I left Michel on the train platform in Rye, so lonely and fretful, I said, "If you're interested at all in men, give it a try." And he said, "No, I like women. And besides, if it would have been anyone at all, it would have been you." I *don't* think we miss things in this life, but you wonder how much love is lost because of fear of what the neighbors will think, and of course they don't think at all.

I'm sure homosexuals live through what everyone would live through if they weren't proscribed by a rigid middle-class world. Homosexuals have passed the barriers of taboo and so can experience the pain of rejection and loss of beauty as possibilities flicker out, but our need to give and get love remains. Artists survive best because they can at least continue to create beauty.

Paris, Tuesday, June 28, 1994

What happens to love seems somehow disappointing. Even the most conventional heterosexual successful marriage with the children and all the trimmings seems such a poor reward for such heightened feelings.

As I age I feel more and more that I experienced heights and was right in valuing those experiences as the most important events of my life. The rest has been filler and could have been of any quality whatsoever.

And though the objects of my love were only very intermittently able to clamber to the peaks of their emotions, what else is one to do? As you lay down to die, I can't believe you feel as though you lived thoroughly because you mowed the lawn, kept a job, put your kids through school. Those comings-together I felt with Tom and Frank, the frustrated feelings I had for Adam—these were major-league events when I experienced life at its most compelling. Any of the rest of my life I could have missed and wouldn't even have noticed it.

Tuesday, August 9, 1994

I saw the film *Just Like a Woman* last night, and the leading man, who plays a transvestite, has an obligatory bare-butt scene—and he has a beautiful one. A beautiful body, not wonderfully proportioned, but a sexy flat chest and stomach, nice arms, smooth skin. Not the body you see in homoerotic stuff but very sexy all the same. The kind of body a lover can have that obsesses you so that you put up with everything else. His name is Adrian Pasdar.

Paris, Tuesday, August 16, 1995

On the flight over, there was a beautiful Irish-looking guy with a child's skull and clear eyes and only one arm. He offered to help a woman put her bag overhead with his very ugly, scary mechanical arm. Bet he gets a lot of attention. Scary and sexy.

My thought for today: "So many times very sexy men have strong beautiful hands." Warren did. Frank does. Sacha didn't. Guy didn't. It means something.

Monday, September 5, 1994

Last night returning from Pontlevoy, the taxi took me along the quay of the Left Bank. Notre Dame was illuminated, a hefty and ornate pale gray against a sky that was cobalt-blue streaked with purple clouds. So beautiful a sight to remind me again how emotional it is to live in Paris. You become what you look at.

All the news pictures of the escaping Cubans have well-built, good-looking, half-naked men in the foreground. Many people will be glad that they are escaping.

Monday, September 26, 1994

I seem to be in something of a diary mode. Last night I dreamed repeatedly of Dick Troughton's body. White, lean-muscled, blue veins under the skin. The slightly evil, licentious face. (He got that from his father.) He kept reemerging and we twined together. In my dream I said, "I want my hands full of your ass." We were never what you could call lovers, and we last slept together 47 years ago.

Now he is dead. What we learn as we grow old!

Thursday, October 13, 1994

I remembered today that Louise Brooks said, "The trick is to be cool and look hot." And this was in 1925!

At the gym looking about, I thought how we fall in love with how they look and feel, and then we're stuck with who they are.

Jim Provenzano
Un Coin de Table

June 1995, Paris

In my room at Les Deux Continents: A news report showed nude French soccer players in a locker room—and not just from the waist up. The shot continued for more than a few seconds, but I missed getting a picture. I've had dreams like this so many times, moments missed, stunning naked men on TV. I'm here in Paris, and it happens.

The excess of France: That is what I sought from the likes of poets. I got CliffsNotes Rimbaud, all the toxicity of absinthe without the high. Thinking of the scene in *Total Eclipse,* the film version of the Rimbaud/Verlaine affair, when Leonardo DiCaprio whooped it up nude on the edge of a building. I forgave his other excesses. I recognized my mad self in him, and why "lasting" doesn't really matter. S. fell in love with me only because I casually began reading his Rimbaud paperback in French. That little bookshelf above the headboard—very convenient.

In Paris I've gotten used to being immediately recognized as foreign—out for fun, available, wealthy. Play Eros Ramozzotti whilst reading Tennessee Williams's *Roman Spring of Mrs. Stone.* That's my last week here.

So naturally, I had some illusions to shatter. I went out until the map wasn't needed. After visiting Père Lachaise I acquired a clearer sense of direction, of purpose.

The sex clubs? One turned out to be across the street from the hotel. Providence, I would say, if it hadn't taken me days to notice it. Why hadn't I hunted sooner—and better? I'd been getting boners in museums instead. I had long-standing dates with some paintings. I can spot a Rouault at 50 paces.

Going to sex clubs with American porn on the TV while French guys smoke American cigarettes made me feel more like product.

But this is all true—swear on Oscar Wilde's grave.

* *

The doorway was dark as all Paris. (I'll switch to present tense now.) I am greeted. His smile is contrasted by black button eyes, which in turn contrast with his milky skin. The Gaul of him to be so pretty.

His greeting is oddly friendly, a slap on the back while I pay older gents who flirt like nannies. He checks my butt, literally clamps his hand on my ass. I think for a moment he's doing a weapons check. He is, sort of.

He leads me to the bar, he of the sleek French nose, the thick accent. No, I'm the one with the accent here.

He smiles, cups my crotch. *"Pas assez dûr,"* I mumble. He catches the bartender's attention. Beers arrive. We toast. "Welcome." I get it. It's Cock-tease the Yankee Trade Night!

We saunter, all eyes on us. We are getting glances in the way the two near-cutest, youngest guys at any overtly predatory bar always do.

My French and his English collide in the beer, soothing the exhausting full-body ache I've had all day from walking through the famous cemetery. I hate walking. I should have rented a bike.

I stare at his lips, shiny from the first gulp. Change arrives.

"Un coin de table," he blurts, like it's an inside joke. He hikes up his boots on the barstool to show off his ass: two melons in denim.

"Tu t'appelles...?"

"Jean, et tu?"

"Jacques." I know, I'm really Jaime, or how they say my real name—"Zheeem"—but I like the sound of "Jacques" better.

We shuffle back to a leaning wall in the drunken smoke. The glances remind me of a movie where all the patrons are vampires, and they lock the doors between appearances of chum like me.

Jean senses my eagerness, knows he's caught me, pulls back,

smokes, is interrupted by two friends who don't care to be introduced. I touch Jean while excusing myself.

We part. The pissoir offers few followers of interest—not hardly, compared to the porcelain beauty of Jean.

I return to the sex area, watch others gear up to the huddle, the mollusk action. It's in the back of almost all the bars in Paris, it seems. Gorgeous cocks on brutish men, poorly lit. Pant belts clinking. Distorted vision. I see Jean at the center of a herd, inviting me in. I approach, squeeze, feel a sort of car-crash pressure. I hold on, persist, cock out, know I can assert my beauty and foreign arrogance through the thick cloud of breath. Bending down may require effort, acquiescence, but I must taste Jean. I move closer to him, the boy man, no other for me, romantic desire amid pure heat. I reach the top rim of his jeans. My fingers crawl down between the curve of his muscles and the fabric. My hand parks in the warm cleft. His ass ring greets my finger like a kiss.

His cock is in some other guy's hand. His smile pairs with some other mouth kneeling at my crotch, unraveling me. Jean wants me against his butt as protection, a blanket.

My hand scoops down between his legs to feel Jean's scrotum, and the tugging from the other side. His crinkle-eyed grin assures assent. I feel hairs that I imagine are as delicate and black as those of his eyebrows.

I retract my hand, wetting fingers, and submerge again. His anus slurps my finger inside him. The guy in front of him, jacking his cock, resents my pleasing him more. Jean's the grounds of a duel, attacked from both sides.

Men converge around us, but are unable to conduit him. Some spew near me. My belt buckle dribbles with another man's sperm. The men are a jelly-like organism of quivering knees, messy French kisses.

I lick Jean's jaw, my finger burrowing into his ass, as I come on another man's face.

"J'arrive," he purrs, ripping the other man's hand away and shoving his cock into my palm.

Not here, I wish. The hotel is a block away and impossible. I wanted to save his spew in a reliquary vial like the one I saw in Notre Dame.

With the audience, we finish, and finish big, gasping, spurting. I continue my digging, getting him up under the tiny rivulets of my fingerprints, to be saved for later, much later.

* *

Today I strolled about the Musee d'Orsay and saw a painting with a familiar face. Him.

A hundred years ago he had a beard and long hair.

Him.

In a painting, behind a table where Verlaine, Rimbaud, and other dead poets sit, he stands, cheerful, his black button eyes and porcelain skin inviting me.

Luckily, they had a postcard in the museum shop.

He's the last guy on the right.

Shaun Levin
Not Alone Enough

21.7.98, Monday (Envy)

The sun filters through the leaves onto the bench, and the silence is complete. It's my first visit here, and everything is a wonder. I came in through the High Street entrance past a group of drunks sunning themselves in the forecourt. I have no change to give. I've crossed the cemetery to its far end, the wall that flanks Bouverie Road, and I'm here to enjoy the sun. But then the perfect man in tight white T-shirt, denim cutoffs, and flip-flops walks past.

Envy says: "Take me, I want to be you."

Last night I got drunk at a poet's party. I drank chilled rosé and begged a man in a terra-cotta T-shirt to have sex with me. I said I could tell by his beauty that he was a poet. I could tell he'd experienced pain. I could tell he knew his metaphors. He laughed and fed me smoked salmon sandwiches to sober me up. I said I'd lick his come off the walls when he came. I said I'd kiss him right there and then. I said: "These cocktail parties make me want to have wild, unbridled, desperate sex. I don't care if everyone sees me naked."

"I'm not gay," he said.

How wonderful, I thought, *to be desired with no obligation to reciprocate.*

Something to look into: My brother is Icarus and I'm Hephaestus. He's the suicidal rebel, and I'm the foot-dragging maker of arms. We're coming to the end of our myths. From this point on we'll need to make choices. My brother's a circle, the tips of his wings touching when he lifts his arms; I'm the mountain from which I was thrown, a triangle. I need another two people in my life at all times. I need sharp corners. Always.

Now I'm in Abney Park Cemetery. Hackney's oasis. Home to

William Booth, father of the Salvation Army, and to gay men looking for love. The guidebook says that no other cemetery has been better served in English literature. I'm here to explore and to get away from the nagging voices at home that keep me painting just to put me down. This place is a refuge. A sanctuary for the drunk, a haven for schoolchildren and smackheads and couples in love. And me. This cemetery is a haven for me. I'm here on a bench with my sketchbook by a grave with everlasting poppies. The sun has turned the treetops into lace. The wind flips over leaves on the ground, changing them from sharp emerald to dusty green, each time like a flash of light.

There's a man coming toward me, reading a book. I'm over the first rejection and ready with new expectations. He stops, and the tension mounts; his well-trained eye sizes me up. When he passes I am transformed again, reshaped by desire, shame, and envy. I hang onto people like Jacob hung onto Esau's ankle, getting dragged from one place to another. I want a mentor. I want to be shown the way for a change. I want to be led out of here.

"Have you got the time?"

He has returned to bring me back to life. Yes. He has come back with clichés to open up possibilities. I'm going to tell him the story about Jung in Morocco. I'm going to tell him how Jung fumbled for his pocket watch whenever he saw gay boys on beaches or in the Atlas Mountains.

"It must be around noon," I say.

Tell me this: What made Daedalus fly in front of his son and not behind him, like a good father should. Let's face it: You can't keep an eye on your son if he's not in your field of vision. There are consequences to that sort of behavior. Daedalus rebuilt his life after Icarus died, but spent the rest of his days in mourning. Sick with guilt.

And now to Hephaestus. My myth.

24.7.98, Thursday (Compassion)

What I'm going to tell you now might shock you. Something happened a few days ago that put me back on track. I took the guy with the book home and he swallowed my fist right up his pussy. He said it would have been easier with poppers, but he needed to be fucked too much to care. You see, he sat on the bench beside me, feigning interest in my sketches, telling me how he'd always wanted to be a painter. He was sweaty from walking around the cemetery for hours.

"It is hot," I said.

"Can you make me hotter?" he said, tucking his hand under my sketchpad.

He cupped my cock and balls in his fist and smiled at me.

"It's not *that* big," I said.

And he said—he did—he said, "It's big enough for me."

I showed him pictures of the cemetery in the guidebook. We talked about living in London. He was in exile from Europe; I left Africa as a boy and have never been home since. We spoke about families— and penises, cut and uncut. We kissed and licked each other, and I pinched the tips of his nipples with my nails.

"Come fuck me in the bushes," he said.

"I live just down the road," I said.

"But I don't know you," he said.

"We'll just fuck," I said. "It's not like I'm going to kill you."

We left the cemetery laughing, holding hands as if we'd been lovers forever. We bought apple juice from Harvest Wines and fat purple grapes from the grocers by the funeral parlor. By the time we got home I knew everything I'd ever know about him. Except one story. He told me enough names, dates, and places to explain how he could lie back on a stranger's bed, stretch open his arsehole and say, "Look, just like a pussy. Stick your finger in." And as for me, after two years of celibacy, my show was back on the road.

I once had a German lover called Rudolph who brought pastures and isolated farmhouses to our relationship. He was as beautiful as the young Chekhov, taller, equally insatiable. We met on the sofas in the foyer of the National Gallery; his body promised protection, his worldliness offered riches. He was a diplomat, so desperate for love he made me tie him up for hours while I cooked us dinner and spoke to friends on the phone. I was danger and exotica to him. He'd never been loved by a Jew. He taught me that men love to get fucked. And how did it end? It ended when he asked me to slice him open.

"Are you sure you've fist-fucked before?" said the man from the cemetery.

In the silence after we came, I stroked the down on the cheeks of his arse while lying next to him. I ran the tips of my fingers along his spine and put my arm across his shoulder, my elbow nestling in the curve of his neck. I touched his face as if it were a baby's.

"Do you have to work tomorrow?" I said.

"I must go home soon," he said.

"You can stay if you like," I said.

"I need to go," he said. "It doesn't mean I won't see you again."

The sweat had dried on my skin and I pulled the duvet up from the foot of the bed. He wrote his name and number on a piece of paper; I said what I said, and he told me one last story.

* *

I confess: I'm here to find love. Wherever I go I'm there to find love. But I need to hide behind a mission. Love is not its own mission. Every journey needs a reason outside itself. The solitude and green are beautiful here. Can I quote from the guide book again? *"In the spring and early summer the rich variety of bird-song adds to the cemetery's idyllic woodland aura."* It's true. Even in midsummer. My task for the day is compassion. Draw compassion. Two bodies. One standing, comforting the other who kneels, weeping. The comforter holds the other man's head in his hands, soothing his hair, gently touching his nape and the outline of his shoulders. The man in tears leans his head into the other man's body; no matter how hard I try, I can't stop the kneeling man from sucking the other guy's cock.

All creativity is assumption. Take my advice: To create you must pretend to know everything, pretend to belong, pretend your stories mean something to the world. The world, even if it is only one person, relies on your stories for its existence.

28.7.98, Monday (Shame)

Shame was born in the footsteps of love. I couldn't face the cemetery this morning. Don't ask me why. I went to Clissold Park, where I bought a mug of Earl Grey tea and sat on the stairs outside the old manor house. The sun has emancipated the privileged of Stoke Newington, those who don't have or need jobs; the café and lawn are full of mothers and children, and men playing chess with their shirts off, one of them with a guitar on his lap. Gizi sees me and comes to sit on the stairs. She says she misses the coffeehouses in Berlin.

"I'm just grateful for all this green," I say. "I've spent half my life in the desert."

Soon three mothers join us with their children. We're all excited to see each other; it's been over a year now since I left my job at the local nursery school. And why did I leave? Answer: I couldn't stop remembering my own childhood. To love children you must believe in a future. You can't be bound to your own past and care for children at the same time. Every gesture of love on my part was an attempt to remedy my own childhood. Which is what's happening in the park now. I think: This isn't right. All these kids being loved by women. I can't bear witness to this. I am the doe-eyed duckling, pleading: Will you be my mother?

* *

In the cemetery behind the derelict chapel, there's a patch of lawn with a bench. That's where I am now. Alone. The wind in the leaves, like waves, drowns out all other sounds. This is tranquillity. Until he sits down on the grass in front of me and takes off his shoes and shirt. An onion-skin of sweat covers his body and his nipples are dark brown. I can't imagine doing anything gentle to him. Shame and fear turn compassion into cruelty. Stop. Don't. I need trees and grass and silence. Please. I need the sun to myself. But with him here, lying in the grass to be noticed, I can't ignore anything.

I look up, and my eyes are like open palms. I look away, and I'm shamed. Let's assume I do talk to him. What happens then? We go into the bushes, amongst tombstones, fern bushes, clinging ivy, and before we kiss, before we taste each other, before we learn too much about one another from the way our lips touch, he puts his hand up my shirt and recoils from my body.

Wait. A story's about to unfold. A real-life, juicy, smooth-flesh-and-fucking story is about to make its way into the arena. A man with a body like an American porn star walks across the path with his T-shirt tucked into his back pocket. His cock has left a permanent outline on the fabric of his unwashed jeans. What seems like fat is only resting muscle; his skin is browned from being half-naked whenever he can—walking home from the gym, sitting on an old chair in his overgrown back garden, cruising this cemetery for hours to ensure every available man has sucked his cock and massaged his pumped-up tits.

I'll do anything to be next.

My sketchpad becomes a prayer book as I slide off the bench onto my knees. How can men own such perfect bodies? I could draw him. I could put him into words. I could lick him to imprint every pore and hair of his body onto my senses. My mouth is dry. Keep going. Record everything around you. That's why you're here. And then: He smoothes his palm across his chest. His nipples darken like an invitation. The stained-glass windows begin to crack like sugar and crash to the ground. The choir in the chapel sings deafening hosannas. Jesus howls and rips the rusting nails from his aching flesh. Ecstasy is loosed upon the world. Things are happening here, brothers.

29.7.98, Tuesday (Joy):

This is the story of the American porn star at my feet. The man in the grass got up and left, and the porn star settled down on a fallen tombstone by the running water near the main path, his body catching the sunlight. I could tell he was a regular in this cemetery—and in demand: the kind of man men notice. The kind of man who can pick and choose. You see, men with bodies like his can hide their inner worlds with greater ease; they can get adoration without revealing too much of themselves. I carried on drawing—it's the only way I know how to attract love. Sometimes it works.

The porn star lit a cigarette. I wasn't ready to look up from the page. I needed to be sure he was looking at me and not into the bushes, planning to follow the man who'd been lying in the grass. Did he know I could bring him voluptuous pleasure? Was he aware of the wondrous things I'd done with my penis? Explore joy. Today's task: Joy. Joy goes beyond the self and revels in its own being. Joy is born with the words *I* and *love,* and you string together. Joy is wrapped in the skin of another. Question: Does joy have other forms besides memory?

Wait, wait, wait. There's more. The porn star splashed water into his hair. The strip of sun between the chapel and treetops had narrowed; still, there was room for him to walk toward me, take off his shoes and jeans, and lie naked in the grass, his velvet skin exposed and welcoming me. Then I fell in love.

1.8.98, Friday (Desire)

Desire holds out both hands and says: "Take me. I trust you." "Desire risks being torn to pieces. It can't focus on the day-to-day. This is where Hephaestus comes into the story. No matter how hard his father kicks him, he accepts his mother's invitation to move back in. And there he sits, at home, albeit Mount Olympus, making weapons for the gods, helping others fight their battles.

OK, enough of that. I need to tell you something.

But.

Desire closes down the mind in order to survive. I have no one to share these stories with; I have become Anne Frank, locked in my head-attic, stuck in and cut off from history. If I had someone, I'd ring him up and say, "Do you want to know what happened to me three days ago?"

"Not again," he'd say.

"I met this man in the cemetery, and I fell in love."

"How long does it take you to fall in love?" he'd ask. "The guy's a stranger. How can you love someone you don't know?"

"What's time got to do with it?" I'd say. "I can tell you've never loved before."

And there's still the man with the book and the story he told me while tying his laces. His grandparents owned a travelling theatre company in the 1920s and 1930s. He was a German, she was from France, and when the war came his grandfather joined the Nazi party, which meant they got invited to perform for SS officers. They traveled between concentration camps performing Moliére. When they realized what was going on beyond the officers' quarters, they began to hide Jews and Gypsies amongst the ball gowns in their caravans and drive them out to the partisans in the woods. Some lived to tell the tale, but the French still see his family as collaborators.

I wonder: Did guilt make him tell me the story, or was it that he had no defenses after my fist had been up his pussy? Most men are defensive when you ask them questions after sex. They'll give you their bodies, but they won't let you in further than the length of your cock. His openness was a promise. But our histories kept us lonely again.

With him there was no love, but now there is. The so-called porn star's name is Henrik, and he's Denmark's number 1 rock star; a sex-crazed 6-foot-2 man with jet-black hair who comes to London for the kind and quantity of sex he wants. Once a year he is a regular in the cemetery. This is what I can tell you about him: He smiles without fear and walks everywhere as if he's never been lost. He leaned against the chapel wall while I sucked his cock, his thick pubes damp with sweat and someone else's come; leaning down, almost kissing the top of my head, he dribbled spit onto the root of his cock for me to wet my lips. He wanted to be fucked out in the open, turned on by the possibility of discovery. And while I was inside him, fucking him from behind, watching my cock go in and out of his hairless arsehole, he answered all my questions. That's what made me love him. He knew I could be trusted.

By the time we'd finished, they'd locked the cemetery gates, so we climbed through the hole in the fence by the timber yard and went for a drink at Bar Lorca, a straight pickup joint with live percussionists on some nights of the week. I got us drinks from the bar, half-expecting him not to be there when I turned round.

"I'm going to be in *Hamlet,* the musical," he said when I joined him by the stage.

"Are you Hamlet?" I said.

"Yes," he said. "What do you do?" (Hadn't I told him in the cemetery?)

"I'm a painter," I said.

"I paint sometimes," he said. "I spend two or three days painting, and when I go out again, I feel like the loneliest man in the world."

"That's how I feel every day," I said.

When they called for last drinks, I suggested we go for coffee. And each time he agreed, I felt braver, like a god-fearing Christian in the lion's den, charming the beast with divine encouragement. We bought coffee at the kebab house and walked down Church Street, stopping to look at children's clothes in the window of a secondhand shop. He leaned in toward me, thinking I wanted to whisper in his ear, me thinking he wanted to be kissed.

"I don't think I can return that kiss," he said.

"I didn't think you would," I said, the lion's claw marks across my cheek.

"I'm just tired of quick sex," he said. "I've had a boyfriend for nine years."

"I've only had sex twice in the past two years," I said. "And last week was the first time."

"You're not looking for quick sex," he said. "You're looking for someone to love."

I walked him to Defoe Cabs because he wanted to go to Heaven and I had to get up early. I had things to do. He left without giving me his phone number. We made no plans to meet up again, but I am a rottweiler when it comes to love; I called the Danish Tourist Board and got them to send me information about all the musicals in Copenhagen.

7.8.98, Thursday (Humiliation):

On the day of the premiere, I sent him flowers with a postcard of a stone angel on a tomb in Abney Park Cemetery, saying: "I miss you." A call came two days later.

"Thank you for the flowers," he says.

"Do you like them?" I say.

"Can I see you when I come to London next time?" he says.

Every thought of him is nails across raw flesh. Every heartbeat threatens to leave me with nothing. I'm in the cemetery again and I want sex. Watch me, I'm becoming an addict. The two of us are strangers in a forest, jerking ourselves off—his eyes are blue and his skin aging, loose and hairless. He says he'd like to see me again, that I look like the serious type. I tell him to keep flicking his fingers like that over the tips of my nipples. I come into my hand and offer it to him to drink. He wiggles his tongue over my open palm, as if it was scalding hot water, saying: "God, I'd love to swallow it," until he comes too. I wipe his come off my thigh with a tissue and throw it into the bushes. We don't share smiles, just the sheer exhilaration of disgust.

* *

Humiliation is on the floor. Head in palms, heart against knees, arsehole and spine exposed. Humiliation couldn't give a fuck. It says: "Protect me, violate me; do anything as long as I don't have to take responsibility."

10.8.98, Sunday (Glee)

I want to make every entrance with glee. Blindly, hopefully, ready for anything. OK, so what if I'm drunk? I've fallen in love again. Twice in one month is not a lot compared to adolescence. But you're 35. No, I'm not. I'm five or 15, never more. Falling in love is addictive. All that promise. All that license for abandon and danger. Am I just addicted to the pain of disappointment? It's too cold for the cemetery; I'm going down to the river.

Walking through Covent Garden on the way to the South Bank, I stop at Tesco's for a tub of hummus with roasted red peppers and two olive ciabatta rolls. I cross Hungerford Bridge and walk along the Thames to Gabriel's Wharf where an international festival of street performers is in full swing. I can be anonymous here. I lean against the railings eating my hummus and watch a young man in a kilt and heavily tattooed legs balancing on the handlebars and back wheels of his mountain bike. He jumps from one side of his bike to the other, like some cowboy acrobat, his skirt exposing black boxer shorts whenever his legs are in the air.

"This is my only job," he tells his audience before his last trick. "So if you like the show, please support it."

Which I do, by going up to him and telling him he was brilliant, amazing, and because I'm beyond caring and out of my element, I say: "Can I buy you a drink?"

"You sure can," he says. "My fucking girlfriend didn't turn up, and I'm vexed."

Ripples lap against the embankment wall, echoes of waves crashing on African shores. It was on a day like this that Icarus drowned. On a day like this, Hephaestus sat at the bottom of the sea making rings and bracelets with nymphs.

"I don't like it when people I love see my work," I say.

"I don't love her," he says. "Not anymore. Besides, I need to be looked at."

"I'll look at you," I say.

"Let's go and get a drink, then," he says.

11.8.98, Monday (Disappointment)

Disappointment walks away, expecting nothing.

12.8.98, Tuesday (Detachment)

Who gave birth to detachment? Pain. And who gave birth to pain? A good slap in the face. Eyes rolled back, seeing nothing, not even its own insides, detachment is never where it is. The weather's improved. I'm on the bench again beside the plastic poppies. I can convince myself of this: I'm here to explore. I've given up on love. All I want is to survive these days.

How come it's so impossible to find love? Why don't I ever find love in supermarkets and at bus stops? Why don't I have the kind of friends who introduce me to lovers? Instead, biker boy followed me home from the river and asked me to tie him to my bed. Futons are a problem when it comes to bondage, so I strapped his wrists to my writing desk, lifted his legs over my shoulders and fucked him. He kept telling me to fuck him harder, to look at his face while he was getting fucked. I made loud noises until he said: "Did you come already?"

And I, plopping out of him, said, "Yes."

* *

He wants to be buried with his mother. This is what they tell him: We need to put a rod in to check how deep the grave is. We need to see if there's room for you. This is all happening in the offices of Abney Park Cemetery while I wait to speak to the conservation officer. She'll be able to fill me in with anecdotes about the cemetery once she's finished with the old man. She tells him the price depends on the grave's distance from the path. If it's too far they'll need to dig by hand. That'll cost anywhere up to £500.

By the 1850s, according to the guidebook, monumental stone-masons had set up shop around the High Street entrance. You can spot their work in discreet but visible positions on pedestals and curbstones.

Matt Bernstein Sycamore
Breakthrough

Sunday, March 12, 2000—8:25 P.M.

Of course I haven't been out of the house yet. Yesterday I didn't get out until 11 P.M.—that's fucking crazy. I need new sinuses—too much time in bars, I guess, but then what else is there to do when you get out of the house @ 11 P.M.? Yesterday was ridiculous. I spent Friday night at Stephen Kent's because I had a trick there @ 1:30 P.M. on Saturday, so I figured why not just spend the night—Stephen Kent's out of town. Got up in time for my trick—actually, the phone rang forever around 12:30, just like a wake-up call.

I was exhausted—did I get up early on Friday for something? No, that was yesterday—right, I got up @ 12:30 and I was exhausted. But why was I so exhausted on Friday? Oh—because I drank tequila in Tompkins Square Park and then went dancing @ Centro-Fly—that was AMAZING: DJ Cajmere from Chicago layering one funky song after the other with lots of that clank-clank-a-clank—not as hard as I usually like it, but unbelievable anyway. Badis and I got there and just stayed on the dance floor for 2½ hours, until I was about ready to pass out.

Oh, but anyway, Saturday—maybe Saturday starts with that trick on Friday. He called right when I got to Stephen Kent's—2 A.M. and I was ready for bed but horny too, so it was perfect timing: I got a hard-on in my pants just talking to him. Funny, right? Rushed over, hoping he'd be hot, and guess what?—he was hot. Really great meaningful green eyes—I don't know what that means, but that's the way it was. Just started making out and I was creating the passion, but I think it was there too.

Then we got undressed and into bed. He wasn't exactly in shape but not out of shape either. And pretty young—30s. Plus he knew how to touch. He wanted to cuddle, and then we were making out, and pretty soon I was sucking his dick, which stuck straight out, and then just the head curved down, which was kind of weird for my throat. Then he was on top of me—I was on my back, and then there was his dick poking @ my asshole, pushing in.

Now, the dick pushing in without a condom thing is nothing new for me, right? Doesn't even scare me anymore, really. Well, I do think, *What if he just shoots? What if his fantasy is all about shooting in my ass without asking?* There was something about this guy's attitude that kind of felt that way. He was fucking me, and I was thinking, *Why am I doing this no-condom thing again? Especially after last Sunday when I had that breakthrough.* Did I even write about that? Shit, I'm so behind in this journal.

So the guy was fucking me for a minute—or maybe it was two or three minutes. When I'm getting fucked, time is strange and slow, so maybe it was only 30 seconds. Anyway, after that time period, I pulled away and said, "You should put a condom on." Which he did. But, oh, the breakthrough: Well, now I'm not sure it was a breakthrough— last Sunday at the Cock when that guy was just pounding me in the middle of the room: so fucking hot hot HOT. The point is that I felt like finally I can just get used like that—and it was with a condom for the whole time. I didn't need the raw part to relax my asshole. But I'll talk about that later.

So then Friday night's trick put on a condom, and he was fucking me. He went right into POUNDING, which was hot but too painful, really. I said, "Let's change positions." I got on my knees, and he got behind me. I sat on his dick, and he grabbed my chest—yes, that was the way to do it—I got really loud, just moaning and grunting. He said, "Did you come?" I said no, so he kept pounding, but then it was too much, and I pulled away. He said, "Do you like getting fucked?" I said, "Yeah, but sometimes it wears me out quickly." Which was a simple answer, of course. Sometimes I feel like I should just go right into the pain. I'm totally turned on by the idea of being an insatiable bottom—fuck me harder HARDER, right? But then when it comes to the physical act, it's more difficult.

Anyway, then I was sucking the guy's dick in all different positions for a while. Then we were lying down, and he was holding me (that part was hot), and then he was trying to stick his dick in my ass again without a condom. This happened a few times, and I pulled away—that whole routine. Guess I was sucking his dick after it had been all the way in my ass—is my ass what I tasted? I don't know. Finally, he came with me sitting on his chest and jerking off too—I really needed to come, because otherwise I knew I'd be up on the phone sex lines as soon as I got back to Stephen Kent's. I said, "Just grab my balls"—and then I came on his chest, but yuck, it wasn't satisfying except for a second. He'd totally left as soon as he came, wasn't turned on @ all by me coming, I don't think. I hate it when I get all crazed and just NEED to come—it's spring approaching, I guess—but I think I would have felt much better if I hadn't come.

I walked back to Stephen Kent's, beyond exhausted—stopped by Hollywood Diner but no vegan soups again. Bought canned split pea soup, ate it when I got back, and of course I didn't end up in bed until 4 or 5—I can't remember. That's why I was so exhausted when I dragged myself out of bed @ 12:30, plus I'd been waking up every hour to make sure I hadn't overslept.

Then Saturday's trick arrived, which is quite the rarity with all the in-call flakes I've gotten recently. He was this huge guy—not fat, just tall and big—6 foot 6 or so, stale cigarette smell. He was fine— nothing special to report, nice enough, brought his luggage, went back to Texas. Afterward I was so tired, I had to lie down and sort of meditate. Then I used the computer for hours, and before I knew it, it was dark. Didn't really matter, because it had been raining all day and I didn't want to go outside.

Called about seven people to make plans after Scott flaked (we were supposed to do dinner and/or a movie)—still no plans, so I just waited, waited, waited. Hoped for a trick or SOMETHING to do other than the East Village bars, but no luck. Went out around 11 P.M., too hungry and spaced-out to decide where to go, walked around the West Village and then over to Cafeteria because it was late and I couldn't deal with another diner. Sure, Cafeteria's a trendy Chelsea hellhole, but it's perfect every six months or so. The music's good, and it's relaxing to sip a cocktail and stare out the windows.

Got the veggie burger, of course (nothing else there to eat), plus Stoli Vanilla on the rocks—which I didn't want, but I was forcing myself. I just felt so horribly depressed, and I wanted some spark of happiness before bed, figured alcohol would give me that. It wasn't really working. I had a second cocktail and I just stared out the window feeling totally vacant and dead—Scott called me on the cell phone, Jose called, but still no plans.

Then this woman came over and said, "Me and my friends were watching you all by yourself, and we thought we'd invite you to join us." That totally changed my mood. Sometimes it's so easy. They wanted to know what I was doing all alone, what I did in New York, did I come here often—the usual bougie questions, but they were soothing. Two Mexican women who were sisters and a friend of theirs, all in their 20s. Somehow it came up that I was a whore—oh right, they asked me what I wrote. I brought out my book; they wanted to know how I dealt with old men. I said I focus on something that turns me on.

I had another cocktail, and they wanted to go to Serena, the new bar in the basement of the Chelsea Hotel—it's for straight fashion victims. So we went to Serena, but there was a line; they left in a cab, and I walked over to Barracuda. Kind of dead, but I got a cocktail anyway, went into the bathroom, and on my way out this guy was watching me while he was pissing. Cute.

The guy came out of the bathroom, and I went over, said, "Hi, my name's Matt." His name was Matt, too, and he was cute—seemed sweet but smashed. I kissed his cheek and rubbed his head and sent him other not-subtle hints, which felt good (my confidence), but he had to get up for work @ 7 (it was about 2 by then). Though he did ask if I had any coke, then he left and said, "I hope I see you around," and I wondered whether I should grab his head and start kissing him. But I figured I'd already made my point. The bar was boring, so I finished my cocktail and decided to go to the Spike. I was ready to get on my knees and suck some dick, figured that would work there.

But you know what I also haven't written about? That porn video

I was in two weeks ago. Steve had said, "You better write it down before you forget it." So let me just put in a few notes. It was called *College Cock 101*. I was the college boy, and then there was the coach and two guys @ the gym (one didn't show up). I had this great line @ the beginning, "Coach, when am I gonna get big like that?" (pointing to the guy working out). I accidentally said, "When am I gonna get to be a bitch like that?" It was a double accident, because I meant to say "butch" because they kept asking me to make my voice deeper. But it came out as "bitch," which sent me into hysterics.

This one really cute guy was working as staff for the video—I fantasized about him while I was having sex with the actors. I assumed he worked at the spa where we were filming, but when I asked him later on, he said, "No, I have a degree." Whatever for him. Of course, me and the other two guys were Viagra'd out, but they still couldn't get hard, which was perfect because I was supposed to get fucked, but instead I got to fuck them both.

It was weird: I totally felt like a stud—in the breeding sense—guy with a hard-on. OK, do these dudes. But it was hot too, not sexually but emotionally or something. Then @ the end we all took forever to come—one guy couldn't come @ all, so one of the guys on the crew shot all over Coach's chest as a stand-in (the video just shows come shooting). Actually, two different guys tried—the producer was even going to do it.

Wait it's fucking 9:45 P.M. now—I've gotta get out of the goddamned house, so back to Saturday night: What was going on? The Spike was crowded, but no one was turning me on. I figured if someone's dick was out, though, I could suck it, be his boy or something (I was probably the youngest guy there). But no sex @ all going on— not even in the back area. Then I was kind of dancing to some cheesy song, so I thought, *Why don't I go to the Roxy if I want to dance?* Yale put that idea in my head, tried to get me to go when I called him and I was like, "No way in hell, honey."

But all of a sudden the Roxy sounded OK—got there and ran into Feraz, whom I went home with from the Cock way back (yes, I went home with him—remember that k-hole and everything). He was with the same boy as when I first met him, but tonight that boy was fully working Diana Ross—yum, yum.

1:47 A.M.

OK, I got all wired and had to run out of the house. Actually went all the way to Manhattan to get contact solution and food. It's FREEZING out too. But now I feel better—just as exhausted but a little more calm. I almost went to the Cock, was walking around just about getting hard thinking about it. Seriously. I could feel my dick getting bigger, pushing against my corduroys. Well, I had to piss, but it was something sexual too. But then I kept thinking, *I'm exhausted, I need to rest; I'm exhausted, I need to rest.* Like a counterargument: Of course, it doesn't matter how exhausted I am at the Cock on a Sunday—it's almost always fun. And sometimes transformative. But a week off will make it better.

More tomorrow—I'm getting ready for bed.

Monday, March 13—2:45 A.M.

Too tired to write much, but I HAD TWO TRICKS TODAY—it's about fucking time, right? The first one was @ the Penn Club, which was FANCY in a very old-money sort of way. The guy was one of the ones where I'm thinking, *Oh no*—tan and flabby and @ least 60 I'd say, maybe 70. His ass was the scary part, almost twice as wide as the rest of his body, and it was sag, sag, sag. Plus that ass smelled— I don't even know what it smelled like, but when I was massaging his ass, his asshole kept making popping noises.

But whatever—I got hard massaging him, he played with my dick, I jerked him off—he was nice enough. The second trick (11:30 P.M., after I went out with Scott and Stephen Kent for dinner)— he was sort of hot, long hair and 30s, very shy and kind of straight surfer-looking, but he had a huge rainbow flag for a curtain. He was sweet, once he loosened up. We smoked a hit of pot, and then I was getting all into him sucking my armpits—yum, ready to fuck, horny. Got him off sucking until the very end, then jerking him off— wanted it in my mouth, of course, but sometimes I've gotta resist, right? If I could just believe it's totally safe, I'd swallow all the time, but really I always freak out @ least a little bit.

Oh, the funny part was the guy burned his nose with his poppers. Then I left—that hit of pot was STRONG (I can still feel it—no way). Oh, the fucking landlord is coming over tomorrow to tear down walls—guess I got three months free rent, right? That piece of shit—gotta get my computer out so he doesn't run off with it. Gotta go to bed so I can leave as soon as the crew gets here (2 P.M., I guess). The good side is that it will get me out of the house—focus on the good. OK, time for bed. Love—

What's today?—Tuesday, March 14 @ 2:59 A.M.

I had three tricks, count them—one, two, three—hello—hopefully I'm in the money for the rest of March because, honey, I sure NEED it. Two themes for the tricks: wanting to fuck (me), loving my head. First one smelled like way too much stale sweat—I said no way to getting fucked. Second one kept shoving it in, but he couldn't stay hard. Well, he stayed hard when my head was falling off the bed, but that wasn't working either. But he gave me a $40 tip—that's the way it should be. Third one liked to say things like "Dude, you suck cock so well...man, you like sucking cock?" Duh. Then he did fuck me, and actually that was hot, but a few minutes was enough. Wanted me to come, so I pretended to try really hard.

The third one was actually fun, plus he had a great apartment—big loft on E. 16th. The bathroom was the best part—reddish slate (?) tiles and old fixtures. Afterward I went over to Stuyvesant Park to see if anything was going on, ran into Craig, sat and talked to him—he's so fucking cute. Petted him on the head right when I sat down, then touched him every now and then—we talked for a while and that was fun, but he pretended he wasn't cruising, even after I said that of course I was. Walked him to the subway and got a great hug, then went to meet Eric for food. Came home, and the landlord hasn't torn any walls down yet, & I don't have the energy to move more stuff. Gotta go to bed, get up by noon again, get out in the SUN—it's supposed to be 60 tomorrow: delicious.

Yes, once again it's 3 A.M., honey.
Thursday, March 16, 2000

OK, well, the get-up-@-noon thing is working, I guess—though I was way too exhausted today. Walked to the gym but couldn't go up. Then it's all crazy coming back here with the walls torn down, dust everywhere, and this is my home—well, for another two weeks, shit.

OK, the money is still rolling in, YES—and it better KEEP rolling 'til the end of the month because it's about fucking time. OK, it's about fucking time. Just got back from these two guys who really turned me on. One guy fucked me with his huge dick in a condom, and it barely hurt—though when his dick slid out I made him stop anyway—habit, I guess. The other guy was kissing me—and I was sucking both of their dicks, and both of them were rubbing my chest—one guy grabbed my neck; he was so perplexed that that turned me on.

Earlier this guy from Long Island came to Stephen Kent's, but he was too nervous. Then he wanted to leave. I said, "All right, just give me $50"—the bitch wanted to leave without giving me a cent; he gave me $20. Piece of shit—made me RUSH back from Blake's opening, which had BEAUTIFUL mosaic work and was in a nice space too.

Oh, and yesterday I had two tricks, but who the hell were they? Oh, one was the young guy who was kinda hot—he fucked me too, didn't he? Wow, I'm turning into the bottom I've always dreamed of becoming. He wanted me to fuck him too, but for some reason I only had Trojans in my bag—I can't ever stay hard in those fucking things. And he was tense, worse than me on a bad day. Then he wanted to watch porn—good thing we were @ Stephen Kent's because that's porn central, right? Then after he came, he went on about how he wished his girlfriend could know—or something like that. I said, "Why not?"

Then he had a moment of pure brilliance: He said, "You know, I think I'm attracted to both." Hello, Bisexuality 101. He actually seemed surprised that I agreed with him. He said, "You don't think bisexuality's a crock?" But who was the other guy?

Friday, March 17, 2000—3:47 P.M.

All right, the noon thing is sort of working, I guess—got up @ 12:20 today.

Oh, a few things I forgot to write about last night's trick—@ first there was this whole dynamic of one guy paying for the other to have fun, because he'd just broken up with his boyfriend, but pretty soon (after about one minute) that dynamic collapsed. Then it was funny how they both kept saying "Tyler's so hot, isn't he? Tyler's so hot"—like I wasn't in the room—that kind of turned me on.

Anyway, I know I wanted to write something about last Saturday, plus the backroom @ the Cock a few Sundays ago—there was supposed to be some great significance to it all, but I'm not sure I know what that is anymore. So Saturday I ended up @ the Roxy, which kind of got me high for a few minutes—that here I am, I'm radiant, I'm alive, I'm the center of it all club energy—then I was walking around, and believe it or not, I found a backroom. What?

Yeah, it was upstairs in the back, not so many guys, but the room was DARK, and I was craving someone's dick in my mouth, which of course I got. It was funny, because every now and then a Roxy employee would turn up the lights, and then someone would turn them down. Plus it felt like most of the guys—especially the more built ones—had disappeared from their friends for a few minutes, like "I'm going to the bathroom." There was a great moment when the Roxy guy turned up the lights, and then a woman came by and turned them down—hello, solidarity.

But anyway, I don't remember the order of things. At some point I was rubbing this guy's chest—very hard, yum—reaching down for his cock, and he said, "I don't even know what you look like." Then the lights came on, and he was more into it but shy too. We sat down, and I started sucking some other guy's dick while the first guy rubbed my chest—perfect—and the other guy grabbed my head good, and eventually he came in my mouth, which was definitely what I needed. Then he kissed me and all the guys nearby before getting up to leave.

Then the first guy was asking me, "Don't you worry about

swallowing?" I said, "Yeah, but I do it anyway." He said, "You like it too much, right?" And then I was sucking his dick until he came in my mouth, and wow, he had a lot of come—so delicious. Then I was jerking off; I'd been ready to burst for at least a half hour, ready for that amazing orgasm, and it started, but some guy reached over to feel my come, which was annoying because it totally fucked up my orgasm. Oh well. Held the first guy, and he held me; we were boyfriends, and then we left; he went home.

So I went out to dance, but let me tell you, the music was so unbelievably bad that dancing was impossible. Every other song was a fucking fade-out. I found Feraz and a group of what passes as club kids these days—youngish and not all Chelsea'd-out like 99.5% of the rest of the crowd. I kept saying they need to ship that Victor Calderone DJ-person out to the Bermuda Triangle. I kept going up to random people and saying that was the 14th fade-out in a half-hour. But no one really got it—I fled.

So the way-back-now Sunday thing @ the Cock started with sucking dick and swallowing, of course—gotta get my vitamins. I was on my knees, and the guy had a beautiful dick—but he wasn't so beautiful. I got up and leaned over to touch this other guy who was hot, but only our hands could reach (there was someone in between us sucking the hot guy's dick—oh, and someone was sucking my dick too). We were massaging each other, slowly pulling closer, and BOOM— when we got together it was so charged. He was grabbing my face, and we were making out making out, making OUT, grabbing each other's bodies and dicks and grinding into each other. Then as I was sucking his dick, he started kind of slapping my face, which was delicious, I nodded, "Mm-hmm, yeah, uh-huh"—kind of like to make those noises now to let someone know what I'm into. I stood up and said, "You can come in my mouth if you want to." He said, "I'm not ready yet," and then we were pushing each other around. He sucked my dick but not for that long.

Then I was sucking the hot guy again, getting into that bottom role but all aggressive of course, pushing his dick into my throat, then standing up again and kind of smacking his face too. He was grabbing my chest, and someone behind me was pushing his dick against my asshole. I've got the technique down now for appreciating the sensation and then angling slightly away so it doesn't slide in. Then the guy said he needed to take a break; I said, "You better give me your number before you leave. "OK," he said. "The guy behind you is really hot." I looked back, and he was really hot. I felt his chest (hard), he had a preppyish look: short, curly hair maybe, or I don't know—he was hot, that's all.

I felt his dick, and wow, he actually had a condom on—that's DEFINITELY a first time for the Cock—hello for progress. I lubed his dick up with my spit, and then just like that, his dick was in my ass— wow, it was hot. Pretty soon I was bent over, and someone was sucking my dick; I was sucking someone else's dick and sometimes making out with someone else. And the guy was just pounding me in the middle of the room like in my best fantasies. I was just relaxed, getting pounded, and wow, I was LOUD with all the moans coming out of me when someone's dick wasn't gagging me. One guy came in my mouth, and then I was spitting his come into his mouth, and then I slid away from the guy who was fucking me because now it was hurting.

But the guy leaned over and said, "Can I come in your ass?" I said, "Are you close?" and he said, "Yeah." I said, "All right," felt for the condom, and then he was fucking me again. Now I was practically screaming. The guy who came in my mouth was rubbing my chest and kissing me, and wow, I was just going with the pain and the pleasure—yes yes yes YES YES! That's all there was: me getting fucked in the middle of the room. And I was collapsed against the other guy, and the guy fucking me shot. I jerked my dick with him in my ass, then I came, and he pulled away.

Leaned back to kiss the guy, but he turned away, wouldn't even say anything; I just LAUGHED because it was perfect anyway, went out to the front and DANCED so hard—my body gets so centered from that backroom. I was turning it out and then inside out and then all over the place. I *was* that bar, and at the end I was dancing for Michael (the hands guy), and eventually we were making out again—

that was just the night, THE FUCKING NIGHT...well, I guess it was also the fucking night, right—because it relaxed me or something, now I'm getting pounded all the time.

WOW—that's all, just wow. You know, I'd only slept four hours the night before because Jason's friend Hrod came home with me. He was nervous, I was nervous, and we talked and then ended up having sex @ like 4 A.M. or something, and I had to get up @ 10. But the Cock just did it for me, healed me and sent me to the sky. Sometimes that place is heaven—amazing sex and then dancing like my life depends on it—wait, my life does depend on it. Sometimes the Cock is a hell-hole too, of course, but wow, writing about all that makes me need it—I might have to go on Sunday, maybe forget about this new schedule.

David Serling
Phone Sex

April 21, 2000, 11:30 P.M.

I can't take my eyes off the phone. What was I thinking, giving out Deb and Carl's phone number to a total stranger? If the psycho calls back, I'm cutting him off.

I was lucky they didn't notice anything strange in their bedroom when they got home. Or that I'd been rolling around in their bed. That's how I got into trouble in the first place—snooping around their bedroom earlier today while they were out. I'm just so hot for Carl. I wanted to imagine where his butt had touched the mattress. His pillow smelled so musky I could almost taste him. Then, I *saw* him smiling at me across the room. He was *actually there*—on his computer's screen saver. It was a slide show of his honeymoon photos. The solo shots of him spun around until I was dizzy. I wanted to lick the screen.

Where were my manners? I'm a houseguest, and Deb is, of course, such a good friend. But I was already out of control.

I crawled over the bed to his desk, and bumped the keyboard. Carl's face disappeared, and up came the Internet. I thought a little X-rated chat would work off this lust. So I logged on with one of Carl's guest screen names, and right away I met this stud, a dead ringer for Carl named "CUTUPJOSTR8." He sent his dirty photo, and I went bananas. It showed him lying on a bed fully clothed but with his stiff dick towering out of his open fly. He had Carl's thick, prematurely gray hair. Lips that were full, but not pouty. Deep-set eyes with a steady romantic gaze. So much better than the shifty-eyed losers I've been dating.

I started typing in porno shit, but he didn't want cybersex. He wanted phone sex. That's when I really got excited. Maybe he *sounded* like Carl too! He asked to call here, but I didn't see how I could let him. And he couldn't take calls because he was in Hong Kong on business—with his wife. Hearing about her was the *pièce de résistance;* the thought of cheating with him—simulating adultery— was too arousing. I began pumping lotion out of a hand cream jar on Deb's boudoir, lathering it over my dick just above Carl's keyboard.

A message flashed up announcing that "CUTUPJOSTR8" had left the chat room. I thought I was going to die. My shame was burning, hormones raging. I needed to let it out. I should have given him the damn number. What kind of an asshole was I? As if sensing my remorse, his message box reappeared.

HIM: *Sorry my computer froze.*

ME: *No prob. Can you call me, Bro?*

I never say bro. But this archaic jock lingo made me feel younger and dumber. What other self-respecting 40-year-old would give out his friends' number to a chat room stranger? I knew this was wrong. I should have listened to my instincts, but I never do. Why start now? If I listened to my instincts, I'd be in a decent relationship and not jerking off with strangers.

HIM: *In about 5 I'll have the room alone, I can call you then.*

I was even turned on by his lousy typing skills. It made him seem less cultured and more brutish. Like some big dumb animal. Or, maybe, he was just in a rush.

ME: *That'd be great, tell me when to log off.*

HIM: *Send your pic first. Or no deal.*

He drove a hard bargain—and he was asking for the impossible; I had no photo. I'd lost him once; now it looked like he was slipping through my fingers again. Unless I used one of Carl's honeymoon photos. I could download it from his computer's screen saver photo files. I wrestled with my conscience for about two seconds. Then I sent off a sizzling honeymoon photo of Carl in wet surfer shorts, riding in the Maui surf.

Like me, he fell for Carl right away.

HIM: *Cool, I'm looking for a cocky str8 badass top to fuck my muscle ass back.*

I'd have preferred being the submissive one. But either way was fine. No skin off my back.

ME: *I'm your man, dude. Gonna treat you like a pucking younger frat bro.*

ME: *I mean "fucking," not "pucking."*

HIM: *Now your talking, that what I like.*

The truth was I'm a pussycat, a marshmallow. He started talking about rape and shit like that. It was so wrong, but something sick happened to me.

HIM: *Fuck, rape me like that bitch we gangbanged at my house.*

I should have been repulsed. I'm a male feminist and love women. I supported my mother's right to burn her bra. But, God help me, the "bang" aroused me. My dick sprung up harder and bobbed against Carl's keyboard. I remembered that time in the third grade when I was locked in a basement by a group of bullies. It was nothing sexual, but I was terrified, humiliated, ruined. I always wanted to be a part of them, to join their sexy mean asses. This felt like my chance. I'd had enough bad boyfriends to know a little something about abuse.

ME: *Gonna give it to you every which way till you're sore.*

HIM: *I like it real fuckin rough.*

ME: *Fuckin rip your legs up around my shoulders, and fist your hot ass.*

HIM: *Oh yeah…fuckin humiliate me while you shove that fist in my ass and make me beg for mercy…*

ME: *Crack the back of my hand against hour face if you scream.*

ME: *Your face, not "hour" face.*

HIM: *That's right…no fuckin mercy.*

I stopped typing and stroked myself long and hard; a drip of pre-come oozed out, lubricating Carl's space bar.

ME: *Bro, I'm getting really hard. Ready to call yet?*

HIM: *Total sexual rough abuse.*

ME: *That's right, you fuckin whore bitch.*

HIM: *Dude, I'm gonna need like 5 more minutes, then I am 100% sure I can do it…sorry.*

ME: *No prob, you cunt pig. Tell me about the gangbang.*

HIM: *Well, I gangbanged a bitch, but I have never been used by more than 2 guys...and I want that bad...I want to get fuckin beaten used, abused, dumped in...but only by str8 muscle boys, no fags.*

ME: *Very cool. Ready to fuckin rough you up, you little piece of shit fag boy.*

HIM: *What is the biggest group you've done?*

ME: *I've done about a 14-dude bang. One guy we raped landed up bleeding with a broken leg.*

This was vile and a lie. I wouldn't even consider having a three-some. I'm too jealous. And I've never even been punched, too afraid of getting hurt or bruising my delicate features. But I wanted to jump his bones and whip his hot ass—now, now, now.

ME: *Call me now.*

I gave him Deb and Carl's number without even blinking.

I logged off, and a few tense minutes later he phoned. Right away, I knew he was a keeper. I loved his voice. It had the same cadence as Carl's, that bland midwestern monotone. I affected a similar heartless tone.

"What are you wearing?" I asked.

"Nothing."

I paced the bedroom and gazed out the open French window with the view of their driveway, backyard, the swing sets, and maze of hedges. Like I was lost somewhere out there.

"I'm gonna knee your ass and throw you to the floor," I said and flopped onto Carl's side of the bed.

"Oh yeah!"

"I'm swinging your legs over my shoulders and sticking my arm up your hole." But I was facing straight up on the bed, one hand on the phone, one feeling up my own ass.

"Oh yeah, hurt me."

"You want my 9.5-inch cut dick?" I flipped over and plunged my 7- inch dick into the fold of Carl's pillowcase.

"Oh yeah, I want your dick."

"You little fairy pussy boy."

"Oh yeah, I am."

"You want me to stick a gun up your ass and shoot you?"

I didn't know where all this crap was coming from. I should have stopped there. Anyone else would have stopped long ago. Anyone with a grain of sense.

"You want it deeper?" I yelled. I was thrusting into Carl's pillow-case. My T-shirt was getting sopped. I listened for noises of anyone coming home.

"Yes." He sounded so masculine and yet so helpless.

"You want to die?"

"Yes, I do." He was nearly crying. This was shame taken almost to the nth degree. The nth degree would be death.

"When you go to the hospital what are you going to tell them?" I asked him, sounding sinister.

"That I got into a car accident."

"You're not going to show them my come dripping over your ass?"

"No." I hopped off the bed and looked out the window for any signs of them. Carl had built his daughter a tree house, and I thought of that dreamy, screwed-up porno star who, the tabloids claimed, in a fit of self-loathing, had thrown himself from a building.

"You want me to throw you out a 20-floor building? All your bones are going to be shattered at the bottom." I flicked on the TV to drown out the rest of this filthy conversation so the neighbors wouldn't hear. *Oprah* flashed up on the screen with a show about household clutter.

"Yes, oh yes!" He sounded enthralled, like I'd just offered him a vacation for two to the Bahamas.

"Lie back, I'm squatting with my muscular straight ass on your face," I said.

His tongue made clucking sounds into the receiver.

"Ever since I saw you fucking your girlfriend I wanted to eat your ass," he said.

"Eat it now. Can you taste my breakfast down there?"

"Yes."

"While you eat my ass, you want me to break your dick off?"

I was just appalled at myself. But I closed my eyes as if entering another world, where dicks were casually chopped off and shit was served as food. I drew away from the bed, wandered over to Carl's slat closet door and took in the cardboard smell of his laundered shirts.

"Oh yes," he said with a whimper.

"You want me to snap it off so there's just blood coming out of it?"

"Oh YES!"

"So you walk around with only a pussy, like a girl?" I rubbed my face in the crotch of Carl's pants and wrapped one of the pant legs around my neck.

"Yes."

"And you'll walk around in a dress—"

"Yes."

"And bra and panties for me?"

"Oh yes, sir." He was crying now. Tears of miserable joy. A pair of Carl's wing tips toppled from a shelf. My heart skipped a beat, as if he had come home and was angrily tapping me on the shoulder for his phone.

"I'll take you to dances as my girl, but my buds will find out you're a guy and rape you. We'll dump you in an alley with our come all over you."

"Yeah, oh yes."

"Keep eating my ass."

"I love eating your ass, sir." More tongue clucks.

"You'll be so beat up, you'll have to put makeup over your face to hide the bruises, right?"

"Yes, sir. Oh yes!"

I was out of my mind turned on, I could come any second. I grabbed one of Carl's carefully folded fuzzy polo sweaters and shoved it up under my shirt as I stroked myself.

"OK, take my 9.5. You feel that big mushroom head going in?" The way the words came out, 9.5 reminded me of the hours of a typical work day.

"Oh yes, I live for your dick."

"Got half of it in," I said, holding my dick in my hand, ready to shoot at any moment. This was so visceral, I could almost feel his tight walls opening.

"Suffocate me."

"Putting my hands over your mouth so you can't breathe."

"Oh yes," he quivered, "Can I come?"

"Yes," I said. I thought he'd never ask.

"Yeah, coming in your ass," I said and shot all over my hand, barely missing the white pony logo on Carl's crew neck.

"I want to die today," he said, and we both moaned our orgasms.

My hands were shaking, like I'd just come out of a trance. I quickly wiped the come onto the lining of my pockets. Then I scrambled to fold Carl's sweater.

"You're hot, man," he said, back to his old buoyant self.

"That was hot." I retained my bad str8-ass voice and stuffed Carl's business shoes back into their box.

"Can I call you again?" he asked. He sounded so sweet, as if we'd just been on a nearly perfect first date.

"Yeah, this is hot." I said *this*. Not *you*. Like a good selfish pig. As I flattened out Carl's row of mussed pants and folded back a cuff, I snapped back to reality. Of course he couldn't call Deb and Carl's again. "When are you calling?" I blurted, hoping I hadn't lost him already.

"Any time...I'll surprise you. When you least expect it. Just be waiting."

"No!"

"After midnight."

"You can't ever call here again."

"Oh yeah? What are you going to do to me if I do?" he asked, nearly purring.

Kill you was my first thought, but we'd already been down that road.

"Destroy that phone number!" I ordered him.

"I've memorized it..." he murmured, "by heart."

"You fucking rip it up! Now!"

"I love it when you talk rough. Talk to you later, dude," he said, then hung up.

I staggered back to the computer to log off. The phone receiver glistened with my sweat. I quickly mopped it with one of Deb's pink tissues.

This was when I heard the car pulling into the driveway. On the TV, *Oprah* had been replaced by news—a story about the "I Love You" computer virus. I quickly tried to delete my screen name but deleted Carl's sexy photo instead. I heard Deb calling my name; their daughter marched down the hall humming a nursery rhyme. I slapped at the bedcovers, scrambled into my pants, and dashed out to greet my hosts as nonchalantly as I could manage.

Saturday morning, 12:50 A.M.

Tried to sleep, but can't—still waiting for the psycho's phone call. He has the phone number; he could call any time, long after I've left. Wonder what time it is in Hong Kong? Did he mean my midnight or his midnight?

I've gone around the house unplugging phone jacks, except for the one in my room. I feel nauseous, and to tell the truth, my dick hurts. When I tried to pee a minute ago, it stung.

1:30 A.M.

My heart's still pounding. *He called.*

Just as I was almost nodding off, the phone rang. I knew it was him. If I didn't answer, it would only turn him on more, add fuel to the fire. He'd be calling all night. On the other hand, I couldn't let it just ring and wake everyone up.

His voice had a drained lovesick tone. For a moment, I felt mildly flattered. It had been so long since a man wanted me badly enough to call in the middle of the night.

I told him right away that he couldn't phone here ever again. His response was to offer me his name (Mike) and his hotel phone number in Hong Kong (was he *really* there?).

For a brief insane moment, I actually thought of giving him my own home number. But I needed to end this now. Long-distance jock-impersonation wasn't going to get me a boyfriend.

I begged him to go away. Somehow or other, the words "Honey, please" slipped out of my mouth. Instantly, I felt an energy drain on his side of the phone. His breath slowed down. "Darling," I added. "Angel." "My pet!" The syrupy words just kept flowing out of me. With each endearment, I felt him vanishing. Then it hit me. Be nice. Be more than nice. Be loving.

I smothered him with sappy phrases about hearts and flowers, taking long walks in the woods, and spending our lives together, introducing him to my folks. Nectar of romance poured through the phone. With each adoring word, I could feel him slipping away. His breath got lighter, he was fading. Melting, melting. Until finally the line went dead.

All that was left was the sound of my own voice trailing off. A persistent busy signal took over, but it sounded like a heartbeat racing up.

Kevin Bentley
Reasons to Live

March 3, 1996

Yesterday was clear and warm after a cold, rainy week, with the automatic lift of spirits the sun brings. I'd been browsing the *BAR* personals to scope out the competition, but instead saw one I wanted to call. I dialed this guy's mailbox and said something, probably all the wrong things. Then, natch, I imagined every time I came in the message light would be blinking. Maybe he's simply away pedaling a mountain bike somewhere. For a while I was all 'up,' certain I was on the verge of some new development, instead of looking at the date on the *Examiner* and thinking: *Three years, two months, and ten days since Richard died; seven years, eight months, and three days since Jack.* Not so fast, cowboy.

March 5

I've stalled for the moment about placing my own ad, not getting called back by the one *I* called having taken the wind out of my sails.

On the other hand, Sunday's adventure, though fruitless, overall brought me up a bit—I think I could try Eros again at a more ambitious time. I'd gone into the steam room and sat on a top ledge; pretty soon there were about six to eight guys spread about, mostly fiddling with their dicks to get them hard. A rather fat, mean-looking fellow sat against the wall to my left with his arms crossed over his stomach; a young, longish-haired guy—hot body—sat just below me stroking his dick, which quickly grew erect; to my right, quite close, a nondescript 30-something guy: shag hairdo, short beard, and a horse face looked at me and—yes—stroked his short, fat dick. The steam came on periodically with a noisy blast, and when it stopped and you could see again, people had made their moves: somebody was sucking dick on the other side of horsey; hippie, his mouth hanging open, was jacking the impassive fat guy's hard-on. I half-heartedly groped horsey's big-headed shorty, which he allowed, just, but turned his head away from kissing, and he removed his hand as if from a hot stove when he found I was only half-erect. My problem: I get hard from someone's interest, implied or physical, but I can't just get an erection for a general audience and wait for comers. And then I'd been in the scalding steam room for 20 minutes, and my heart was racing and my dick did not leap to its customary position when I bent to suck horsey's cock. I halted a bit awkwardly, and horsey seemed so uninterested in me—horsey thought I was what, piggy?— I left to get some air. I wandered the dark cul-de-sacs upstairs; nobody stopped in his tracks for me. One wiry, dark-haired guy caught my eye but hurried on. It was like a nightmare airport, and I didn't know my gate.

March 31, 1996

Weird gun-metal–blue rain clouds spread over the east horizon, sultry almost, the sun shining hot through the gaps. I walk home down Market Street, shaky-legged, oiled up and slick as a seal, jaunty, drinking a tropical protein shake through a straw. Thirty minutes earlier, a pink, fat dick with a gold ring through the tip was pulsing in my mouth. I feel tired and emotionally raw now. It's love and the aftermath of sex I want too, of course, so I'm a little sad at the same time as I'm exhilarated and sated.

I'd decided yesterday to call and book a massage with this guy whose ad in the massage section of *BAR* appealed to me; he looked attractive, nicely built, and comfortable, like he wouldn't be all weird and creepy about the sex part.

The first thing I noticed when he buzzed me into the second-floor Victorian flat and leaned smiling over the banister was that his short hair and goatee, dark in the ad, were now blond or reddish-orange. He showed me into a room set up with burning scented candle, boring New Age music, and a professional massage table with the towel-padded keyhole at one end to stick your face in.

I hadn't asked over the phone, though his being casually naked in the ad had seemed to indicate so, if this was sexual or nonsexual; I asked now. "It can be," he said, smiling. "It depends on the client and how I feel." I got hard just taking my pants off, but he began with me on my stomach, so I didn't have to worry about that immediately. He gave a long, thorough, strong-handed massage, really digging between the tightened muscles in the backs of my legs and shoulders. When he ran his fingers down my arms and laced his hand through mine in that way they do, tears sprang to my eyes. I realized how I've ached for that kind of touch as well.

By the time he asked me to turn over, I was quite jellied and no longer had a raging erection, but when he touched the insides of my thighs, boom—my dick shot to attention. He'd been using lotion all along, and after maybe 20 minutes of working on my legs and arms, he ran his fingers lightly up the shaft of my dick, put more lotion on his hand, and began to jack the head. I was shaking; I felt like I was going to fly off the table. I moaned discretely and started thrusting into his fist, opening my eyes and looking up at him. Unlike in the ad, he was clad in some loose swimming trunks and a tank top. I reached around and cupped his very nice round ass, and began reaching up the open legs of his shorts and stroking his sweaty crack. He pulled off the tank top. I palmed his chest and touched his pinkish nipples but didn't pinch them, unsure of the boundaries. He was rubbing his crotch, clearly hard, against my side.

"Can I touch your cock?" I asked politely. He stepped out of the trunks and went back to pumping my dick, bending and sucking the head with that sloppy, smutty popping sound, and suddenly a fully erect, upward-curving, fat white cock—with, yes, a gold ring through the dripping glans—was bobbing in my face. I sniffed, kissed, and then took it into my mouth and sucked enthusiastically, the ring clicking as it passed my front teeth. Now he was moaning and deep-throating my cock unabashedly. I reached into the wet crack of his ass and stroked his silky-haired chest. "I'm going to come—" he breathed, and I made a quick judgment call ("Cinderella *shall* go to the ball!") and continued blowing him till he shot copiously in my mouth and I shot dramatically past my head in four or five porn-quality jets, my butt arched off the table. He actually continued the massage, doing my face and chest—then went away and returned with wet, hot towels with which he wiped me down from head to toe.

I emerged feeling euphoric, trembling, strange—because I'd been made so vulnerable and then ejected back out into my single life with a hug at the door.

April 12

Dreamt this last night: I was sitting in a theater waiting for a play to start, and there was Jack's friend Charlie, who died last November, sitting beside me. When I looked over and stared at him, well aware of why his being there was so surprising, he smiled and *beamed* at me, and I put my hand on his chest, then over his terribly thin, gnarled hand. I must have stuttered out something like "So, there *is* an afterlife?"

"Oh yeah," he said, nonchalantly.

"So then you've seen Jack?"

"Sure," he said, like he'd just left him at the corner. "He's very worried about who you're going to be with…"

April 18

Ninety years post–Great Quake this morning. The afternoon paper will have a photo of some very old people spraying a new coat of gold paint on that Dolores Park hydrant that saved the Mission.

Speaking of earth-shaking, I agonized over and finally called in and recorded my mailbox greeting last evening. Just now I called and listened to it, and I sound nasal, hesitant, hopeless. *BAR* comes out today with my ad: *Books and sex—are reasons to live.*

April 27

Arranged to meet Jerry for a beer yesterday at 5 o'clock. Earlier in the week he'd left a long, sensible message reacting to some of what I'd said in my ad—which made him stand out from the more typical ones left by men with slurry voices and ice cubes chattering in highball glasses in the background.

I was first to show, which meant I had to sit in the sunny window at Pilsner's wondering each time a cute or awful figure came through the door, *Is this him?* And then someone walked up, saying, "You wouldn't be Kevin, would you?" He wore a sort of baggy Lacoste shirt and Levis; he was 'older,' that is, he had a lined face, graying pale-brown hair, pretty eyes (blue?)—looked like he'd been outdoors a lot. He had a tendency to squint several times quickly in succession. He was nicer than his phone voice.

We went to dinner. He mentioned having a spiritual teacher, "Omni Ra," whose goofy-jacketed books I remember selling at Bonanza Books (didn't one have a psychedelic gorilla wearing a party hat on the front?). But he didn't spout spacey New Age stuff. I wasn't sure of my physical attraction, but thought it worth a try; I asked, sitting back here on the couch after dinner, would he like to neck a bit?—and he "reluctantly" agreed, and then of course we were going to town. He'd hauled my hard-on out, and I reached for his, and hooray!—it was of a good size and hard. When I came, it was one of those shotgun blasts.

May 7

Met Paul, whose Italian last name I can't recall, on Wednesday night next to Clean Well-Lighted Place for Books before the reading I felt duty-bound to attend (my work on this particular book consisted chiefly of leaving the author endless messages hounding him for the overdue manuscript). Paul's also 40, dark, husky, and hairy; gold chain, ring, fancy watch, fancy boxer shorts—looks like a sexy middle-aged straight Italian man. A bit taciturn, which seems part of his butch nature. Nice blue eyes and a handsome smile.

We had only a moment to talk before hurrying over to the reading; as we wove through browsers, I pulled him into an alcove between two bookcases and told him, much-abbreviatedly, of Monday's nightmare meeting with Bachelor #3, when I'd knocked over my chair fleeing the human Gila monster who'd been spitting on his hand and grooming himself. "If that's how you're seeing me, you can escape right now and no hard feelings—"

"That's not what I'm feeling," he said, smiling sexily and pulling me against him.

May 13

The Jerry thing has ended awkwardly. Essentially, he's a pleasant, fairly intelligent person—but he's not, and the sex isn't, what I'd want all the time. He's totally into *my* dick, sucking and jerking me off, which is nice in a purely selfish way, but not enough emotionally. I didn't fall in love with him at first sight, and I never could. There's a certain occasional saccharine tone ("You're a beautiful man.... Mmmm, I love the direction this is going in!") that made me sure deep down this couldn't go on. For chrissakes, his license plate says "LUV4RA!"

In the midst of the last slow, sparsely populated, surreal waiting-for-layoffs afternoon at work today, I thought of Paul, the guy I spent Friday and Saturday nights with, and found myself having a surprising rush of feeling for him. I never, not for a second, had a natural, emotional feeling like that with Jerry. I'd expected to be thinking, *Great, Paul's off for his previously planned three weeks in Europe, leaving me free to size up the remaining "bachelors,"* but instead I feel sad that he's left.

May 29

The Sunday evening of little brother Mark's first weekend here, Rick Jimenez (Bachelor #2) came with Bob and us to see Blossom Dearie. Rick's a tall, olive-skinned Latino, slightly fey, but sexily rangy at the same time. At the Great American Music Hall, when Mark and Bob roamed for a closer stage view, Mr. Jimenez and I held hands and groped. (I got an erection in baggy jeans and put his hand on it; he set about pressing and squeezing it, while staring toward the little wizened woman with a pixie cut warbling "Peel Me a Grape.") Oddly, though, he evaded my attempts to kiss him in the backseat later; if he considers kissing unsafe, there's a problem.

Paul returns from Europe in a week, and that may heat up to a degree that will preclude other contenders. Today a postcard from Paris: He went to Père Lachaise and gave my regards to Oscar, as I'd requested (and ran into two queens from his gym on his way from Oscar to Gertrude).

June 2

Movie with Rick. We'd talked on the phone the night before. "I've got a kind of quandary." Seems someone he'd dated who wouldn't make a commitment has now decided (with me as stalking horse?) to "make a commitment." Since I'm privately counting the days till Paul's return, I could hardly feel put out. I explained that I was dating others as well and not to give it another thought. We went to dinner and a stupid alien movie he chose (having nixed *Cold Comfort Farm*).

Afterward he moaned about his long drive back to Concord, so I said, not thinking he'd accept, "Well, you're welcome to sleep over on the couch or whatever." When he promptly said yes, I realized he wanted to try it on with me after all. (The boyfriend to whom he's freshly committed is out of town.) When we got into bed, stripped to jockeys, he placed himself against me, and after about 10 seconds, made a big show of pulling off his underwear beneath the sheets ("I'm so *hot!*"). OK, I thought, me too, and tossed my own on the rug. Then followed a bizarre cock tease, the likes of which I haven't encountered since last July, parked out front at 2 A.M., necking with work pal Isaac in his car. He'd rub his size-large boner against my butt and brush his hand over my aching erection, but when I reached for his dick or attempted to roll over and kiss him, he'd stop me: "Oh, you're really trying to tempt me, I don't want to do this—" Then, 10 minutes later, as I drifted off to sleep, his hand was back on my cock.

I sat up and turned on the light. "Look, do you want to have sex, or do you want to go to sleep?"

"No, I told you, I can't have sex with you. I *promised*." But all night long I woke to him lightly stroking my dick, keeping it hot and hard. Around 4 A.M. I woke from a sexual dream to find him jacking me off in earnest, and I rolled over and enjoyed it, finally ejaculating so intensely it burned on the way out. I jacked him off then, sucking and biting his nipples while he whined, "No, I can't. Stop, I mustn't." (I thought this kind of "you're bad, we mustn't" rap went out with Lana, the older girl I'd finger-fucked in my VW after the junior prom.) When I woke to his fingerings at 7:30, he stopped me when I slid down to blow him: "I don't feel comfortable with that."

Whether these strictures were psychotic "safe sex," or whether this was his way of staying half-true to his new husband I don't know. I only went ahead out of pragmatic horniness, thinking, whether or not we remain pals of any sort, I'll never stoop to sex with him again.

June 6

Home from the gym last evening, happily exhausted, reading the paper. The phone rings; it's Paul, whose postcard from Italy had just arrived, home again. "What're you doing tonight?"

"Waiting for you to come over and fuck," I said.

"I'll be over in an hour."

He looked real good when I went down to open the door; he has a sort of downcast, "aw, shucks" way of glancing up from his feet that's quite appealing—eerily reminiscent of 1980s bad-news boyfriend, Ray. We'd both had three weeks to think about what we'd done and might like to do when next given the chance. It was very nice, setting aside my glasses and putting my arms around him and kissing like I meant it (I did). I felt awash in a sort of timelessness—teary-eyed and cock-hard, greedy and bursting with joy at finding it: love.

"Let's just lie on the bed and kiss for a minute," I said, pulling him by the arm, believing this. "Then we'll sit on the couch and talk." But then we were hard and panting, and that was that for the evening. I felt incredibly turned on to him, to his specific body: hairy belly, funky crotch, red, very hard dick. He was talking some smutty sex talk—a thing I've always laughed at, but I wasn't laughing. We ended the second time around with him jerking off straddling my chest— *"Yeah, shoot in my face"*—and he did, turned-on and staring back at me as the warm drops hit my forehead, nose, mouth, and I came jerking myself.

June 10

Yesterday was another of those long, swell blossoming-of-romance days. Nice morning sex; we'd dressed to go out but started necking on the couch. I pulled off my T-shirt and shorts, leaving on jockeys and high-tops; Paul sucked and batted around my hard-on through the cloth. We got back in bed. After some wrestling around dick to dick, he started putting fingers up my ass, slavering on the lube, working his way up to sticking his condom-sheathed cock in. Difficult at first, as usual, but then I was crouched and backing into him, jerking him off with my asshole and pumping at my own well-lubed cock, and I crossed the threshold about the time he began talking dirty about what he was doing, and I began telling him what I wanted (*"Yeah, all the way out and back in, slow..."*). He was fucking me the best I've ever had; I was aiming my ass at him trying to get it in at the best angle. Just as he pulled completely out, waited a beat, and shoved it brusquely back in, the yells of teenagers playing basketball in the court across the street wafted in on the hot breeze, like a gang cheering on a gang bang, and we both came, over-the-top with pleasure.

We cleaned up and drove to breakfast, then to the Castro for film festival tickets. We agreed on all our picks except for the three-hour B&W documentary on the elderly deaf Swedish lesbian World War II resistance fighters, but I decided I could always rent it later.

The day being clear and beautiful, we drove down Highway 1 to Gray Whale Beach; not until we were climbing down the hillside did I recognize it as the same beach Richard and I drove to in our first glow of meeting in September '89, taking photos of each other naked—me sitting on a log, Richard walking into the waves.

We pulled off our clothes and lay on a sheet; I requested "The Paul Story," everything up till his moving to San Francisco. Not having brought sunblock, we both got a bit burned, and my butt's doubly sore. Driving back to the city, watching the blur of greenery spinning by alongside the freeway, hand in Paul's lap, sun streaming in the sunroof, I had a moment of pure happiness I couldn't have told without sobbing. I hadn't thought I'd get to have this again.

November 30 (Guerneville)

Yesterday, in the wake of Thursday's feasting, we drove up Highway 1 to Fort Ross and walked up a trail past the Russian cemetery, across the highway, and over a fire road to a deep forest and stream. I came on to Paul, talking dirty and dick hard, standing beside a toppled redwood, aroused by the forest, the mulchy leaf odor—remembering adolescent sex in the woods at Fort Rucker. He'd expressed concern about being caught when I'd hinted about it earlier—but after a glance or two around, he pulled his dick out, and I crouched and sucked his swollen cock, very excited (memory of being unable to breathe during the penultimate scene of *Deliverance* sophomore year)—pumping my own cock. I stood, and while he pinched my nipples, I kissed him sloppily and jacked off, shooting onto the mossy stones, and then he beat off while I stared and smuttily encouraged him till he shot. We kissed and held each other, cold, noses wet, breathing hard, a little sunlight filtering down through the trees.

We hiked back. Paul was for some reason jokily singing the Barney song (*"I love you, you love me…"*) as we rounded a bend in the leafy trail back nearer Sandy Cove and abruptly came upon a young couple and toddler sitting off the path on a blanket, the adults clinking glasses of wine—and we all laughed. A bit later we passed a group of older straight couples heading out. "Is it worth it?" one asked.

"Yes," I said.

Don Shewey
Eugene

5.4.95

Yesterday I had a session that I worried about in advance. This was with Eugene, the affluent black businessman who's going through a divorce. He turned 44 recently and decided it was time to do some of the things he had always dreamed about but never done. Being with a man was one of those things. He'd gotten massaged at his health club, but he called me for a private session out of curiosity to see what might happen.

I quickly discovered Eugene's pleasure spot was his butt, especially the tender pink skin around his butthole, stroked by a finger or a tongue or the firm head of a hard cock. What really surprised me, though, was how eager Eugene was for hugging and kissing and friendly affectionate interaction. He didn't seem to have a shred of sex shame or body shame. I couldn't bring myself to think of him as heterosexual; he was just sexual, period.

Eugene was full of euphemisms. I enjoyed hearing them and liked to torture them out of him by asking point-blank, "What is the experience you would like to have today?" Eugene was much too polite and respectful to say, "I want you to chow down on my joint" or "Put it up my ass, baby, the way you know I like it." No, no, no, no, no. He'd say things like, "Well, I like part one of the massage, and then I'd like to move to part two." Or he'd say, "Depending on how you're feeling, I'd like to have an 'interesting' session rather than a conventional one."

Since our second session, he's been nudging me about "going all the way." I've resisted that mentality and tried to convey to him that erotic massage/bodywork/sex can be lots of different things besides penetrative-intercourse-to-ejaculation. But in our last session we found ourselves in a place of experimenting. He was feeling especially aggressive and horny, and that afternoon we were lying around in bed rather than on the massage table.

There's a particular moment that I love. It's when a guy is sprawled invitingly on my densely patterned Australian comforter in front of my architecturally splendid bay window, either in his underpants or completely naked with a healing boner pointing up toward his navel. I love walking slowly toward him and draping myself over his body, as our arms and legs find just the right position to interlock like jaws. That coming together feels great. I like to wrap my arms all the way around his back and bury my face in his neck. I like it when he stretches his legs around my hips and we lie there, a happy clam. The thing about Eugene, too, is that he loves to kiss. He has big fleshy lips that are fun to chew and suck. His mouth tastes good. He knows how to use his tongue. He's sweet and warm and never uptight about his body. He has an open curiosity about his body and mine and a taste for affection that seems neither desperate nor chary.

In our last session, he pretty quickly slid me onto my stomach and lay on my back with his knob resting in my crack, the way I usually do with him. He nibbled on my neck and the top of my back. I took a couple of his fingers in my mouth and sucked them deep into my throat. He leaned back and put some spit on the end of his dick and then lay back on top of me. We were heading into the danger zone. He seemed intent on sliding into me without benefit of either lube or love-glove. Uh-unhhh, baby. I rolled onto my side, and we had a little chat.

He was happy to have that chat, happy to agree to using rubbers, happy to go slow—but mainly happy that I seemed to have consented to letting him, you know, put it in me. Eventually, I did roll him over onto his back, put a rubber on him, lube myself up, and slowly lower myself onto him. It took a while, and it went pretty slowly. He's really big, and I'm not Miss Loose Pussy by a long stretch. We never really got to the point where he could let go and fuck me the way a guy likes to fuck—long strokes, bang-bang-bang, with abandon. I hovered on the threshold between pain and surrender. I kept trying to relax, which generally made my erection wilt. Then I'd work myself up to full hardness again. I know that's a way to override the sensations in my butt, to go a little numb and avoid the feelings, which I'd rather not do. But it does keep me interested in prolonging the process.

Every time I would start jerking myself fast, Eugene would say, "Don't come yet! Don't come yet!" Finally, I had to stop and dismount. It wasn't pleasurable anymore. I took off the rubber. We switched positions, him on top butt-surfing me, and I introduced some sacred hot chat. I told him I imagined him entering me and fucking me and coming inside me, and blam! He shot till he was wobbly in the knees.

It's funny, you know—during that session I found myself feeling like a cheap ho, wondering what time it was, wondering when he would come and we could stop. I wasn't getting much pleasure out of this interaction the way that I do sometimes when I'm sucking cock or simply holding someone, lying around cuddling and being close without moving. Afterwards I felt like it was time to have a conversation with Eugene and try to steer him away from the straight-guy mentality: that all our sessions were building up to some version of "fuck the pussy till you squirt." That's why I was nervous.

When he came in yesterday, we spent 45 minutes fully dressed talking. He told me that our last session was very meaningful to him. Fucking with a man was something that he'd thought about doing since he was a teenager, and he had always suppressed the desire. To act on that desire at last, in a slow and conscious way with someone who's intelligent and able to talk about the experience together, showed him a piece of himself that he was grateful to have.

So we weren't as far away in our thinking as I imagined we were. Nevertheless, I made it a point to talk about my interest in interrupting the pattern of upping the ante with every session: progressing toward intercourse, or defining our sessions as checking off a list of sex acts to perform. He admitted that he's a pretty linear thinker, but that he truly didn't have that agenda in mind.

I did have an agenda for the day. I didn't want to launch right into erotic play with him. But I knew that "just a massage" wouldn't do today. We only had 45 minutes left, too. So I decided I would introduce some classic Taoist erotic massage with conscious breathing, which I'd never done with Eugene before. At first he didn't like the idea of a session predicated on not ejaculating.

"I'd be lying if I didn't say that I do like a sense of completion" was how he put it. But I explained it to him this way: Taoist erotic massage is not about denying pleasure but about expanding your capacity for sensation and making contact with spirit. It's hard work breathing vigorously for 25 minutes nonstop, especially the first time you do it, before you know that there is an ecstatic experience on the other side of your initial resistance and discomfort. I worried the whole time that I wasn't allowing enough time for this experience. Trying to cram it all into half an hour might give Eugene a bad impression of this kind of energy work. But he was erect throughout the massage and kept going with the breathing. I led him into a Big Draw, even played the corniest Body Electric post–Big Draw music (from the sound-track to *The Mission*) and gave him a few minutes to simply luxuriate in that feeling.

When I asked how it was for him, he said he liked it. It did feel like a spiritual experience to him, more so than an erotic experience, which surprised him. "I think I really needed this today."

After he got dressed, I gave him a copy of my article about Joe Kramer that was published in the *Voice*. He called me this morning to say he'd read the article and wanted to take me to dinner to discuss some of the ideas in the article, which he found very exciting. All of which is to say, I guess I'm doing good work. It feels scary to me because I'm making it up as I'm going along, this combination of holy whore and hot hairy horny priest.

* *

I want to stop and register all the things I'm not saying about my relationship with Eugene. How do I feel about being with him? I am, among other things, intrigued with getting to know a black man who is upper middle-class, who's a successful businessman. I have met entertainers or people in show business who meet that description, but I've never had any friends who did. Although I never show it or talk about it to him, I'm fascinated to hear about his "lifestyle"—taking his two sons on a skiing trip to New Mexico, flying to Washington for a date with a woman, living in a town house near Gramercy Park. His life has the external appearance of a successful white businessman. Yet he doesn't deny his blackness. His (soon-to-be ex–) wife is black, and his friends fix him up with black women. I suspect that most of his business colleagues are white, but I don't know. Aside from comments about his dates and that everyone thought he and his wife were a good match, he has never talked about his life in terms of race. And yet it's always in the forefront of my mind that Eugene is a wealthy black married man exploring his bisexuality.

I am mystified by my role in his life. I may be in denial about what it is that attracts him to me. I'm youthful but clearly not a kid. I consider my maturity a plus; it means I have more to offer as a person. I'm open and friendly, and I'm inclined to see the best side of people. That makes me a little naive, I guess. I take people at face value, which means I will listen to miles and miles of bullshit before challenging someone. Anyway, if I were a married man in his 40s looking to experiment with homosex, I'd be thrilled to encounter a handsome smart guy who's willing to give me the experience I want for $100 a pop.

So the money. What do I feel about this? I know that Eugene has money—he knows how to tip, he appreciates me. Does it make me more willing to go along with things he wants to do that I don't especially enjoy? That's not it, really. But I do go out of my way to please him. I do feel like a geisha with him.

Here's one thing that I accept about him: his closetedness around his bisexuality. I'm pretty sure he has never told anyone that he goes to see a male masseur for erotic touch. I wonder if he has told anyone that he has experimented with cocksucking and butt-fucking.

I have refrained from pushing him toward coming out. I try not to let egregious assumptions about gay culture go unchallenged, but I haven't said to him, "Eugene, instead of going out with women, why don't you try going out with men and having a relationship with a male peer?" Oh my God—I guess I'm it. I guess by agreeing to have dinner with him, we're having some version of a date. This will be his experiment with being in public with a handsome (slightly) younger man that he knows is gay. What should I wear? Should I be real swishy and obvious? Wear my pink fuzzy sweater? Or should I be really butch and obvious that way? Leave my three-day stubble on my face and wear my motorcycle jacket with a long, dangly human-skull earring? Or should I go really straight and mainstream: khaki trousers and a button-down shirt?

What do I like about Eugene sexually? Well, for one thing, I do find him physically attractive. I like his body. In some ways, I acquiesce to completely erotic-play sessions because I'm lazy. Rolling around in bed is more fun and less work for the money than giving a massage, that's for sure. Eugene has a giant dick that gets hard easily and stays up. It's delicious to slurp, and I've managed to take it all the way down my throat, which excites both of us. The fact that he's never had any experience with men makes me extremely tempted to drain his ball juice, to get my long-desired forbidden jolt of male protein. I do like kissing him. He has a great butt that responds to touch wonderfully. It makes me really hot to butt-surf him. I would love to just slide my dick in his ass and fuck his butt good sometime until I deliver my squirtage deep inside him.

As the kid asks in Bill Finn's musical, *March of the Falsettos,* "Is this therapy?" Yeah, I have to say, this is clearly an invaluable initiatory experience for him. He gets to explore forbidden desires, and so far nothing has happened to say, "Stop! Bad! Danger! You shouldn't do this or have this!"

What am I getting out of working with Eugene? The pleasure of intimate touch with a handsome man isn't new or urgent to me. What is new and valuable and challenging is the opportunity to improvise each session. I really don't know what we're going to do or what's going to work.

Don Shewey
Fun at the YMCA

5.16.98

Sex is such an opportunity to experience freedom. In the steam room at the gym, I eyed a big beefy bottom bear boy, redheaded with a nipple ring. When the room emptied out for a moment, he moved to sit next to me, showing me his stiff little widget. Then someone came in. We both hung out, and the next time we were alone, I walked right up to him and started touching him. He sucked me for a little bit as I stroked his bristly buzz cut. After 10 seconds someone else came in, and the room filled up, so we left and showered.

As we dried off we exchanged names. He walked out ahead of me and was drying his hair as I walked by. I asked if he wanted to continue what we'd started. He said, "Possibly." He'd already let me know he was staying at the Y. I followed him to the elevator and asked, "Is this an invitation?" He said, "Yes, but it'll have to be quick." He emphasized that several times. His partner was due back at 5 P.M. It was now 3 P.M. He said we have an hour, tops. Sounded like plenty of time to me.

When we got to the room (tiny, with bunk beds, for $75), I got naked. He was really nervous, lest his lover walk in on us. They live on the coast of Maine; his lover was on a buying trip and attending a show at the Javits Center. He said he was into everything, but when I moved in to kiss him, he brushed me off—I established that he liked everything but kissing. He wanted me to suck his dick, fairly small and uncut but delicious. He got hot really fast, so I took a break and let him suck me. I suggested sixty-nine. He said then he'd really come fast. He seemed reluctant to lie down on the bed and very nervous, so I said, "Hey, I'll just suck you off." (We'd established that we were both HIV-negative.) He came in about a minute. Then we hurriedly dressed.

I gave him my card and told him to call me. He said he would—his partner has to work all day Sunday and Monday. He's young, maybe 30, quite fat and solid but still sexy to me in a butch beefy bottom redhead way. A couple of times he said he'd "make it up" to me. So I walked down the street with a hard-on and imagined licking his big hairy butt, sucking him off immediately to take the edge off and sitting on his dick while I unloaded mine. Mmmm. Such a good fantasy.

4.4.93

This morning at the gym I got a headache fast and didn't feel like going thru my workout: too mental. Went to the steam room. Instant erotic vibes, boners on display. A big older man and a wild-haired guy it took me a minute to recognize: the guy I'm always turned on by, the one who shaves his balls in the shower. We had the place to ourselves. I immediately started touching myself and sprung a boner. They showed theirs. The older man hesitated only slightly before getting on his knees before me and taking me in his mouth. Quite bold and quite hot—I liked having the other guy watch this because I know he likes to watch. As he was sucking me, the older guy slowly lost his erection. He drew back and jacked me off for a while. Then I said to him, "Play with your own cock." So he sat back on the bench and wanked himself.

Ballshaver waved his own hard cock. Then the older guy stood up and jerked himself really fast till he squirted, then immediately grabbed his towel and left.

Ballshaver, who had moved from halfway down the bench to the corner, now got up and stood right in front of me with his hard-on in my face. He'd never offered himself to me like this before. I gratefully accepted his offer and took his yummy-sized uncut cock in my mouth, played with his smooth balls, and ran my hands all over his belly, legs, and butt. He liked it, especially when I took him deep in my throat. But we were both very cautious about doing this, looking toward the door and pulling away at the slightest sound. He took hold of my dick a couple of times, seemed to like feeling it with no inclination to do anything more. I would have liked the time for a leisurely, worshipful blow job, but that's not possible in the steam room at the West Side Y. What we were doing was about as wild as I've seen in that space. I leaned against him, stroking his butt and jerking his dick fast. He seemed on the verge of squirting when someone came in. He immediately wrapped his towel around his waist and went to the window and stood there whistling. I sat back on the bench, one foot up, hiding my Pan-dick boner. A second new guy came in and sat down next to me and said hi, a friendly older guy with white hair and worked-on nipples with whom I've chatted and semi-played before. We sat there contentedly shaving with our disposable razors as the steam went through its cycles.

After I showered, I walked to the sink to complete my shave and passed Ballshaver, dressed to leave. I nodded at him, and he made a click sound back at me—such is male camaraderie at the West Side Y.

4.12.93

Dutiful report of romping at the Y this morning: early morning workout (arrived at 8:30), shaving in the steam room around 9:40. A couple of guys there; eventually it's just me and R.P., whom I've played with before and have had fantasies about. He's short and angry-looking but very muscular, always wears his bathing suit in the steam room, gets hard easily. I stroked myself into a big erection; he edged closer and closer to me until we could touch each other, then quickly and firmly pushed my head down on his raging uncut hard-on while he reached around to play with my butthole. It was hot and exciting but definitely made me decide I don't actually want to make a date to fuck with him—another guy who has trouble taking his time. Of course, outside the steam room, where everything has to be fast and furious, who knows what his style would be? I went to nuzzle his nipple, but someone else walked in, and we leapt apart.

Then I went into the back shower where there was only one guy who'd been in the steam room briefly and who'd clearly been working his fat dick. Average-looking Joe, slightly hairy chest, younger than me, chubby face, blue eyes. We stroked ourselves and soaped ourselves up and showed hard for a while, slowly walked closer and closer (there was one shower between us), and groped each other's hard-ons. He leaned forward and kissed me on the lips, but that's as far as I wanted to go with that. He has one of those dicks with a little pointy flap of skin at the end. I turned around and leaned against the wall and stroked my butt cheek. He walked up and stroked it with his hand and waved his dick around in the vicinity of my butthole, which got me very hot. Then we stood back and admired each other for a while. It truly felt like my ideal of warrior sex/spiritual practice, daily charging the cells of the body with breath and erotic energy.

I noticed he was holding his breath as he jerked himself nearer and nearer to climax, so I made a little more noise breathing. I leaned against the wall again and stuck my butt out; he moved up and humped me from behind a little bit; again I got so hard and hot I nearly came, so I stood up again after only a few seconds, and we modeled for each other quite a while longer. I thought he might have wanted to squirt, so I would hang in there with him. But I realized he was waiting for me to go. So I just stopped and leaned over to his ear and said, "Instead of shooting, why don't you keep that energy in your body all day long?" He said "Yeah."

12.29.92

My friend Steve told me that the new renovation at the Y had removed all the opportunities for fun. But I've had adventures nearly every time I've gone.

One day a very red-faced Irish-looking guy I've nicknamed Thomas sat down with his legs wide apart, and when the only other person in the steam room left, all I had to do was touch myself for him to leap up and push his cock into my mouth. Seconds feel like minutes in a public place, where anyone could walk in and object or have us thrown out of the gym, but this seemed to go on for at least five minutes.

He talked dirty, I moaned appreciatively. He seemed confused when I walked away without anybody coming. After the initial burst of excitement, my erection always wilts when the action is so fast, furious, and one-sided.

This morning when I walked into the sauna, the only person there was someone I used to play "mutual show-hard" with in the old sauna. After a minute we started playing with ourselves and got mildly hard before someone else walked in.

He went to shower. After a few minutes I did too. I glanced into the sauna (the new one that has massive picture windows—no hanky-panky there anymore) and saw a youngish guy sitting there who I could tell was cruising for action. I watched him for a while— he must be new at the gym, because he wore his towel everywhere, to the sauna, all the way to the shower, into the steam room. When I finally got a look at him, I noticed that he seemed to have a bit of an Xmas-in-Hawaii sunburn, stocky hairy body, cute butt, and a very attractive oak log–like uncut dick (not huge but with a copious foreskin).

He came into the sauna as I was leaving for a shower. While I was drying off, I saw him go back into the steam room, followed soon by the first guy. I imagined they were alone in the steam room. I imagined that the new guy might feel shy about fooling around at the Y with one other person. I imagined that he'd feel better about it if First Guy and I modeled some steam room homosex moves.

I was done with my workout, thoroughly done with my toilette, ready to go home. But why deny myself this pleasure? So I hung up my damp towel again and walked into the steam room.

I was wrong—there were three other guys there besides my two pals: a big slow old man, a bearded redhead who I think is queer, and a tattooed guy in a bathing suit who pretty clearly likes the sexual vibes at the Y without wanting to stop anything or to participate.

One by one these guys left; the tattooed guy did what I've seen him do before, which is vacate the premises when a couple guys seem to be gearing up for some dickplay.

As soon as he walked out, New Guy and I were left by ourselves in the steam room. New Guy started furiously working his meat. I fondled myself too, but slowly, taking my time. He had very intense eyes and big red juicy lips.

After a minute or two, someone else walked into the steam room, and we stopped, covering our dicks with our hands. It was First Guy, though, so I uncovered myself. New Guy quickly realized First Guy was cool too. First Guy sat right next to me, his thigh touching mine. We all got hard pretty quickly, especially me. I showed off my proud Pan-dick. First Guy reached over and grabbed it. I took his cock in my hand, not very hard. First Guy reached over and took hold of New Guy's cock for a little bit—a cock-hungry pig after my own heart—while I stroked his smooth butt. New Guy reached for First Guy's cock and got only a slight brush of it before First Guy sat back on the bench next to me.

I knew what New Guy wanted. I gave it to him. I stood up, and his mouth went right onto my cock. He worked his own cock furiously while he sucked me. I stroked the back of his wet head and murmured sacred hot chat. First Guy stroked my butt and thighs and back.

One or the other of us kept a constant vigil to see if any dark shapes loomed outside the steam room door—someone about to walk in, or the locker room attendant peering in.

Any time the steam went on or off, New Guy flinched, frightened. We reassured him by continuing our playing. I sat down for a moment. We took a breather.

I stood up again so New Guy could suck me. He's obviously like me, an incorrigible cocksucker. First Guy stood behind me, embracing me from behind, rubbing his hard cock against my ass.

This tight three-way action is unusual in my experience at the Y. It's not so hard for two people to pull away from each other and look "innocent" to a newcomer; a little harder for three. (But who are we kidding after all, with our obviously distended penises peeking out from under our oh-so-casually draped hands?)

For a moment I engaged in a fantasy of the impossible (or at least improbable): bending over and sucking New Guy while First

Guy slipped his cock in my ass. But I've never observed butt pene-tration at the Y. Instead I leaned over and kissed New Guy on the lips. I wasn't sure if he would like that or respond. He did. I chewed his fat lower lip for a second. He pulled away quickly, as if someone was coming in. But I saw there was something more tempting he wanted in his mouth: First Guy's dick. Each of us touched and tasted each other's dicks.

New Guy looked at his watch. It was 10 o'clock. Time for work? Without speaking, we concluded our festivities. We'd been at it for quite a while—a good five minutes or so at least (an eternity in public-sex time).

First Guy left. I stood up and stroked New Guy's head: a blessing. I headed for the door but stopped and stretched, looking out the picture window to the toweling-off area.

I let New Guy leave before me, and then after a couple of minutes I left myself. The steam room was empty. Thank you, Steam Room Sex Temple! New Guy was showering in "the back showers." I show-ered next to him. The only other person in sight was an ancient man in the farthest corner, a guy I've known to participate (at least as a voyeur) in sauna sex. I didn't care to continue the steam room encounter, but I did take a good look at New Guy's cute butt. When the old man showering turned his back to us, I leaned over and stroked New Guy's beautiful bottom. He thought I was leaning to whisper something to him and perked up his ears, but I just smiled, turned off the water, and walked away.

When I went to toss my towel in the laundry basket, First Guy was standing there pulling on his red bikini bathing suit. "Now he swims," I said to him. He grinned and offered his own rationale for steaming first: "Inspiration!"

Stephen Greco
Simon's Chair

11-17-99

I don't know what the fuck is up with Simon. For some reason, he's not returning my calls or E-mails—which is hugely inconvenient, because I don't know how I'm supposed to get the cum out of my body.

I've come to depend on the little cocksucking "salon" that Simon hosts over at his apartment on weekends when his boyfriend is out of town. Sure, I like the guys I meet over there—the very hot, straight- and bi-identified janitors and schoolteachers and bartenders and doctors and high school soccer coaches whom Simon meets mainly online now, as well as the plain old gay guys who have been referred to Simon by other serious throat addicts. Moreover, especially now that my relationship with KJ is getting serious, I like the convenience of a fairly strings-free opportunity to get my nuts drained, which provides a welcome supplement to my program of combined romantic lovemaking, group-scene sex sport with Chelsea muscle boys, and masturbation. Simon's like a doctor. He just gets the cum out like a pro, without shame or social fuss. With him on his knees in front of me, I feel safe, relaxed—and I like being in the company of other guys who enjoy the same kind of recreation.

Simon lives a few blocks away, and I've been seeing him once or twice a weekend for many years. There are often a few other guys over there, either sitting in that legendary chair (lined with a fresh towel for each occupant), or resting on the sofa between rounds, or just arriving or leaving. When Mark came back to town a few weeks ago, I knew that Simon was occupied with him alone. That's the way Simon and Mark are together. Though Mark is married and has a grown daughter, I know that Simon is totally boyfriends with him in some corner of his mind, though Simon's been with his real boyfriend, Joe, since the '70s (when Simon was this superhot number and Joe was a Marlboro model or something). Simon gets off on: (a) those Navy stories Mark tells, (b) the fact that Mark is more completely addicted to having his cock sucked than anyone else on the planet, and of course, (c) Mark's nine fat inches and his explosive skull-fucking technique, which always propels him out the chair at the last minute, all poppered up, grunting gutterally, knocking furniture out of the way, to pin Simon to the wall, clamp down on his head with both arms, and pump a load down his theatrically gulping and choking, though nonetheless supremely capable, mouth hole.

But Mark's gone back to England, and Simon's still not returning my calls. I need to figure out why and get back in that chair. Like many of the 15 or 20 guys who will be invited to sit there during the course of a weekend—to have a cocktail, to smoke a joint, to watch videos "over the top of Simon's head," as it says in his online profile—I usually achieve nirvana in my sessions with Simon. Though I'm not at all explosive. Unlike Mark, I stay seated during my blow job. Simon's talent and dependability have granted me the space, as it were, to contemplate and explore in depth dimensions of sensation and physical response that had previously been unclear to me, even though before KJ (who is great sex) I'd had a lover for 15 years (who was also great sex).

Simon is something else. He's not particularly hot by the superficial standards of contemporary gay party culture. I always tell guys to whom I try to pimp Simon that he's "a Grizzly Adams type"—6 foot 3, maybe 220 pounds, husky (not fat), 40-something, dark hair with a bit of gray. I mean, he is a handsome guy, but to me, the most attractive aspect of Simon is that, like some kind of spiritually advanced sex Buddha, he is so fully uncondescending to this cock hunger of his that he has set up his whole life accordingly. (And his scene is not about drugs, either. He did a lot of Quaaludes and cocaine in the '70s, but doesn't do that stuff anymore.) I was not attracted to Simon the first few times I encountered him, late on summer nights years ago, in a nearby neighborhood park where lots of guys, straight and gay, would go to get their cocks sucked and hook up with other guys cruising in cars. He would nod hello, then watch as I hooked up with somebody; he would maybe hook up with somebody else nearby and attempt to indicate in that wordless, universal gay language of outdoor cruising that if I liked good head I would certainly be interested in meeting him. Then one night, Simon mimed an invitation I couldn't refuse. I had gotten out of a cab at the park, smashed after some party, and needed to dump a load big-time. No one else was around, and there was Simon on the other side of a fence of metal bars. He sank to his knees and braced himself by grabbing the bars. It was right out of a porno movie set in prison. I figured, *What the hell? Might as well try it out.*

I went nuts with ecstasy during that first session, and I make it a point of some kind of erotic philosophy to say that the pleasure has been amplified tenfold each time we've done it since. I have learned that such multiplication is possible for the human body and mind. And Simon and I have done it together almost 500 times, I was reminded by Tony, another of Simon's customers. Tony and I have gotten friendly after running into each other occasionally at Simon's. (He'd be resting on the sofa, freshly de-loaded, playing idly with his soft cock whenever I arrived; I'd get in the chair, start up with Simon, then see Tony restiffen, get up from the sofa, and bring his cock over to my chest, where he'd make his piss slit "suck" my right nipple. I swear he can get his cock, which is huge, to make a true sucking action. This has happened a number of times.) Tony told me that Simon once confided that he keeps count of everyone who visits him and how many times they shoot. The historian in me was relieved to hear that some part of Simon's extraordinary practice is being recorded, but the mouth-hound in me was a little disappointed to learn that I still hadn't deposited a thousand loads of sperm in his body.

It was Tony who suggested that Simon might be punishing us both for not taking our pimping responsibilities seriously enough. Simon hasn't been responding to Tony's calls or IMs either. Simon likes being pimped. Actually, he kinda demands it. From Tony, Simon has wanted a picture of that huge cock, to help lure other guys over—

but Tony is slightly phobic about having his cock photographed and has repeatedly refused. From me, Simon has wanted a hook-up with a long-haired bodybuilder who's been connecting with me and KJ. Now, I send a lot of men Simon's way, but the flip side of his admirable single-mindedness about all this cock traffic is that he doesn't seem to understand that the bodybuilder is just not interested in him—I did ask once—and that there's nothing I can do about it.

Anyway, I suppose this'll blow over in a week or two. Little tussles that have arisen between me and Simon in the past—like the time I let somebody else suck my cock at his house: a big no-no!—have always been resolved soon enough. This connection between us is too strong to lose.

Stephen Greco
My Favorite Porn Star

12-4-99

I had sex with Vinny LoMaglio the other day—KJ and I did together. It was fun, though probably more so for me than for KJ, who did all the work. KJ was on suck detail. Vinny likes a specific kind of blow job that requires a very circumscribed range of motion, degree of pressure, and pacing, let alone ancillary hand action—all of which can be difficult to coordinate and ultimately a little boring for the person doing the coordinating, except in the case of somebody like Vinny, who happens to be a porn star.

KJ has one of the most talented mouths on the planet. He thinks that hands are for amateurs, but he uses them with Vinny because Vinny's hot: body by God and a big, friendly attitude. I got nipple detail. Vinny's needs there are as circumscribed as those of his cock, and though I am usually embarrassed for the kind of guy who gets off only on constant tit-squeezing at this or that angle, somehow I didn't mind in this case, because it allowed me to cradle Vinny in my arms as KJ worked and to speak quietly into Vinny's ear what all top guys wanna hear about: bottoming out.

Vinny lives in my neighborhood. Last Sunday morning at the gym where Vinny, KJ, and I all work out, I had spotted Vinny bench-pressing, and I mentioned that fact to KJ when I called him afterward. "Come over and we'll sit on my stoop for a few minutes," I suggested. "He always walks by on his way home." I was still horny from the night before when KJ and I had gone to a sex club. I had watched KJ suck off two or three really hot guys while I served as narrator/coach—meaning that while KJ worked I stood next to the guys getting sucked off, felt up their pecs, lats, and delts, and periodically said things like "Yeahhhh." I told KJ in the cab on the way home that I could have used some cock myself. He smiled exasperatedly, "Then why didn't you drop that daddy-top thing you do," he said, "and get down on your knees and shove me out of the way? Have you ever thought about how much fun it would be to suck cock together?"

The next morning when KJ arrived, we decided to get some coffee from a shop located between my house and the gym. As we were about to enter, there was Vinny coming up the sidewalk right on schedule, strutting amiably, open denim jacket barely covering his popped-out shelf of tank-topped pecs, striped stretch leggings straining to contain his snaking-to-one-side cock, looking massive though soft. I'd never seen any of Vinny's movies. He and KJ have hooked up a few times at the gym in a "secret" bathroom off a back stairway that I still can't find. To tell the truth, it took me a few weeks to finally figure out from KJ's spooge-laced descriptions exactly which "big, tattooed, muscled porn star on the workout floor" he was talking about—and once I knew, I never said hello myself, because there's something about a gym that still, decades after high school, makes me shy.

KJ said hi, and the three of us stood outside the coffee shop conversing genially about the movie Vinny's currently working on, which KJ had asked about. Vinny beamed and said, "It's goin' good. I'm gettin' a lotta great head." As he described (and partially mimed) a one-on-one scene he'd just shot—"I was holding this guy's skull like a melon, using his mouth like a fuck toy!"—I noticed that Vinny's cock had begun to bulge outward a bit more. Yet it was his large, intelligent-looking hands that kept my attention. I wondered how would it feel to have those clamping my head to his crotch. Through the coffee shop windows, we could see all these nice folks enjoying their after-church breakfasts, probably with no idea of what devotions we three faithful were cooking up. Finally, KJ said something like "So what are you up to, man?" Pause. "Well, I don't know," Vinny said. "Guess I'm headin' home." Another pause. Trying not to smile, though clearly knowing what everyone had already agreed to do next, KJ said, "You wanna...fool around? My buddy lives just down the block." "Yeah," Vinny smiled. "Always up for a BJ."

Now, I know you've never heard of Vinny LoMaglio. That's because I made up the name. Even though Vinny has sex for a living, I don't want to use his real name since he has boyfriend—a well-known furniture designer whom I met once at an art opening—and I don't know what kind of agreement they have about seeing other people. My agreement with KJ obviously does include the possibility of threesomes. I knew that the moment we got to my apartment—even while I slipped into the bedroom to try to select the right music—KJ would go straight for Vinny's cock and start chowing, spermhound that he is. And I felt a little silly when I rejoined them moments later and realized how completely nonessential music is (even DJ Cam's *Mad Blunted Jazz*) to a Sunday morning hook-up.

Vinny was spread out naked, on his back, propped up with pillows on the daybed. He was moaning, as KJ kneeled between his legs and throated him hungrily. Like in a movie comedy, I bumbled quickly out of my sneakers and sweatpants and hopped around to the side of the daybed. Perching next to Vinny, I put an arm around his shoulders. Somehow, until that point I hadn't really noticed how incredibly tattooed he is—with dragons, angels, flowers, scimitars, a bar code, and a motto (in Latin) teeming over that naturally smooth musclescape. And it was only when KJ paused for a sec that I got my first close look at Vinny's cock, which I want to describe with a word that straight men use when they talk about a sexy woman with a really fantastic body: stacked.

Vinny pulled my free arm up to his chest so I could work his nipples. Each time I let it wander over his bumpy-defined abs down to his pubic area, which he keeps shaved except for a neatly trimmed 1-by-3-inch "mustache," he pulled it back up. It took KJ about 11 minutes to get Vinny's load out—time I spent not just doing the nipple thing and whispering secrets about my favorite muscle-bottom boy, but figuring out whether there was any way to reposition the three of us gracefully so that I could get my tongue around Vinny's cock or meaty nut sac—or into his pretty, shower-fresh butt. There wasn't. Suddenly, Vinny was pulling out and shooting his load onto his abs, while KJ's face hovered close.

KJ thinks that wasting loads is for amateurs too. But Vinny wants his money shot.

The sight of a big cock gone soft after a blow job always turns me on. So when Vinny came back from cleaning up in the bathroom, I was hoping I might get it—dangling so friendly!—in my face as KJ went to work on me. But Vinny pulled his gym stuff back on, chatting, and KJ and I stood up to act the good hosts. Goodbyes at the door were warm. I suppose it shouldn't surprise me that Vinny is such a nice guy. After all, I've fucked around with enough porn stars since coming to New York, and they have all been princes: "Big Max," whose real name was Sam, the first really huge body-builder I ever had sex with (and a writer who did an article for me about being a sex object, when I edited a gay magazine); "Frank Vickers," whom I knew as Roger, whom I found in a straight sex club one summer night, begging a straight couple to pee on him (I watched them pee on him, then got him to pee on me); "Bruno," a.k.a. Herman, who used to live a few blocks away from me and patronized the same dry cleaner; "Peter," a.k.a. Armand; "Eric," a.k.a. Craig. There were others. What impressed me about them all was this porn-specific quality of their stardom: a generosity of spirit that translated in nonsexual circumstances as, well, something really decent, like camaraderie.

"So don't be a stranger in the gym, OK?" Vinny said to me as he left, winking. He kissed KJ.

Of course, since then I haven't seen him at the gym at all. And I am so ready to transcend my shyness and slap him on the back like an old friend, maybe even ask how things are going, in audible—no, booming!—tones, just like the straight guys do with each other. Maybe Vinny will even show me where that secret bathroom is. 'Cause now I'm fixated on having that cock in my mouth, and I kinda got the impression that he wants mine in his.

Stephen Greco
The Sperm Engine

12-30-99

I don't fetishize cum, but I do take my responsibilities for load production seriously. I like to have enough for all the guys who wanna feed on it, and since I am a real blow job addict, that means a lot of guys. I also want my load to taste good and have a nice consistency. So I eat well, work out, get plenty of rest, and take lots of vitamins. If somebody told me that taking castor oil would improve my cum production, I'd be taking castor oil every day.

Same goes for load manipulation. I like to be able to put on a good show, even if only for myself, whenever I shoot somewhere other than into a throat or a rubber. That requires controlled aim and thrust, so I practice a lot. Seeing cum is very special to me, a pleasure that has intensified as I have gotten older. When I masturbate, alone or with one of the sensitive JO freaks I know, I get to experience my load as a very particular substance or event, rather than a blind injection into a hidden place that, now matter how well I feel it, I cannot really know. Recently, I met a guy I call "the best cocksucker on the planet." His technique is flawless—from breath control to popper bottle manipulation—and though there's nothing like depositing a cumload in his esophagus at the end of a session of quiet but intense massage of my cock by his pharyngeal muscles, I love that he knows how we both sometimes want to watch as my sperm emerges from the inner world into the outer one.

Which often means sperming up his face. I love having him sit on the floor, nestled between my legs as I recline in my favorite armchair. There's a point when he slides up off the shaft and starts making love to the underside of my cock head like it was the neck of a new boyfriend. I sit up a bit then and bow over him protectively.

"That's right, show me my load," I whisper, as he lovingly turns a blow job into a scum show.

His name is John. When I say that he's the best cocksucker on the planet, I am taking into account that I say the same thing about two other guys I see regularly, one of whom is my boyfriend. The other guys worship cock; John worships cum. He works from a very deep love of the substance that allows him, like an opera star, to coordinate all the consequences of talent into a performance that goes beyond any rational accounting. When John has me in his mouth, building my third or fourth orgasm, his cheek resting on my thigh, breathing contentedly through his nose, he positively whimpers when I narrate the progress of my cum toward his tongue.

Actually, I don't like the word *cum*. It sounds too *Penthouse* to me, too cheesily heterosexual in its origins. But since the word clearly has become useful in gay male erotic writing, I don't avoid it entirely. I just try to use it compounded with other words, to give it some spin: *cum addict, cum freak, cum dump*. Forget *come*. As a verb, it reads weakly; as a noun, it's a disaster. I like *sperm* for the substance itself, though obviously I know the difference between sperm and semen; and I like *load* for the substance in action, the idea of semen as a by-product of recreation. *Seed* is OK, though I wonder if its resonance can be adequately felt by those who have never taken the Bible literally. I love to use *sperm* as a verb, both transitive and intransitive; I also like the verbs *dump, lose, waste, produce, trade, leak,* and *feed* in connection with sperm. In fact, I like all talk about eating and feeding on sperm: It sounds so sacrilegious, yet of course it's only a healthy, gratifying practice that should probably be taught in elementary school. *Creamy* and *thick* and *sweet* and *salty* are OK adjectives to describe sperm, though as in all written and verbal expression, it's best to avoid clichés. If you're lucky enough to be free of the kind of sexual ick that can lock your imagination into clichés, you might agree that *chunky* and *fragrant* and *weighty* are interesting for describing certain kinds of loads.

Some cum words find their power in the smart side of adolescence—the anti–status quo bad-boy side. Some, of course, reflect the dumb side of adolescence. Like *wad,* which I've always thought silly. Or *jizz,* ditto. (Though, inexplicably, *jizzwad* is fine, as is either *jizz* or *wad* used to describe something spermy other than sperm, as in, "Waiter, what's up with this jizz on my string beans?") As a teenager, I was weirded out by guys who were too focused on sperm. Back then I was repelled by all that talk about producing it and cleaning it up, eating it and freezing it, defrosting it and putting it in omelettes and such. It was AIDS, I guess, that pushed sperm mechanics beyond adolescent fixation into the realm of adult manners, as the sexual negotiation surrounding the once demonized stuff gelled into etiquette.

"I'll take your first load before people get here," John once said to me, before a group scene I had set up for him at my house, when I asked how he wanted to cum. "Then I'll drain everyone else's load one at a time. Repeats welcome, of course. I'll cum once at the end by jerking myself off as I take my last load, which should be yours again. And I'd like your cock to be coated with at least one other load at that point, so if you could get someone to jerk off on you..."

These days, I often find myself thinking about my body and its busy sexual life in terms of scum husbandry, the biggest result of which is that after years of bonering out power-blast after power-blast, I really love cumming soft. I'm grinning as I write this too, because I'm kinda pleased with myself for learning how to pee a rope of warm cum out of my big, floppy soft-on. Heightening the sheer body-enveloping pleasure of this practice is a nice transgressive feeling, since my ability to cum soft is both the result and the cause of my rethinking the function of orgasm and the purpose of pleasure— a process I first began during day-long group sex scenes in which no one could stay hard because of drugs, yet everyone kept...trying.

I don't do drugs anymore, but I brought a lot of sexual understanding away from those scenes. The reason I continue to pursue the soft orgasm is that it's more like the sex I want than any sex I've ever had. It feels like truly making love—conjuring love out of nothing—as opposed to that pounding, invasive thing that feels to me more like work in sexual form.

My number 1 imperative now is this: play with sperm. Sperm play is where we start getting into divine territory—which is, for me, the goal of sex. A vision of John's has burned its way into my mind: men walking around invisibly, except for sacs of semen floating a yard above the pavement. It sounds funny, but there's something in this vision that is surprisingly consistent with the orthodox understanding of men's bodies as precious reserves of fuel for the ancient engine of human reproduction. Only I see this engine as giving more to our species than plentiful offspring. As a big scum cow, I can tell you that dumping load after load, day after day, somehow makes me the beneficiary of an evolutionary system designed to protect men whose sperm is obviously in demand. Nature seems to bless champion scum-bringers with health and youthfulness, and if they happen to write books, arrange flowers, mentor the young, and enrich life in other ways as well as reproduce it, well, then let the textbooks be revised.

Sometimes when I am sperming up John's lips, I find myself deeply moved. It's more than affection, more than respect. I think it's the feeling that we are close to life's font. It's a holy feeling that I think was often there for me during sex but lost among coarser, porno-consistent sentiments that gay pop culture tells us we're supposed to feel. John believes in this holy/sexy thing as much as I do—and I sense that we're right on the edge of some new, freaky-good, pseudo-religious scum-prayer territory that could really get us beyond...

On second thought, I do fetishize cum.

Contributor Biographies

Tom Ace was an editor, writer, and envelope licker at *Diseased Pariah News,* a magazine by and for people with HIV disease. He's glad he got the desire to work on a magazine out of his system. Nowadays when he's not writing erotic diary entries, Tom prostitutes himself as a mild-mannered engineer, writing software for start-up electronics companies you've never heard of. He lives in a remote Western desert area, complete with coyotes and roadrunners.

Kevin Bentley is the editor of *Sailor: Vintage Photos of a Masculine Icon.* He wrote the text for *The Naked Heartland: Itinerant Photography of Bruce of Los Angeles,* and his creative nonfiction has appeared in *ZYZZYVA, The James White Review,* Beliefnet.com, and the anthologies *Bar Stories, His 2, Flesh and the Word 4,* and *Obsessed.* His solo volume of diaries, *Wild Animals I Have Known,* will be published by Green Candy Press in 2002. He lives in San Francisco.

Jack Bissell (1962–1995) was an artist with a particular talent for illustration and portraiture. He also worked in silk-screen production, overlaying up to 40 color plates to recreate the work of Erté, Thomas McKnight, and other artists. When he passed away of AIDS complications at 32, he left behind 10 notebooks of diaries. These selections were edited by his lover Jerry Rosco, author of the biography, *Glenway Wescott Personally.*

Eric Brandt is the editor of *Dangerous Liaisons: Blacks, Gays, and the Struggle for Equality.*

Jim Buck is among other things a writer, thespian, amateur astronomer, absinthe drinker, and professional dilettante. He is also an erstwhile porn star and received awards for Best Newcomer, Best Actor, and Best Overall Performer during his brief stint in the biz. His journalistic endeavors have been published in *Unzipped, All Man, Skinflicks, Eclipse,* and elsewhere. He lives in New Orleans with his partner Jonno and their menagerie of hounds and kittens. He's never been happier.

Richard E. Bump (a.k.a. REB) is a writer, photographer, filmmaker, and activist who has used his voice to inspire and challenge the queer community and its allies since 1972, when he entered activism immediately following his first entry into a tearoom. Since 1992, he has published *Fanorama,* which has been hailed as the "granddaddy of queer 'zines." He is currently inspired by the Radical Faeries and is working on the next issue of his 'zine and various Super 8 film projects. He lives in Cranston, Rhode Island, the home of Ali MacGraw's doomed character in *Love Story.*

Clint Catalyst is a Southern-fried, Goth-damaged spoken-word performer. After an extensive career in degeneracy, he has settled in Los Angeles, where he released his book, *Cottonmouth Kisses,* through Manic D Press.

Clifford Chase is the author of *The Hurry-Up Song: A Memoir of Losing My Brother* and editor of *Queer 13: Lesbian and Gay Writers Recall Seventh Grade.* His writing has also appeared in *Newsweek,* MSNBC.com, *Book Forum, Nerve,* and *Poz* as well as in literary journals such as *Yale Review, Threepenny Review,* and *Boulevard.*

Mitch Cullin is the author of four acclaimed novels: *Whompyjawed* (1999), *Branches* (2000), *Tideland* (2000), and *The Cosmology of Bing* (2001). He short fiction has been previously anthologized in various collections, including *Best American Gay Fiction 2* (Little, Brown) and *Gay Fiction at the Millennium* (Alyson). He currently resides in Tucson, Ariz., where he lives and collaborates with the artist Peter I. Chang.

Kevin Dax is the pseudonym of a much-published Bay Area author and artist. In 1996 he published a now defunct, well-reviewed 'zine called *DOC (Drunk On Cum)*, which recounted "the real-life E-mail romance of two cock-hungry man-sluts" and was recently published in book form by Green Candy Press. He can be reached at Kevnpaul@aol.com.

Anthony Ehlers is a 29-year-old freelance writer born and raised in a town near Johannesburg. After high school he received a diploma in journalism. For the last seven years, he's done freelance advertising and also worked full-time as a personal assistant. His real passion, however, has always been writing fiction. He's written many short stories and hopes to publish an erotic thriller in the near future.

Stephen Greco's short stories have been anthologized in the *Flesh and the Word* series. His story "Good With Words" is included in the 1996 collection, *The Penguin Book of Gay Short Stories,* edited by David Leavitt, and his story "The Last Blowjob" appears in *Best Gay Erotica 1996* (Cleis). Excerpts from Greco's diaries have been collected in *Personal Dispatches: Writers Confront AIDS* (Stonewall Inn Editions, 1990), *Gay Widowers: Life After the Death of a Partner* (Harrington Park Press, 1997), and anonymously in Boyd McDonald's *Straight to Hell* series. In collaboration with photographer Brian Moss, Greco is at work on a new book, *Bodybuilding, U.S.A.,* to be published in 2001.

Don Hatch frequently reflects on his checkered past in New York and San Francisco, where he worked as an actor, market researcher, and book-jacket designer. He now lives a quiet life of contemplation in his native state of Massachusetts, where he is embarking on yet another career—writing.

Mike Hippler (1951-1991) was for 10 years a columnist for the *Bay Area Reporter* in San Francisco. His *BAR* column earned him three consecutive San Francisco Cable Car Awards for outstanding journalism; his writing also appeared in *The Advocate*, the *New York Native*, the *San Francisco Bay Guardian*, and the *San Francisco Chronicle*. He published two books, *So Little Time: Essays on Gay Life* and *Matlovich: The Good Soldier*, and left behind three unpublished novels. His diaries, covering the late '70s to his death, are preserved with the Mike Hippler Papers at the Gay, Lesbian, Bisexual, Transgender Historical Society of Northern California in San Francisco.

Doug Jones recently found the following biographical data: First Year of Life: "very shy." Second Year of Life: "doesn't eat well. Very loving to family but shy with strangers." Third Year of Life: "afraid of dogs. Loves cuddly toys." Sixth and Seventh Years of Life: "unusually artistic. Prefers adult company." None of the above now applies.

David Leddick began his career as a dancer at the Metropolitan Opera of New York and subsequently worked as a creative director for Revlon and L'Oréal advertising. He is the author/editor of the photo books *Naked Men: Pioneering Male Nudes 1935-1955; Naked Men, Too; George Platt Lynes; Men in the Sun; Intimate Companions: A Triography of George Platt Lynes, Paul Cadmus, Lincoln Kirstein, and Their Circle;* and the novels *My Worst Date, Never Eat In,* and *The Sex Squad.*

Shaun Levin lives in London, where his short stories have appeared in *Does the Sun Rise Over Dagenham?, The Slow Mirror: New Fiction by Jewish Writers, The Gay Times Book of Short Stories,* and in the journals *Stand* and *Kunapipi.* In the U.S. and Canada, his work can be found in the *Queer View Mirror* anthologies, *Bad Jobs, Quickies 2, Best Gay Erotica 2000, Slow Grind, My First Time II,* and in *Mach, Indulge, The Evergreen Chronicles, Venue,* and the *Harrington Gay Men's Fiction Quarterly.* He also has stories on suspectthoughts.com and Mind Caviar.com. He runs Gay Men Writing, a creative writing workshop for gay men.

Joseph Manera is a strapping 5 foot 7 and weighs 135 pounds (for now), a fountain of hot, eager Italian manhood. He recently graduated from Dartmouth College with a BA in English, and enjoys sugary drinks, holding hands, and talking about feelings. He resides in the Haight-Ashbury District of San Francisco and is at work on a novel.

Robert Marshall is a visual artist whose work has been exhibited throughout the United States and Europe. His memoir "Notes on Camp" appeared in the anthology *Queer 13*. He lives in New York City, where he is completing his first novel, *Ixtlan*.

David May was a nice boy from a good family who fell in with the wrong crowd. He is the author of the S/M-oriented *Madrugada: A Cycle of Erotic Fictions*. His work, both fiction and nonfiction, has appeared in *The Harvard Gay & Lesbian Review, Advocate Men, Cat Fancy, Drummer, Frontiers, Honcho, Inches, International Leatherman, Lambda Book Report,* and *Mach*. His work also appears in the anthologies *Kosher Meat; Bar Stories; Midsummer Night's Dreams: One Story, Many Tales; Cherished Blood; Flesh and the Word 3; Meltdown!; Queer View Mirror;* and *Rogues of San Francisco*. He lives in San Francisco (with his husband, a dog, and two cats) where he is (of course) working on a novel.

Steve Nugent has kept diaries in England and Australia. Now living in Toronto, he has contributed to the *Lambda Book Report, fab* magazine, the *Church-Wellesley Review,* and the anthologies of short erotic fiction *Quickies 2* and *Exhibitions*.

Dan Perdios is a freelance writer living along the Russian River in Sonoma County, California. His previous stories have been published in *Manifest Reader, Manhood Rituals, Diseased Pariah News,* and *Atrocity.* He also writes a column for *We the People,* the gay and lesbian newspaper for Sonoma County. He can be reached at danp@Inreach.com.

Felice Picano is a best-selling author of fiction, poetry, and memoirs and other nonfiction. Notable recent titles include *Like People in History* (1995), *The Book of Lies* (1999), and *The New York Years* (2000). He's received many literary award nominations and awards, and his books have been translated into six languages. He also writes for the *San Francisco Examiner* and is an online reviewer for Barnes&Noble.com. He now lives in Los Angeles. The selection included here comes from Picano's diaries covering the years 1970–1989, which are in the process of being edited for publication by Kevin Fries.

Jim Provenzano is the author of *PINS* (Myrmidude Press), the acclaimed novel about gay wrestlers. His short fiction is included in over a dozen anthologies.

Andrew Ramer is the coauthor of *Ask Your Angels* and the author of *Angel Answers, Revelations for a New Millennium,* and the Lambda Literary Award Finalist *Two Flutes Playing.* Interviewed in Mark Thompson's *Gay Soul,* he has also published stories in the anthologies *Best Gay Erotica 1998, Best Gay Erotica 2001,* and *Kosher Meat.* He lives in Menlo Park, California.

David Serling is a fiction writer, journalist, film critic, and actor living in Los Angeles. His work has appeared in E!Online and *IN Los Angeles* magazine. As an actor, he played a recurring role on *Days of Our Lives* and starred in various national television commercials. In his upcoming one-man show, he portrays 20 characters, including quadruplet brothers. Also in the works are the novels *Cabin Fever* (a mystery) and *Pressure Points* (a romance).

Don Shewey has published three books about theater: the biography *Sam Shepard* (1985); *Caught in the Act: New York Actors Face to Face,* a collaboration with photographer Susan Shacter (1986); and *Out Front,* an anthology of gay and lesbian plays published by Grove Press (1988). His articles have appeared in *The New York Times,*

The Village Voice, Esquire, Rolling Stone, and other publications, and his writings have been included in a wide variety of anthologies, including *The Politics of Masculinity, Contemporary Shakespeare Criticism,* and *Best Gay Erotica 2000.* He grew up in a trailer park on a dirt road in Waco, Texas, and now lives in midtown Manhattan halfway between Trump Tower and Carnegie Hall.

Matt Bernstein Sycamore is the editor of *Tricks and Treats: Sex Workers Write About Their Clients* (Haworth 2000). His writing has appeared in numerous publications, including *Best American Erotica 2001, Best Gay Erotica 2000, Best Gay Erotica 2001,* and *Best American Gay Fiction.* He is currently working on a nonfiction anthology, *Dangerous Families: Queer Writing on Surviving Abuse.* He recently finished a novel, *Pulling Taffy,* and is looking for a publisher. He just moved back to San Francisco, and can be contacted at tricksandtreats@hotmail.com.

Acknowledgments

Thanks are due to Clifford Chase for his early encouragement of the idea for this book and his helpful comments on the draft, Scott Brassart for his immediate enthusiasm for the project, Matthew Van Atta for his careful copyediting, Kevin Stone Fries for his help in obtaining the excerpt from Felice Picano's diaries, and Jerry Rosco for sending me the late Jack Bissell's tender passages. Special thanks to the Gay, Lesbian, Bisexual, Transgender Historical Society of Northern California for allowing me to read and select from the Mike Hippler diaries. Most of all, I'm indebted to the contributors for their honesty, bravery, and generosity.